The White Indian Series
Book VIII

AMBUSH

Donald Clayton Porter

Created by the producers of
White Indian, Children of the Lion,
Saga of the Southwest, and
The Kent Family Chronicles Series.

Chairman of the Board: Lyle Kenyon Engel

BANTAM BOOKS
NEW YORK • TORONTO • LONDON • SYDNEY • AUCKLAND

AMBUSH

*A Bantam Book / published by arrangement with
Book Creations, Inc.*

*Produced by Book Creations, Inc.
Lyle Kenyon Engel, Founder*

*Bantam edition / October 1983
6 printings through April 1990*

ISBN 0-553-25202-X

Published simultaneously in the United States and Canada

---

*Bantam Books are published by Bantam Books, a division of Bantam
Doubleday Dell Publishing Group, Inc. Its trademark, consisting of the
words "Bantam Books" and the portrayal of a rooster, is Registered in U.S.
Patent and Trademark Office and in other countries. Marca Registrada.
Bantam Books, 666 Fifth Avenue, New York, New York 10103.*

PRINTED IN THE UNITED STATES OF AMERICA

RAD   12 11 10 9 8 7 6

AT A TURNING POINT IN AMERICAN HISTORY, REVENGE AND PASSION BATTLE FOR A WILD, UNTAMED LAND.

GHONKABA—The young Sachem born to inherit the mantle of greatness worn by his grandfather, the legendary white Indian, Renno. The mixed blood that beats in his warrior's heart may make him the savior of a mighty new nation or its most dangerous enemy.

TO-SHA-BE—Lusty, half-French captive of the Senecas. Unless a fearless act of bravery wins her freedom, her seductive beauty will doom her to a life of forced degradation in the white man's world.

LUDONA—Chief warrior of the savage Erie, traditional adversaries of the Seneca. Shamed before his people, only one act can bring him new respect—the murder of Ghonkaba.

BETH STRONG—The lovely, but tempestuous first love of Ghonkaba. By promising her heart to another man, she has forced a proud Indian to vow a ruthless and unrelenting revenge.

COLONEL TOWNSEND WHITING—Ghonkaba's British-born rival for Beth Strong's love. Fate places his future—and that of an entire nation—in the hands of the man who hates him most.

GENERAL MONTCALM—Commander of the French forces in the New World. His genius and his nobility make him an ally to be trusted, but for the mighty Seneca, he is a foe to be feared.

The White Indian Series
Ask your bookseller for the books you have missed

Chapter I

Ghonkaba, inheritor of the proudest and most distinguished tradition in the Seneca nation, was the only member of his illustrious family to be of mixed Indian and white blood. A tall, athletically built warrior with dark hair, who had earned his senior rank in his nation's armed forces by distinguished conduct in battle, he was the son of Ja-gonh, the white-skinned sachem, or leader, of the Seneca, and of Ah-wen-ga, daughter of one of the most revered of Seneca war chiefs.

But Ghonkaba's ancestry was even more honored than his parentage alone could indicate. His grandfather, father of Ja-gonh, was none other than Renno, the mighty Great Sachem of the Iroquois League, the powerful group of six nations that dominated the English-speaking colonies of North America. Renno, in

1

turn, was the foster son of Ghonka, one of the first Great Sachems of the Iroquois. Countless songs and legends recounting Ghonka's deeds and character passed down to each succeeding generation, as they had about Renno.

These ancestors of Ghonkaba had been courted by kings of England intent on seeking the Iroquois, and particularly the Seneca, as their allies. And their leading generals likewise saw the military advantages to be acquired in obtaining Iroquois collaboration in wartime. Active in that tradition, Ghonkaba had formed a close friendship with Colonel George Washington of the Virginia militia, for whom he had acted as a scout in the previous year of 1758.

But Ghonkaba now was filled with uncertainty and self-searching. Never had he—or any member of his renowned family—been subjected to such an insult as he had experienced at the hands of a lovely young colonist from Boston, to whom he had openly given his heart. To him, it had seemed inconceivable that an honorable offer of marriage from a brave such as he would have been spurned. But Beth Strong, daughter of the commander in chief of the Massachusetts Bay Militia, had turned from him after encouraging his interest. Even worse, it was a dandified, handsome English officer to whom she turned—Colonel Townsend Whiting, a special representative to the Iroquois. Ghonkaba little knew or cared that Whiting's patron, a politician named William Pitt, was a leading candidate for the office of prime minister of the British government.

That Beth, born in the colonies and thus privileged to call herself a native American, actually preferred Colonel Whiting had seemed an outrage that set Ghonkaba's blood boiling. He felt he must act to retrieve his honor as well as the honor of his family. His target was within reach, since Whiting, together with Beth and her father, Major General Kenneth Strong, just happened to be in the main town of the Seneca, where they would be spending two days and nights. The general had come to confer with Ja-gonh and the aged Renno. Beth was his interpreter; Whiting brought a message from London that reassured the Iroquois about the British commitment in their struggle with the French for control of North America.

But as he plotted to kill Whiting, the manitous had sent him a message. The manitous were the spirits who acted as intermediaries between the gods and human beings. As he sat near his lodge that night, a hawk feather had floated down before his eyes. The hawk itself was totally invisible, no matter how diligently he searched the sky, but the feather was unmistakable. The unusual event must be a sign, he recognized—the manitous' signal that he should reconsider his hasty resolve to take Whiting's life.

Having accepted the presumed purpose of the feather that fell from the sky, he still was unsure as to what other direction he should take. How could respect for him be restored in the eyes of his people? What must he do to regain his own self-respect? The manitous certainly had not made any of this clear. Rather, they had created confusion and upset within his mind.

Often in the past, when confronted with the need to wrestle with a serious problem, he would retreat deep into the limitless forests as his ancestors had done. There he might be able to ask the manitous for a clearer sign. This he would do now.

Speaking to no one, he gathered his principal weapons—his tomahawk, a bow, and a quiver of arrows—and with his sharpened knife in his belt, he left the town. After crossing the fields where the town's women grew their crops, he plunged into the thick forest. Here, as always, he was at home.

Running silently, swiftly, he smiled to himself as he heard the chittering of chipmunks in a grove of trees. Slowing his pace slightly, he watched four or five squirrels searching for nuts.

Becoming aware of a brown speckled deer not far away to his right, Ghonkaba impulsively increased his pace until he was running parallel to the buck, which was headed in the same direction. He was not in search of food, so he had no intention of shooting the deer; he and his tribesmen did not kill for sport.

He was enjoying a game that he had played ever since his early teens; he was still able to keep pace with the deer as his long strides matched its fleet ones.

Tiring of the contest, perhaps growing distrustful of this two-footed animal who was challenging him, the deer finally veered off and vanished into the wilderness.

Continuing without letup, Ghonkaba speculated on what the encounter had meant to the deer. Like all Indians, he attributed full reasoning powers to animals and felt them capable of analyzing any situation as easily and completely as a human.

His rapid pace brought him shortly to his destination. Here, the grass was thick and lush, especially near a small stream flowing through the center of the field. A dozen huge oak trees surrounded the meadow, and between them thick brambles discouraged intruders.

A sacred grove, it was known only to male members of the Bear Clan. Since time immemorial, Seneca warriors had come to pray to the manitous. Never was this grove used for frivolous purpose. Now, with his arms raised above his head and his eyes lifted toward the sky, Ghonkaba begged the indulgence of the manitous and asked them to give him a new sign of what to do.

His failure to show them sufficient respect by fasting for many hours, he explained, was caused by the presence of the man whom he had come to regard as his enemy. That man would soon be en route back to Boston, and if the manitous decided Ghonkaba should kill him he wanted to know as soon as possible.

He went on to relate how he had come to know Beth while serving with General Strong and how, over a period of time, he had gradually begun to assume that they would marry. No wide gap separated their civilizations. His father had taught him the language of the English, and from his mother he had learned French, and he was as fluent in speaking, reading, and writing in those languages as in his native Seneca. He was familiar, also, with the customs of people from the far side of the Atlantic. When he dressed in their attire, he was invariably mistaken for a colonial.

All these elements contributed to his surprise and dismay when Beth told him she intended to marry Whiting. Finally, Ghonkaba related that he had given full and proper consideration to the incident of the hawk feather and had, as the manitous apparently intended, delayed any action until they clarified their intent.

After unburdening himself fully for at least an hour, Ghonkaba stood silent, his arms still lifted, and waited expectantly for a sign.

His faith in the manitous was boundless. He believed with all his heart that somehow they would give him a further signal that would make clear their wish for him. Never had he prayed to them in vain, nor had his father, grandfather, or great-grandfather.

In the distance, Ghonkaba discerned a sudden crackling noise in the dry leaves. Someone was coming toward him through the underbrush. His hand crept to his tomahawk's handle, but he refrained from making a belligerent gesture before he knew who approached. The manitous required this courtesy.

A chill shot up and down the young warrior's spine when he saw a huge, brown bear push through the underbrush and enter the clearing. A female weighing at least a thousand pounds, she was shepherding two small, frolicking cubs that paused briefly to eat some berries from surrounding bushes.

Immediately alert to his grave danger, Ghonkaba knew that a mother bear escorting her cubs was the most ferocious of all animals. The safety of her cubs was paramount to her, and she could be expected invariably to attack any alien who might represent even a remote threat.

But Ghonkaba quickly recalled an often-related incident in his family's history that brought some hope. His grandfather, as a young boy, had been saved by a bear that defied its natural impulses by forming a close friendship with him that lasted for years. In fact, Ja-gonh, Ghonkaba's father, was named in loving remembrance of the bear.

Consequently, Ghonkaba felt no fear but stood very still, lest the mother consider his actions hostile.

The cubs approached him, sniffing his moccasins and buckskin trousers, then returned to their mother's side.

The mother bear, too, seemed satisfied that Ghonkaba was harmless. Perhaps, he thought, she could recognize him as the grandson of Renno, befriended by Ja-gonh, the great bear.

Whatever her reason, she allowed the cubs to eat their fill for some minutes, then cuffed them, sending them head over heels. When they scampered off into the wilderness, she followed, never looking back. The trio crashed off through the forest; then all was silent again.

Deep in thought as he reflected on the incident, Ghonkaba reached a quick conclusion: the manitous unreservedly approved his original plan to kill Townsend Whiting. Clearly, the mother bear and her cubs represented the manitous themselves, and their lack of concern about Ghonkaba indicated he was free to act the way he felt was best.

His spirits much improved, Ghonkaba returned to the town at a rapid "Seneca trot," a joglike pace that, when necessary, he and other warriors could maintain for an extended period. Now the road ahead seemed clear, and he was better able to analyze his outlook and emotions. To his surprise, he realized he had not been in love with Beth. He liked and admired her, to be sure, but now he recognized that he had thought of marrying her only because it seemed a natural and expected progression of their friendship.

Still, her rejection had deeply hurt his pride, as sensitive as it was ferocious. His solution would restore his honor, along with that of his people, who shared the insult that had been directed his way.

In high spirits when he reached the town, Ghonkaba spontaneously decided to visit the Quarter of the Captives. It was his way—and to his parents, his biggest shortcoming—to act impulsively, and right now he felt like visiting the Quarter and spending an hour with his favorite prostitute. Certainly the killing of Whiting could wait a little longer.

Surrounded by a high wooden palisade, the area consisted of huts, each containing a single room. Here, captured young women of the Erie, Ottawa, and Huron lived in enforced prostitution. Their sole companion was a Seneca brave who had shown cowardice in

7

battle; his punishment was to dress as a woman and submit to the taunts and mockery of his former comrades-in-arms.

Ghonkaba was familiar with the district because on occasion he visited Toshabe, a young woman captured two years earlier from the Erie, traditional enemies of the Seneca. Toshabe, like Ghonkaba himself, was a half-breed. She had confided one night that, though her mother was an Erie, her father had been a French fur trader. She had lived in Quebec until ten years of age, attending school, learning French, and being reared in accordance with the customs of the city. Then, after her father died, she and her mother were no longer accepted, and they returned to the mother's people, though her mother, too, had not long survived.

Toshabe's misfortune, after living for eight years in a wilderness town of the Erie, was to fall into the hands of Seneca raiders who brought her home with them and presented her to their people as a captive.

A realist who accepted adversity without complaint, she had a perennially cheerful good nature that helped to attract Ghonkaba to her pallet from time to time. He was subconsciously motivated, too, by a far more subtle reason: because Toshabe was a half-breed and therefore regarded by many as a white Indian, like himself, he felt they shared a special bond.

When Ghonkaba entered her hut, Toshabe parted her heavily rouged lips in a welcoming smile. She was very beautiful under all the makeup, with shining, long dark hair and big black eyes. She was taller than most women, with full breasts and long legs. As was her habit, she wore, without self-consciousness, her abbreviated costume—a short doeskin skirt. Her nipples were rouged, as were her earlobes and the palms of her hands, all signs of her enforced servitude.

They engaged in little conversation and even fewer preliminaries. Their strongly felt chemical attraction impelled them to hurl themselves into each other's arms, and their lovemaking was lusty, violent, and mutually satisfying. But Ghonkaba's manner was considerate, his touch gentle. Unlike almost all of the callous braves who visited her, he cared about her reaction. Toshabe was very much aware of his concern and consequently enjoyed his lovemaking.

Ghonkaba did not analyze the reasons for their success in making love; he knew only that he thoroughly enjoyed his relationship with Toshabe and that she seemed equally pleased. Toshabe, more inclined at this moment toward introspection, suspected that she might actually be in love with Ghonkaba. But she quickly put the thought out of her mind. The difference in their stations meant that contemplating genuine love would be a futile waste of time.

Only after they were satiated did they begin to talk, and then, as he invariably did, Ghonkaba spoke freely. Toshabe always had been closemouthed, never revealing his confidences, and he trusted her implicitly. So he told her freely all that was in his mind.

As she listened, Toshabe's blood seemed to freeze in her veins when he casually mentioned his intent to kill Colonel Whiting. Their nudity was forgotten, irrelevant to the serious aspect of their conversation.

Not wanting to cause him to become defensive, she tried to match his casual air. "You must love Beth Strong very much if you are willing to kill for her sake."

Ghonkaba laughed as he held her and gently stroked her thigh. "You are completely wrong," he assured

9

her. "You mean more to me than Beth means, and you have more sense. I am sure you would not reject my offer of marriage!"

That much, Toshabe reflected, certainly was true.

"My honor and the honor of my family have been compromised by Beth Strong's action," he went on. "This I cannot tolerate."

"If you kill one who is a guest under your roof," Toshabe insisted, "you blacken your name for all time."

Ghonkaba grinned complacently. "Colonel Whiting is not a guest under my roof," he said. "He is lodged in a guest house near the council chamber."

He was being evasive, she thought, and his excuse was feeble, but she was too diplomatic to point this out. In spite of their momentary equality, she was a captive of the Seneca, and he was the son of the nation's sachem, the grandson of the leader of the entire Iroquois League. If she forgot the great gulf that separated them, or tried to bridge the distance, she could expect to encounter great difficulties. "Ghonkaba," she said at last, "knows best the ways of his own people and the ways of the English, to whom he is related. My only concern is that I would not wish to see Ghonkaba in trouble once again. He was punished last year when he defied authority by rebelling against orders, and I fear he would be dealt with even more severely if he offended his people now."

Ghonkaba felt the heat rise at the mention of his punishment. "I will not offend them," he said. "The manitous approve of what I do." He described the incident with the mother bear and her cubs.

Now Toshabe was confused, but had the presence of mind to ask, "When will you put your knife into Whiting?"

"I had intended to do away with him tonight," he

10

replied, "but I now plan to wait until tomorrow night, the last night that he will be here."

That seemed to close the discussion. As they stood and embraced, Ghonkaba ran his hands appreciatively over her again. Then he dressed swiftly and took his leave after promising her the pelts of the three foxes that he would hunt and kill tomorrow, though one would have sufficed. Her attraction for him was evident, but Ghonkaba himself seemed unaware of its full significance.

Once he was gone, she acted quickly. Daubing fresh red berry stain on her lips, nipples, and earlobes, she donned her short skirt and a cape and quickly left her house. Although she was not supposed to leave her own quarter, she had made herself familiar enough with the town's layout to be able to go straight to the large building that was the home of the sachem of the Seneca.

There, gathered around an open pit fire outside the house, she found Ja-gonh, the sachem, and Ah-wen-ga, evidently ready for their evening meal. And then, immediately, she knew that the manitous favored her cause. Opposite the sachem and his wife, clad in his magnificent beaded buffalo robe, sat the majestic, white-haired Renno, Great Sachem of the Iroquois.

Ah-wen-ga was startled by Toshabe's brazen appearance. "What do you want here?" she demanded.

Now almost overcome with shyness, Toshabe forced herself to speak boldly. "I am Toshabe of the Erie," she said. "I have been a captive of the Seneca for two times ten moons and six more."

"And what brings you to the dwelling of the sachem?" Ah-wen-ga insisted.

"I fear that the son of Ja-gonh and Ah-wen-ga, whom I humbly regard as a valued friend, may be in serious trouble and may cause grave troubles for all of his people."

Renno decided to intervene. "Sit!" he ordered in his deep voice. "You have eaten your supper?"

In response to her negative reply, the Great Sachem picked up an empty gourd and dipped it into a pot that contained the typical Seneca stew of venison, beans, squash, and corn. Without comment, he handed it to Toshabe.

Ah-wen-ga decided to take control of the situation. Herself a well-kept woman of over fifty who looked little more than half her age, she was annoyed by the way her husband eyed the lithe, ripe figure of this unduly naked young woman, and she felt dismayed surprise upon recognizing the gleam of appreciation in Renno's eyes. She had considered the Great Sachem too old and austere to note such physical beauty.

Rising swiftly, Ah-wen-ga went into the house and brought out a long cloak of doeskin. She draped it over Toshabe's shoulders and fastened the thongs at her throat. Now, concealed from neck to toe, Toshabe no longer represented a potential threat to her.

Grateful to have been given the covering, Toshabe was able to relax enough to speak slowly and carefully as she related what Ghonkaba had revealed to her.

When she had finished, Renno and Ja-gonh exchanged a long look, without need to communicate in words. No warrior among all the Seneca was more courageous than Ghonkaba. But similarly, no brave was sometimes more lacking in common sense.

Only Ah-wen-ga was agitated. "Whatever shall we do?" she inquired.

With his customary tranquillity, Renno proclaimed: "Thanks to this young woman, who has placed the good of the Seneca nation above her own good, we have been warned in ample time. I shall attend to the matter myself." He raised his voice slightly. "See that Ghonkaba is summoned and appears before me at once."

Ja-gonh rose and departed immediately.

Ah-wen-ga, still perturbed, insisted, "The girl should return to her own dwelling immediately. If she is here when Ghonkaba arrives, he will know she has spoken to us out of turn and he will resent her for it."

Toshabe started to rise, but Renno gently but firmly waved her back. "You will stay," he ordered. "By the time I am done speaking with Ghonkaba, he will appreciate what you've done for him, and he will share our feeling of gratitude to you." Folding his arms, he silently looked off into the distance.

Ah-wen-ga wanted to argue the point, but not even she had the temerity to flout the Great Sachem's will. Trying to conceal her concern, she told Toshabe, "Eat your supper before it gets cold." Despite her nervousness, Toshabe did not dare disobey in the presence of the leaders of the entire Seneca nation, and she began to eat. So tense she could scarcely taste the food, she silently concentrated on keeping her meal down. Ghonkaba surely would resent her intrusion into his private business, she feared, realizing that she had no right to come to his family with his wild plan.

Ja-gonh returned, reporting tersely, "Three junior warriors are searching the town for Ghonkaba. They will soon find him and he will be here." He filled a long pipe, then lighted it with a coal from the fire.

Slowly, Toshabe became aware that Ah-wen-ga was studying her, openly and candidly, dark eyes penetrating, expression inscrutable.

Such an inspection ordinarily would have made her nervous and apprehensive. Ah-wen-ga, after all, was

13

the squaw of the sachem of the Seneca and daughter-in-law of the Great Sachem, the most powerful Indian leader in North America. But even under such scrutiny, Toshabe felt completely at ease. She was thankful that Ah-wen-ga showed no signs of a condescending attitude toward a prostitute. Rather, she seemed only curious about her, and appeared to be trying to fathom why Toshabe would have interfered in Ghonkaba's affairs though she would have found it so much easier to keep his secret.

When Ghonkaba appeared at last, he raised his left arm in a rigid, formal salute to his grandfather, and then his father. His eyes widened slightly when he saw Toshabe in the borrowed robe beside his mother. As was proper, he refrained from acknowledging her presence and devoted his attention only to the Great Sachem.

Renno came to the point at once. "Is it true that Ghonkaba intends to put his knife into the body of Townsend Whiting, the representative of England?" he demanded.

His grandson was equally blunt. "It is true." With an effort, he concealed his resentment and anger at being betrayed.

"What is the reason for this?" Renno was unyielding, but Ghonkaba stood up to him as no one else dared. "He has disgraced me and has disgraced the Seneca nation. He has stolen the woman of Ghonkaba and dares to make plans to marry her."

Ah-wen-ga glanced at her father-in-law with an expression suggesting that she wished to take part in the questioning. Trusting her, though he could not know what she had in mind, Renno immediately deferred.

"Was it the intention of Ghonkaba to make Beth Strong his squaw?" she asked in seeming innocence.

"It was!" Her son was still strident.

"I am surprised," she said mildly, "that my son, the son of Ja-gonh, would wish to marry a woman when he has no love in his heart for her."

Ghonkaba immediately became belligerent. "How can you make this claim? How can you say that I have no love for Beth?"

His mother's expression did not change, and her voice remained calm. "He who loves one woman," she remarked, "does not couple with another, as my son does with Toshabe."

Color rose to the young warrior's face, but he could offer no reply. Toshabe, feeling her cheeks burn, avoided looking at him.

Ah-wen-ga glanced again at Renno to show that she was returning the interrogation to him.

"The grandson of Renno," the Great Sachem said, "appears to be very certain that the path he has chosen is the right one."

"I am certain because I have received a sign from the manitous telling me that I am right."

Leaning forward, Renno accepted a long pipe from his son and puffed it reflectively. His attitude suggested deep interest in the subject. He seemed willing to accept his grandson's words as the truth. Encouraged by such an apparently open-minded response, Ghonkaba mentioned the incident of the hawk feather and then launched into a detailed recounting of his encounter with the bears.

Ja-gonh despaired; he could think of nothing more catastrophic for the Seneca nation than what Ghonkaba was contemplating. Ja-gonh felt a desire to shake his son until his teeth rattled.

Renno, however, saw the solution. With a glance, he assured Ja-gonh that he could resolve the troublesome

15

matter and understood clearly how to bring Ghonkaba under control. "The meeting of Ghonkaba with the bears this day is of vast importance," he said. "We are of the Bear Clan, so any meetings with the bears are vital to us."

Seeing the point his father sought to make, Ja-gonh promptly picked up the theme. "The life of my father was saved by a bear whose name I carry," he added, "and we have had in our family ever since that time a special rapport with bears. I can see little doubt that the mother and her cubs who appeared before Ghonkaba in the sacred grove today were sent by the manitous."

Toshabe's long discipline in concealing emotion enabled her to hide her amazement. The elders of Ghonkaba's family, instead of discouraging his mad scheme, appeared to be encouraging him.

"I am certain," Renno now went on firmly, "that the bears were sent to Ghonkaba by the manitous. It grieves me, however, that my grandson has misread the sign that the manitous sent to him, in a way similar to his interpretation of their intention in sending the hawk's feather to him."

Startled, Ghonkaba remained silent, prepared to listen to the elders' wisdom in fascination and wonder.

"The mother bear," Renno told him, "represented Great Britain, and the cubs represented her colonies in the New World."

Ghonkaba would not dream of disagreeing with how his grandfather interpreted the meaning of the manitous' messengers. Too many miraculous experiences had occurred to permit any question of the accuracy of whatever interpretation the Great Sachem put on the encounter in the forest.

"What would have happened," Renno asked quietly, "if Ghonkaba had struck one of the cubs?"

"I do not like to think about such things," his grandson answered with a slight smile curling his lips. "The mother bear would have attacked me. And if I were not very quick, as well as skillful and courageous, she surely would have killed me."

"What would have happened had Ghonkaba attacked the mother bear herself?"

The smile faded. "I would not be here now. The furious bear would have clawed and chewed me until I died."

Now his father offered a telling observation. "In my counsels today with General Strong and Colonel Whiting," Ja-gonh reported, "Whiting promised on the word of William Pitt, a man who is to be the next prime minister of Britain, to send many firesticks, together with gunpowder and bullets, to the Seneca. If he were to be destroyed by the hand of the grandson of the Great Sachem, the son of the sachem, Great Britain would hardly honor that promise."

Seemingly tranquil, Renno puffed the long pipe as he looked into space. "Colonel Townsend Whiting," he said, "ranks high in the war councils of Great Britain. If he is killed by a warrior of the Seneca while visiting our town, we would be guilty of breaching the hospitality for which we are famous. Never again would our word be trusted. And that is not all. The British would become our enemies, go to war against us, and punish us for our transgression against one whom we pretended was our friend. They can put many warriors into the field for each warrior that the Seneca can send into battle. Each of their braves is armed with a powerful firestick. One firestick is worth twenty of the best bows and arrows that the Seneca can make. The arms of the British are potent beyond belief. They could destroy the Seneca nation, kill our warriors, and take our women and children to their own land as slaves. The Seneca nation would be no more."

A shudder ran down Ghonkaba's spine.

"That," Renno concluded emphatically, "is the true meaning of Ghonkaba's meeting with the bears!"

Toshabe marveled at the Great Sachem's mental agility and cleverness. He could not really believe that the great Seneca nation would be impotent and easily vanquished by British soldiers led by the same kind of generals who had proved so unworthy in wilderness warfare. She understood that he was making up a plausible tale to dissuade his grandson from perpetrating a dangerously foolhardy act.

"I can think of nothing that might befall this nation that would be worse than the death of Colonel Whiting at the hand of a Seneca warrior!" Ja-gonh declared with a long, hard look at his son.

Willing to admit the wisdom and validity of these arguments, Ghonkaba nonetheless saw his own dilemma. Folding his arms, he spoke in a low tone. "I freely admit all the Great Sachem has said," he said. "I bow to his greater knowledge of the manitous and to his interpretation of my meeting in the sacred grove with the bears. But this does not affect the situation that I face. When Whiting marries the woman I expected to make my squaw, I will be disgraced. The name of the Seneca will be sullied, as well."

Ja-gonh's patience was tried by his son's stubbornness, and he was on the verge of retorting angrily when a look from Ah-wen-ga silenced him.

"I believe," she said, "that we should allow Whiting and the woman he will marry to work out their own destiny together, with or without the guidance of the manitous. Ghonkaba has more important matters that concern him."

"And what are these matters?" her son asked boldly.

Turning to Toshabe, Ah-wen-ga smiled broadly. "This woman," she said, "deserves full credit for saving the Seneca from a catastrophe that could have destroyed our nation."

Renno was quick to seize on her point. "You are right!" he agreed. "Toshabe had nothing personal to gain by coming to me regarding Ghonkaba's intentions. But thanks to her intervention, the air has been cleared and a terrible miscarriage of justice avoided. She has spent two years as a captive of the Seneca and has more than paid the price for the perfidy of the Erie in making war against us. So I grant her freedom, unconditional freedom, as of this moment forward."

The declaration was so unexpected that Toshabe was stunned. She cherished her freedom and welcomed it with all her heart. No more would she be required to give herself to crude warriors who wanted to use her body. But a worry nevertheless lodged in her mind. Her familiarity with the customs of the Erie led her to doubt that they would accept her back into their tribal fold. Having been a prostitute among the Seneca, even though in enforced servitude, she would be regarded as unclean by her own people, and she could expect to be rejected by them.

She faced a critical dilemma: if she admitted her fears to Renno, he might think it best to rescind his order setting her free. It was best, she quickly decided, to accept her freedom, saying nothing about any problems. She would have to take her chances on how she would be treated in the land of the Erie.

Ah-wen-ga was not yet finished distracting her son from Beth Strong. "I'm sure that Ghonkaba will want to return the favor of one who has been so kind to him," she said. "Surely he will wish to escort Toshabe to her own land."

Ghonkaba readily agreed. The mission would be an honorable one, and he could see no reason why he would not find it enjoyable as well as suitable.

Toshabe looked gratefully at Ah-wen-ga, and a rapid, unspoken exchange occurred between them; they understood each other perfectly. They understood that Ghonkaba was drawn to Toshabe; after all, he had come to her frequently for lovemaking. For that reason, his mother was giving her a quiet, private responsibility. She was to help make him forget Beth, with whom he wasn't really in love. The assignment did not seem difficult, and Toshabe accepted it happily. If she had learned one thing during her Seneca captivity, it was to place a properly high value on her femininity. She had no doubt that in her care Ghonkaba would get over what remained of his affair with Beth. In this way, she would be repaying his family for the unexpected gift of her freedom.

Perceiving what Ah-wen-ga had in mind, Renno proceeded to elaborate on her scheme. His grandson, he realized, had to be kept occupied. Already a first-rate fighting man, he needed only maturity to equip him to take his place in the nation's hierarchy. "After you have delivered Toshabe to the Erie nation," he told Ghonkaba, "you will have traveled a good part of the way to the land known as Virginia. You are to go the rest of that distance and report to Colonel Washington, commander of the militia."

Ghonkaba came to life eagerly. "I thank my grandfather for his great kindness!"

Renno smiled faintly. "I do not regard it as a kindness. You served faithfully as a scout in the employ of Colonel Washington earlier in the present campaign. Now that we are formally at war with France, he has an even greater need for your services. I have received a message from him asking if you could be spared to work with him again. I have decided to honor his request."

Ghonkaba could not curb his surging excitement. "How soon do we leave?"

"That must depend on the convenience of Toshabe," Renno pointed out.

Ah-wen-ga promptly came to her assistance. "I have some clothes suitable for wilderness travel that I will give you," she told Toshabe. "So tomorrow you can leave any time you wish."

"I expect that General Strong might want to send a letter to Colonel Washington and will ask you to take it," Ja-gonh said. "Therefore, it would be desirable that you plan on beginning your journey after the noon dinner."

So the details of the departure were settled, and the group broke up for the night. Toshabe reached out and touched Ghonkaba's arm, delaying him as he prepared to take his leave.

With a brilliant, melting smile, Toshabe told him softly, "I am in the debt of Ghonkaba for consenting to escort me through the wilderness to the land of the Erie. My heart overflows with gratitude to you."

Ghonkaba, too embarrassed to know how to reply, ducked his head and disappeared quickly in the darkness toward the longhouse where he lived.

Ah-wen-ga was satisfied and reflected that, by the time the couple reached the land of the Erie, her son would have forgotten Beth Strong's existence. His interest in Toshabe was far greater than he knew.

*   *   *

As a main course for the farewell dinner, Ah-wen-ga served buffalo steaks, pounded to make them less sinewy, sprigs of fresh watercress that had a sharp taste resembling mustard, freshly picked corn, and roasted sweet potatoes. These had been removed from the coals so recently that they were still smoking when they were added to the wooden dishes.

What made the occasion most memorable, however, was the presence of two women from outside the family. That, too, was Ah-wen-ga's doing. She had argued—successfully—that it was only fitting for General Strong's daughter to be on hand. And, finally, she chose Toshabe to help her and also to join in the meal. Ja-gonh correctly suspected an ulterior motive in this arrangement.

Studying Toshabe now, Ah-wen-ga was more than satisfied with her most appealing appearance. Her eyes were accented by a subtle black line drawn around them, and though she had refrained from coloring her earlobes, the mark of a courtesan, her lips were tinted and highlights of color could be seen in her cheeks. The calf-length doeskin that Ah-wen-ga had provided was the first real dress Toshabe had worn in two years, but it hardly detracted from her natural flair—influenced, perhaps, by her life-style in recent years—and the dress looked far from staid. Her appearance and manner were the height of sensuality, though Ah-wenga couldn't be sure how such a result was achieved so effectively.

She captivated both Renno and Ja-gonh as before, and General Strong treated her with a gallantry that was almost exaggerated. Even Townsend Whiting, still looking out of place in his uniform of scarlet and gold, seemed conscious of every move Toshabe made and each word she spoke. Because of the contrary customs of the visitors, the Seneca prohibition on conversation during the meal was set aside.

Ghonkaba was self-conscious; his mother noted that he did not seem to take Toshabe's presence for granted. Acutely aware of her proximity, he followed every movement with his eyes and listened intently to her every word. He compared her to Beth, and Ah-wen-ga only hoped that he saw both for what they were.

To be sure, Beth had a lively wit, an inquiring mind, and a natural charm. At the moment, however, she had to take second place to Toshabe's fantastic appeal. And quite clearly she was thoroughly confused, to Ah-wen-ga's private delight.

It was apparent that even after accepting Whiting's proposal, she expected to receive Ghonkaba's silent adoration, to which she had become accustomed. That admiration was totally absent today. And, furthermore, Beth was astonished to realize she was shining less brightly than a half-breed, even one who seemed equally intelligent and—to all the men—more attractive and appealing.

Ah-wen-ga was amused to see Beth disconcerted and dismayed because she clearly had lost Ghonkaba as an admirer, even though she did not want him as a suitor.

Unaware of the subtle game being played around them, the men concentrated again on the military business that had brought them together.

"Because you must return now so that Colonel Whiting can be on his way to New York and other colonies," Renno told General Strong, "I will not ask you to remain here until the Council of the Iroquois can convene, as I have asked them to do. But when they come here, I will faithfully deliver all aspects of the message that you and he have brought to us. Meanwhile, you may rest assured that I will personally honor a long-standing pledge of allegiance to your cause and to the instructions of your leader in arms, who I understand is to be the valiant General Amherst. Our alliance with you remains firm and solid."

The general bowed, pleased that the Great Sachem was aware of the necessary timetable. To have stayed longer would represent a severe distortion of the time that he needed for his own work, to say nothing of the long mission that still faced William Pitt's special messenger.

Their conversation touched on the possible benefits of the English declaration of war on France. Renno could not see that it would make any substantial difference in the progress of the fighting. Whiting repeatedly pointed out to him that a previous British treaty with France had made it impossible for arms to be furnished to the Indian tribes. Renno, however, remained unconvinced.

General Strong was gratified upon learning that Ghonkaba intended to rejoin Colonel Washington's troops on the Virginia frontier, and as Renno had anticipated, he asked him to carry a letter informing the colonel of recent strategic developments and expectations.

As the time for Ghonkaba's departure drew nearer, incidental remarks made it evident to the visitors that he was to be accompanied in the early stages by Toshabe. This bewildered Beth, who knew nothing about her years of captivity or the freedom she newly had been granted. It appeared that she and Ghonkaba must be connected in some way, but Beth couldn't fathom their relationship.

Toshabe, realizing how much Ghonkaba's pride had been hurt by Beth's rejection, was delighted that, although he didn't even realize as much, he now was upsetting Beth in turn. To demonstrate how close an intimacy she'd had with Ghonkaba, Toshabe made a point of smiling at him frequently and warmly, and as they ate she emphasized her occasional comments by touching his hand or arm.

Ghonkaba remained unaware of these female subtleties, but his mother understood and approved. Even though he had enjoyed Toshabe's favors, she postponed any idea that he might someday take her as his bride. The relationship would have to develop naturally before it would become evident to Ghonkaba. Ahwen-ga could see, however, that her hotheaded and impulsive son might need a woman with Toshabe's qualities to keep him on a straight path.

It was impossible, however, to predict the shape of the future. The Seneca and other nations of the Iroquois League were now at war with France and the Indian nations allied with her. Anything could happen in the months and years ahead.

Chapter II

With Ghonkaba leading and Toshabe following quietly, they traveled without incident through the land of the Seneca and the adjoining realm of their brothers in the Iroquois League, the Mohawk. They journeyed through the area known to the English colonists as New York and into Pennsylvania.

Not wanting to cause Toshabe undue exertion, Ghonkaba set a leisurely pace, but she surprised him. At home in the wilderness and adept there, she easily kept up. Even so, he was traveling far more rapidly than when he was Beth's escort.

Little by little, he increased the pace, but Toshabe continued to encounter no problems and made no complaints. She was familiar with the principles of conserv-

26

ing strength, and she seemed as fresh at the end of a long day's grueling march as at the early morning start.

Always cheerful, she assumed a fair share of the burdens of wilderness travel. When Ghonkaba brought down game, she skinned and butchered the animal, obtained firewood, and cooked the meals. Invariably, she found time to locate edible roots, plants, and berries to augment the main course.

Having been intimate with Ghonkaba, she showed no false modesty now and bathed with him in the streams. When she washed her clothes, she washed his, too.

What Ghonkaba found most likable about her was her companionship. And she was so familiar with the forest that he found it unnecessary to instruct her in the basics of making their way. Toshabe knew enough to keep a sharp lookout for poisonous snakes and for other animals that might be harmful. She was silent on the trail, only making conversation when necessary. When she needed to speak to him, it was in a careful undertone.

She kept security as well as comfort in mind when she selected campsites; yet, when relaxing over a meal, she chatted pleasantly and helped to pass the time enjoyably.

Ghonkaba couldn't help comparing her to Beth as a traveling companion, although he realized that the circumstances in which each was exposed to the wilderness were quite different. Trained in the rigorous, unyielding school of Indians, Toshabe had lived in the wilderness during much of her life. Beth was a civilized, city creature who enjoyed outings but could not blend in with wilderness surroundings and feel completely at home.

When they were within the Pennsylvania area, Ghonkaba doubled his normal precautions. No longer

27

in lands controlled or influenced by the Iroquois League, they knew enemies were everywhere. The scalp of a senior warrior of the Seneca would be a great prize, and the braves of many nations would be delighted to enslave a squaw as attractive as Toshabe. She was as aware of the increased danger, although like Ghonkaba she did not mention it. She kept a closer watch for other travelers and often studied the underbrush for possible traces of passersby. On several occasions, Ghonkaba returned to their campsite to find her pressing an ear to the ground, listening for other humans.

It was Toshabe who alerted him to an impending crisis. They had halted near the crest of a high, wooded hill, so that Ghonkaba could survey the ground ahead, when suddenly she dropped to her hands and knees.

Ghonkaba turned and saw that she was studying the tall grass several feet away. Quickly he confirmed her suspicion: footprints had been made by either bare feet or by soft moccasins.

Ghonkaba placed an ear to the ground, listening intently, and she did the same. They communicated silently, in sign language, and disagreed: he believed four Indians were in the strange party, while Toshabe detected only three. For the moment, at least, the precise number in the unseen party was unimportant. In any event, they were outnumbered and must exercise the greatest possible caution.

Suddenly the footsteps grew louder, and Toshabe became alarmed. For whatever reason, the strangers were reversing themselves and coming in their direction. Perhaps they had discovered how close Ghonkaba and Toshabe were, and now sought to identify them and assess what danger they might represent.

Ghonkaba quickly studied the nearby terrain for a

favorable defensive position. He found what he was seeking—a huge, spreading maple tree with an abnormally large trunk. As he gestured toward it, Toshabe instantly understood his meaning. While he crouched low, using the trunk of the maple as a shield, she stretched out prone in the tall grass beside him, becoming virtually invisible.

By now they could hear approaching footsteps plainly, and Toshabe looked slightly sheepish as she signaled that indeed four, rather than three, were in the party.

The strangers were drawing nearer. They seemed to be coming from her side of the trunk, so she would see them first. A swift glimpse immediately identified them. With a forefinger, she drew a series of circles in the air.

Ghonkaba, comprehending at once, silently congratulated her for being so clever. The circles were a symbol for the Conestoga, a large warlike tribe that lived in the Pennsylvania hills and valued its independence, refusing to form alliances with anyone. Known for their harsh belligerence, the Conestoga would kill him if they could take him and Toshabe back to their town in triumph.

Grimly, he notched an arrow into his bow. At almost the same time, he felt a tug at his belt. Toshabe was trying to take hold of the handle of his tomahawk.

He knew she carried a knife, which would be useful only in hand-to-hand combat. Even so, she would not stand much of a chance in such a struggle with a male warrior. Though he had no idea whether she could use a tomahawk, he quickly decided to let her have the weapon. If she was skilled in its use, she would prove to be a valuable ally. If not, she was depriving them of half of his armament, and they would suffer the consequences.

He felt her draw the throwing ax but did not glance in her direction again; instead he devoted his attention to the approaching intruders.

All four Conestoga were armed with tomahawks, and two carried bows with quivers on their backs. Their armament was formidable. And judging from their care in walking, they suspected the presence of others in the vicinity and were taking no chances.

Intending to use his advantage of surprise to the fullest, Ghonkaba drew the bow taut. As soon as a husky warrior emerged into the open beyond the trunk of a maple, he let fly. In almost the same motion, he reached over his shoulder for another arrow.

His aim was true; the shaft of his arrow had lodged deep in the base of the throat of the brave, who collapsed onto the ground. Now he must strike swiftly before the other Conestoga could scatter and fight back.

Ghonkaba fired a second arrow, and again his aim was accurate. A second brave sank slowly into the grass.

To Ghonkaba's astonishment, Toshabe let fly with his tomahawk, and the keenly honed edge struck a third brave directly beneath one eye, killing him instantly. She leaped to her feet and, crouching low, ran forward, intending to retrieve the tomahawk. She was breaking a cardinal principle of Indian warfare, that of always maintaining maximum concealment. But it was too late for Ghonkaba to warn her. Again, smoothly notching an arrow into his bow, he caught a glimpse of the fourth Conestoga, and unable to take careful aim at him, let fly quickly. Under the circumstances, his aim once more was remarkable. The brave fell, wounded but still alive.

Too late, Toshabe recognized her error, and she did the only thing possible. Snatching up Ghonkaba's fallen tomahawk and gripping it by the handle, she ran to the wounded Conestoga, who was struggling to draw a knife in order to protect himself. He never had a chance. Coolly, she smashed the cutting edge of the tomahawk into his forehead.

Even then her poise did not desert her. Drawing her knife, she scalped her victim, and as Ghonkaba came up beside her she offered him the scalp. "It was your arrow," she said, "that wounded him and made it possible for me to dispose of him. The scalp is yours."

Ghonkaba was filled with admiration. She was a seductive mistress, a perfect wilderness companion, and a marvelous ally in battle. Never had he known such a woman. "Keep the scalp," he told her. "Take all of them. You have earned them."

Together they scalped the other Conestoga, and Toshabe, displaying no squeamishness, placed the scalps in her belt, then fell behind Ghonkaba as he pressed forward again through the forest.

Neither Beth Strong nor Townsend Whiting wanted an elaborate wedding. Both thought that any display of wealth was very much out of place, since Massachusetts had just gone to war with France. Marriage by an Anglican priest in a private ceremony with half a dozen of Beth's immediate relatives in attendance would have satisfied them. But circumstances forced them to enlarge the number of guests.

General Strong felt he must invite his subordinate commanders and staff members of the militia, and, of course, with them, their wives and children. This forced Colonel Whiting to ask his own military colleagues and their wives. Beth now thought she was required to invite some of her old friends and schoolmates who would be hurt if excluded from a gathering of the sort that was taking shape. Then it was the governor-general of Massachusetts who had to be added, and the same was true of the Strongs' old friend, Sam Adams, the prominent Boston journalist. His cousin, John Adams, a distinguished attorney from nearby Quincy, also had a long-standing friendship with the general; so he, too, had to be included.

Consequently, the Anglican church was filled when Beth, in traditional white, came down the aisle escorted by her father.

Although the wedding had turned into the social event of the year, General Strong made certain that the reception was in keeping with the somber times. The guests adjourned to the Strong house on Beacon Hill, where the modest refreshments included home-baked cakes and cookies, wine from the vineyards of New York Colony, and locally brewed ale and beer.

At the height of the reception the bride and groom slipped away. Colonel Whiting managed their disappearance with consummate skill. Nobody knew where they had gone, but the fact was that they rode to a cabin owned by Beth's father in the deep woods about fifty miles northwest of Boston. There they spent ten days keeping house, hunting for game, and fishing in nearby streams, and then cooking their meals.

They had the time to make interesting discoveries about each other. Beth learned that her husband was far subtler, quicker of mind, and more incisive than she had realized.

Townsend found that his bride was truly a New World product, more direct, blunt, and forthright than any English girl he had known. Perhaps typical of a woman who had grown up on the frontier, she saw every problem from a practical point of view, and was not concerned with subtleties in expressing her thoughts.

One evening, as they sat drinking their after-supper tea at the fireplace, he asked her, intending merely to tease her gently, whether she was really satisfied or would prefer to be married to Ghonkaba.

Beth saw no humor in the question. "I know that some colonial women have married Indians and have led very happy, successful lives. Ghonkaba's grandmother, Betsy, was a member of a prominent Virginia family, and yet she suffered no hardships when she married Renno. From all I've gathered, they got along beautifully, and each was at home in the other's environment. But that couldn't have worked for me; I am very sure."

His teasing forgotten, Townsend was interested in her answer. "How so?" he now wanted to know.

"For one thing," she replied, "I could never feel really at home living in a Seneca village. I'd always feel like an outsider. I marvel at a woman like Deborah Jenkins. As the widow of a Springfield clergyman, she married El-i-chi, Renno's brother. For all practical purposes, she's a complete Indian squaw. She lives and works as one of them, and has adapted totally to their way of life. I couldn't do that. I like the comforts and cultural advantage of civilization too much."

"Are you saying," Townsend demanded, "that such women as Ghonkaba's grandmother and Deborah are simpler than you and demand less out of life?"

She shook her head vehemently. "On the contrary," she replied. "I suspect that they're far more sophisticated than I am and have far deeper characters. They are able to find happiness on a level where I could not achieve it."

"Why can they succeed where you can't?"

33

She smiled at her husband. "There's nothing very mysterious or complex about the answer to that. They're sufficiently in love with their husbands to put up with differences in the way of life that they've known, the making of sacrifices in order to live on a more primitive level. The reason they can do it so easily is because their love for their husbands is genuine. I had no such love for Ghonkaba. I thought he was a fascinating individual, but I didn't care for him enough to make such deep sacrifices for the rest of my days."

The colonel sipped his tea. "I see. You're saying that, for Ghonkaba to enter into a successful marriage, he needs to take an Indian girl as his squaw."

"No, that's where the situation becomes rather cloudy. He's far more sophisticated and worldly than the typical Indian brave. Remember, he can read and write English, as well as French. He can wear English clothes, he's familiar with the customs and manners of colonial society, and if he were in Boston at this moment, he could be accepted in a twinkling as a member of Boston society. So he needs a wife who's able to move back and forth between the world of the Indians and that of the settlers. It won't be at all easy for Toshabe, and I think that Ghonkaba may be making a serious mistake."

Townsend raised an eyebrow but made no comment.

"Toshabe, with whom he seems to be becoming involved, is a handsome young woman—no question about that. But she's rather flashy looking, and in my opinion seems rather cheap. I don't think she's at all suitable for him."

Townsend Whiting wondered idly whether his wife was jealous. That thought seemed to make no sense, and he promptly put it out of his very masculine mind.

* * *

The disguised bird calls and war drums of sentries warned the warriors of the Erie town that a senior brave of the Seneca was nearby in their territory, accompanied by a woman of the Erie. Some of the sentinels recognized and identified Toshabe. She previously had been given up for dead, and her friends now were startled and uncertain.

It was significant that the Seneca, in addition to his war paint of yellow and green, wore a strip of pure white from the center of his forehead to the tip of his nose. He wore similar markings on each arm, on his torso, and on his back. These were assurances that he was coming under a sign of truce. Although his people were their sworn enemies, he bore the Erie no ill will; his mission was a peaceful one. No Erie warrior would be permitted to harm him. He was now under the protection of the manitous of the Erie as well as those of his own tribe. Any Erie brave who violated this code would pay with his life at the hands of his comrades.

The Erie high command was perplexed by Toshabe's impending arrival, and before the visitors reached the town, the sachem called a meeting of his council.

"I find it odd, my brothers," the sachem said, "that a woman we gave up as dead now comes back to us under escort of a Seneca. Is there any among you who knows this man?"

Ludona, the chief warrior of the town, grunted. "The sentries report that the Seneca warrior is pale-skinned. This must mean that he is a descendant of Renno, the Great Sachem of the Iroquois. He is young, so he must be Ghonkaba, son of Ja-gonh."

A moment of uncomfortable silence followed.

"It is very strange that the leaders of the Seneca nation should concern themselves with the welfare of a female Erie captive," Ludona continued, and received the agreement of all present.

"This is especially true," a medicine man added, "when one considers that the warriors of the Seneca surely used the girl as they saw fit."

Everyone seemed to be awaiting Ludona's reaction, particularly as he had a notoriously explosive temper. But he remained outwardly as calm as a self-disciplined senior warrior should.

"There was a time, it is true, when Ludona of the Erie planned to take Toshabe as his squaw," he conceded. "He was prevented from doing this when the Seneca defeated the Erie and a number of our women were captured, Toshabe among them. Since that time, it must be assumed, many of the Seneca have used her for their pleasure. I question that even Toshabe could add up the number. But this is of no matter to Ludona. What Ludona would have done in the times of past moons, he will not do now." A sly, tight smile touched his lips. "Perhaps, if the squaw, Toshabe, is being returned to her people, another use can be found for her."

The sachem, in accord with this idea, proceeded to lay out a strategic plan. "First," he said, "we will find out why Toshabe is being returned to the Erie. Then we will learn why she is being escorted by a member of the greatest of Seneca families. We will keep our plans to ourselves. We are not obliged to repeat them to any outsider. Remember, the wisest of braves is the most silent of braves. He listens always, but never speaks his own thoughts."

So when Ghonkaba and Toshabe came within sight of the town palisade, a delegation of leading Erie came out to greet them. The atmosphere was cool, as was natural enough, since their nations were enemies of long-standing, but certain formalities had to be observed. Ghonkaba laid his bow, quiver of arrows, and tomahawk on the ground as a sign of his peaceful intentions; then Ludona did the same. As soon as this token of amity was carried out, both men reclaimed their weapons.

Escorted into the town, Ghonkaba and Toshabe were taken to a hut for their lodging. The young Seneca quietly demurred. "Toshabe," he explained, "is neither the squaw nor the woman of Ghonkaba of the Seneca."

Toshabe then was led to another hut as the Erie masked their surprise. Their greeting to her astonished Ghonkaba by its coolness. A Seneca returning under similar circumstances would have received an unrestrained welcome.

Several unmarried women approached her, halted about ten feet away, and called to her by name. But they made no attempt to speak to her otherwise, and none came closer. Some other young women, all of them now squaws, extended even more formal greetings, but they seemed to have nothing else to say, and they withdrew as soon as they had called her name and raised a hand in a stiff greeting.

Most significant to her was Ludona's behavior when, as a member of the official greeting party, he, like the others, raised an extended arm. His face was devoid of expression, and even when he looked directly at her his eyes showed no recognition. In greeting, he only muttered something under his breath that she could not understand.

Ghonkaba, who had no idea that Ludona and Toshabe had been betrothed, was not aware of any significance in the incident, but no nuance escaped Toshabe. She was being told by her people that they

37

were aware she had been used as a prostitute, and therefore was not to be welcomed with her rights and privileges restored. Those whom she had known, both men and women, were treating her with studied indifference.

Ludona's approach was even more unkind. He was making it plain that he wanted nothing to do with her. In his anger and jealousy he behaved as though her fate had been her own fault.

Now led with Toshabe to the hut of the sachem, Ghonkaba spoke briefly to him and his military, religious, and civilian advisers.

Toshabe's sensitivity, quick thinking, and tact, he told them, had prevented an incident that would have proved embarrassing to the Great Sachem of the Iroquois and his family. As a result, the Great Sachem granted her unconditional freedom and assigned his grandson to escort her back to her own people. His recounting, in an impersonal, austere manner, discouraged questions.

Calling upon an unsuspected talent for diplomacy, Ghonkaba added his own regret over the enmity between his people and the Erie because he regarded Toshabe as a friend. Even though the tribes were aligned on opposite sides in the war between Great Britain and France, he would always consider her so.

Deeply moved, Toshabe said a few words in response.

Because Ghonkaba long had been her good and trusted friend, she had intervened for his sake alone in the matter that won his grandfather's gratitude. In the years ahead, though their paths probably would never cross again, she would always have a special place in her heart for her comrade, Ghonkaba.

Ghonkaba ended the brief ceremony on a surprise

note. Pointing to the four scalps on Toshabe's belt, he declared that even though she was a mere squaw, her association with the Seneca had made her the equal of the warriors of any nation. She had earned those scalps, and perhaps had just started a career as a warrior.

Uncertain whether they should laugh or be angered, the Erie instead adjourned for a meal at the sachem's private lodge, taking the newcomers with them.

Ghonkaba was astonished to notice that several bottles of French wine were served. As allies of the Erie, the French must have taken leave of their senses. None of the invaders from Europe ever thought of providing alcoholic beverages to Indians, who were unable to tolerate alcohol well and became easily intoxicated. In trying to attract allies by giving them wine, the French were certainly doing them no favors. Nations that accepted such gifts would suffer, as would those making the gifts.

Bottles were passed from hand to hand. Only Ghonkaba and Toshabe refrained from drinking. The effectiveness of the once-powerful Erie would soon be greatly reduced, Ghonkaba thought. They would be fair game for any tribe that chose to challenge them in battle.

As night fell, the party ended abruptly, and the various individuals retired to their own lodges and huts. Ghonkaba, who was to sleep in a small building adjacent to that occupied by Toshabe, bade her and the Erie escort good night and lowered the animal skin flap over the door. He had no doubt that the courtesies being extended to him would be strictly kept, and he would be safe. An honorable nation, the Erie were unlikely to break a sacred truce, for that could cause untold difficulties with their gods and manitous.

Unable to sleep, Ghonkaba was bewildered. Since he was not nervous and apprehensive, he couldn't imagine what was ailing him. Finally the reason dawned on him: he wanted Toshabe. After tonight they would be separated, perhaps for all time, and he wanted to make love to her once more.

He could easily go to her hut, and he was sure she wouldn't turn him away. But he would be repaying her poorly for her friendship. In effect, she would be admitting to the Erie that she was still a woman of the Seneca, available to any warrior of that land who beckoned. Never again would she be able to hold up her head among her own people. He realized that he would do her a terrible disservice if he went to her now. He conquered his impulse and did not leave the hut. Ultimately he slept and the yearning passed.

When the very first rays of light appeared in the sky above the Pennsylvania hills, Ghonkaba was wide awake. He freshened his war paint and prepared to begin his journey to Virginia.

As he let himself out of the hut, intending to begin his journey immediately, the flap of the adjoining hut was raised. Toshabe, standing in the half dark, beckoned to him. Feeling that he was tempting fate, he nevertheless went to her. To his surprise, she had cooked a meal in the pit directly below the smoke hole in her ceiling. She had obtained two large, succulent fish and had cooked them on a willow stick. In the coals were several small sweet potatoes.

"I couldn't allow you to go off into the wilderness without a good meal," she told him.

Ghonkaba devoured the food gratefully. "I'm in your debt for this additional favor you have done me," he said, "but I'm afraid it will do you no good with the Erie. They're certain to know that I came here for a meal before I left, and they'll assume we spent the night together."

Toshabe's laugh was too harsh to be natural. "Those who wish to make such an assumption are certainly free to do so, aren't they? They may think what they please."

"That is not fair," Ghonkaba said firmly. "Also, I overheard remarks yesterday that caused me to wonder whether your people are in fact like the Ottawa. When a woman of their nation has been a captive in another land, she is regarded as tainted and never is accepted fully into her nation again. Can it be that this is true of the Erie?"

Toshabe had faced this problem from the moment that she heard Renno's words that set her free. But she felt she could not ask any Seneca—much less Ghonkaba, of all people—to intervene. Knowing Ghonkaba so well, she realized that he would insist that she accompany him away from the town of the Erie. She believed, too, that her people would refuse, and that he then would fight to free her, engaging in combat against overwhelming odds.

"The stories you have heard are wildly exaggerated," she responded evasively. "As you can see with your own eyes, I have not been mistreated here, and have been given a comfortable house in which to live. What more could I possibly ask?"

He could see truth in what she was telling him and felt somewhat reassured.

"You and I," Toshabe continued, "have not been ordinary lovers or casual friends. I feel sure the manitous would not wish us to part as strangers."

"I cannot argue with the words of Toshabe," Ghonkaba said. "I just do not want to cause her any problems with her own people."

"I give you my word," she assured him, "that your coming here to eat breakfast will not add to any problems I may have." And that, she thought, was the truth. Any difficulties she might encounter already had been compounded by the past, and over this she had no control whatsoever.

He found the fish and sweet potatoes delicious, and thought, as he had on the trail from the land of the Seneca, that it was pleasing to know that she was such an accomplished cook.

"I must leave now," he said, rising and hooking his bow and quiver of arrows over his shoulder. "I must put this town behind me before the Erie decide that my truce has worn out its welcome."

For the first time, Toshabe weakened. "Shall we meet again, do you suppose?" she asked hesitantly.

He stared long and hard at her face, as though trying to memorize her features. "I trust the manitous in all things," he said. "They have been good to me. If it is right, if they wish us to meet again, you may be sure that our paths will cross." He took a step closer to her. "I feel in my heart that it is right," he told her. Somewhat surprised by his own words, he was even less prepared for the impulsiveness with which he reached for her, took her into his arms, and kissed her repeatedly.

Toshabe had not planned such an emotional parting, but she, too, gave in to the sentiment of the moment and clung to him.

As they parted, both were breathless. No more was to be said without creating a scene, so Ghonkaba turned on his heel and left the hut in the early light of dawn.

Toshabe did not follow him to the door. Such a gesture would be a sign of weakness, and she knew that no Seneca woman would ever indulge in such emotion. During her years among the Seneca, she had come to think like one, especially when dealing with a warrior like Ghonkaba. That she herself was part Erie and part French was immaterial.

Unseen by either Toshabe or Ghonkaba, Ludona watched his departure from a safe vantage point in his own hut. He assumed that they had been intimate, and that she felt a continuing loyalty to him. So it was well that Ghonkaba was leaving. If he returned, it would almost surely be without the white paint that enabled him to come and go at will. He would instead be treated strictly as an enemy.

In any event, by then he would be too late to intervene on Toshabe's behalf. Ludona had determined what he regarded as a perfect use for her. Among its benefits would be solidifying the relationship between the Erie and the French, and also increasing his own prestige in Quebec, capital of New France. Waiting until he was certain that Ghonkaba was well on his way into the wilderness beyond the town, Ludona then walked quietly to Toshabe's hut. Entering abruptly and unexpectedly, he sniffed the air, then turned to her. "Ah," he said, "you cooked breakfast for the Seneca before he departed. I trust he enjoyed the taste of fish."

Toshabe, severely startled, recovered her wits quickly. "Yes," she acknowledged calmly. "He ate his entire breakfast."

Ludona looked at her for a full minute, his eyes narrowing to glittering slits. "The time is past," he said, "when you would have become the squaw of Ludona. Your body has been used by too many warriors of the Seneca, and you are unclean."

43

"I have no wish to become the squaw of Ludona," she retorted.

Her tranquil self-assurance infuriated him, and he glowered. "If you think that you'll marry another brave of the Erie, you are mistaken. Every unmarried warrior in the nation feels as I do. You have ruined your chances for a useful life with the Erie."

Toshabe faced him defiantly. "You sound," she told him, "as though I am to blame for what happened to me. Remember how the warriors of the Erie were defeated by the Seneca and fled from the field. The braves of the Erie made it possible for the Seneca to make me their prisoner and to take me off to their land. I was a lone woman there, helpless and afraid. What could I do when demands were made upon me? If I had refused them, I would have suffered a blow with a tomahawk that would have sent me without delay to the land of my ancestors. The braves of the Erie are to be blamed for all that I suffered. Now you would turn the tables and claim that I was responsible for my own fate. But I refuse to accept that cruel and unfair judgment."

Without warning, he lashed out, striking her such a vicious blow across the face that she staggered to the hard dirt floor.

Tempted to reach beneath her doeskin skirt for her knife, Toshabe refrained, knowing that Ludona was far stronger and more agile and, she suspected, might welcome her attack as an excuse to kill her. In her bewilderment she could think only of impending death.

Ludona, however, had other ideas. Seizing a pole ordinarily used to hold open the hut's door of animal skins, he used his tomahawk to drive it into the ground as a stake. He then produced a length of thin, strong rawhide, and before Toshabe knew what was happening, he had secured her left wrist and her right ankle to the stake. She was hobbled, a prisoner who could neither rise nor run away. Try as she might, she was unable to free herself.

"What is the meaning of this outrage?" she demanded.

A thin, half smile creased Ludona's lips. "Toshabe," he said, "has no use in the land of the Erie. She is wasted here. No warrior will want to be her husband, and no squaw will consent to use her as a house slave. But that does not mean that she is lacking in usefulness in other places. Quite the contrary."

She caught her breath, her uneasiness increasing.

"In Quebec," he went on, "soldiers from France are gathering by the thousands for the campaign against the English and their colonies. They are joined by French woodsmen and trappers and farmers, and by their Indian allies of many nations—not only the Erie, but also the Huron, the Ottawa, the Micmac, and the mighty Algonquian. So Quebec needs experienced women to entertain the troops. They need Indian women and French women alike. Toshabe is extraordinary and unique. When she dresses as an Indian, she passes as an Indian. Dressed as a French woman, she also could pass. She not only will earn me a very high price, but will win me the friendship of influential men in New France."

Toshabe was horrified. "You intend to sell me into slavery as a prostitute?" she demanded, her voice trembling.

"Of course." Ludona struck a boastful stance. "You are a juicy wench, as anyone can tell by the way all men stare at you and desire you. You are experienced in ways of pleasing them, and you'll be doing what you know best. You'll be serving me almost as well as if you had become my squaw."

She tried in vain to struggle to her feet, and started to protest.

Ludona kicked her, knocking her further off balance, and then viciously kicked her once more, this time in the ribs.

"You will speak when I give you permission to speak," he ordered. "And you will do exactly as I tell you at all times. You are to be the source of a considerable fortune to me, and I intend to take full advantage of your return. Your friend, the Seneca, is gone, and you have no one left on whom to depend. So bow your head; accept the fate that the manitous decree for you. And be grateful that I am allowing you to remain alive."

Chapter III

Assigned to duty on the wilderness frontier that extended for hundreds of miles through the Appalachian Mountains, the men of the Virginia militia were in awe of their commanding officer.

Colonel George Washington wore the formal uniform of his rank, a blue and buff coat with gold epaulets on the shoulders, white breeches, and well-shined black boots. Even the feather on his bicorne hat invariably was cocked at the right angle. Always immaculate, at a moment's notice he could have led his regiment on an inspection by the governor of Virginia.

As any newcomer to the regiment quickly learned, Colonel Washington was unique. Younger than many who served in his command, he was a curious mixture

47

of aloofness and camaraderie. He kept his distance from his men, never becoming unduly familiar with them. Yet he asked nothing of them that he was unwilling to undertake himself, and consequently he won their complete loyalty. Ranking officers of the British Army who came in contact with him were greatly impressed, finding him competent to be one of their number. Altogether, his reputation was becoming one of which legends are made. Some parts of it almost defied belief, but among the troops no one was willing to approach the rather austere officer to seek authentication of some of the accounts.

Now Colonel Washington sat on a tree stump before a cooking fire at his bivouac, and with impeccable table manners ate a venison steak, using the folding knife and fork that he always carried in the field.

His guest could have used eating utensils, too, but preferred to pick up his meat with his fingers before gnawing at it. Ghonkaba knew from experience that Washington would pay little attention to such small matters and certainly would not judge a man by his habits.

Devoting his attention completely to the visitor, Washington asked him question after question. He had read with interest General Strong's letter but remained curious about several matters.

"All the Iroquois nations will be formally joining forces with the mother country and the colonies?"

"Yes, sir," Ghonkaba replied. "Their stand is a foregone conclusion. My grandfather would not tolerate anything other than complete and unstinting association with the British and the colonies."

"On the other hand," Washington said, "I suppose it's true that the Erie have gone over to the French side."

"They have, Colonel," Ghonkaba told him, "and not because they have any affection for the French. Their hatred of the Seneca is so great that they instinctively join forces with our enemies."

"More's the pity for them. The Huron and Ottawa and Algonquian certainly know better, having suffered severe defeats in the campaigns in which they have been allies of the French. But I suppose they can't resist the lure of weapons and blankets and other gifts."

"Firearms are a very strong lure, Colonel," Ghonkaba reminded him, "particularly for the warriors of tribes that have never had any. I've learned to appreciate my grandfather's attitude. He believes in training our junior warriors in the use of the rifle and the pistol. But when they go into battle, he vastly prefers that they rely on our traditional arms. And I believe he's right."

Washington rubbed his long chin in order to conceal a broad smile. "Surely you don't think that the Indian bow and arrow is as effective a weapon as a long rifle!"

"That all depends," Ghonkaba replied seriously, "on the uses to which either of them may be put. Depending on the circumstances, they're both very effective weapons, and that's the point of my grandfather's whole attitude. For example, a raid on an enemy outpost is far more effective when only bows and arrows are used. A company of scouts is much better off when they are using a silent weapon."

"I get your point, and I must say I'm compelled to agree with your grandfather. In fact, anyone who fails to study his tactics should give up any idea of a military career."

After they finished their steaks, the colonel's orderly brought two mugs of hot tea, sweetened with honey.

Tea was one beverage of civilization that Ghonkaba could really enjoy.

"Our cause begins to look brighter from several aspects," Washington told him. "We've had an excellent response to recruiting in Virginia, and I understand that General Strong in Massachusetts and General Philip Schuyler in New York are experiencing equally good results."

"There's no lack of recruits, Colonel, but you will need a considerable period of time to train them."

"True enough," Washington admitted cheerfully, "but we're in a unique position. This is the first time we've enjoyed a decided advantage over the French—thanks to the farsighted wisdom of William Pitt."

Ghonkaba had heard of some such developments from General Strong's accounts, but he was content to hear Washington's own view of military developments.

"Pitt decided that the army was too old, too conservative, and too confounded tired. So he retired at least twenty-five generals, and promoted younger, more aggressive men with modern ideas into their places. And surely you've heard that Jeffrey Amherst, our commander in chief for this entire continent, has captured the great fortress of Louisburg on Cape Breton Island."

Ghonkaba chuckled. "Yes, Colonel," he acknowledged. "That news did make its way into the remote hinterlands where the Iroquois dwell. I marvel at General Amherst's accomplishment."

"What you very possibly haven't heard," Washington went on, "is that Major General James Wolfe—the youngest general in the entire army—who served as Amherst's deputy, distinguished himself in combat so greatly during the battle that he's to be given an independent command."

50

"That's good news," Ghonkaba exclaimed enthusiastically. It was exciting to hear of competent commanders coming to the fore.

"I've just received dispatches," Washington now told him, "informing me that Fort Frontenac on Lake Ontario has been captured from the French. And perhaps most important of all, a column under General Forbes has taken Fort Duquesne."

Remembering the ignominious retreat from Duquesne the previous year, Ghonkaba was overjoyed. "That's wonderful, Colonel!"

"It's even better than you realize, Ghonkaba. The French destroyed their fort when they retreated. Forbes's men have constructed a brand-new fort at the forks of the Ohio. They're calling it Fort Pitt, and it's as impressive a bastion as ever has been built."

"Then the war is virtually ended!"

"Unfortunately, the contrary is true," Washington told him regretfully.

"But the British regulars and colonial troops greatly outnumber the French. And surely we Iroquois are far stronger than the Indian allies of the French."

"All of what you say is quite true," Washington conceded, "but I gather that Amherst realizes the enormous task that still awaits him. The French are badly outnumbered in manpower, it's true. But they now have a much smaller realm than they once did, one more easily defended in view of their limited manpower and fleet. Let me give you an example of what I mean. The French are certain to launch any number of surprise assaults on us in various colonies. It's inevitable."

"I agree that's a safe assumption, Colonel," Ghonkaba replied.

"I have four hundred men in my command," Washington said flatly. "That's all I have. I can't obtain one more infantryman. But I have a westward frontier seven hundred miles long that must be patrolled against incursions of Indians who are urged on by the French. My four hundred men bear complete responsibility for keeping watch. Doesn't it stand to reason that four hundred men simply cannot patrol an area seven hundred miles long? So attacks are certain to come. We're going to have towns burned and looted and people kidnapped and killed and scalped. I see no way it can be avoided."

Ghonkaba's grimace revealed his impatience and frustration.

"Naturally," Washington now said, changing his approach, "I welcome your return, to say the least. You'll take up your former duties as a scout, responsible only to me. I want you to go where you please and to set your own rules. But even you must expect to be limited in what you can hope to accomplish, just as I'm limited."

"Basically, the French are being forced to retreat into Canada and make a stand there. Am I right, Colonel?"

"Yes. General Montcalm's primary stand now becomes a defensive one. Quebec is a natural fortress, and we have to travel a great distance in order to even reach it. If he could inflict a severe enough punishment on us at the gates of Quebec, the whole tide of war could be turned once again in his favor. His numbers are limited, but he needs no more than he has to defend the territory that he's compelled to hold. He'll be fighting on his own ground, and I'd say that he stands a very good chance of succeeding."

Listening carefully, Ghonkaba realized that Washington was as able a commander as some of the leaders whom he was praising. His analyses were so sharply pointed, so succinct, that it was possible to learn more about the art of warfare from one of these discussions than in actual combat.

Shaking hands and reminding Ghonkaba that he was to report to no one else, Washington sent him to join the special unit of scouts. This was a small, elite group of men who spurned rank and accepted no authority other than Washington's. Living and working together for more than a year, they had formed a close association, forged in war and in the trials that had beset them. Ghonkaba briefly had been a member of the band, and the four scouts, still eating their supper, greeted him with riotous war whoops. His short period of duty with them had convinced them of his skills and thorough competence.

"It's the white Indian!" shouted Muller, the tanner from Prussia, who could travel day and night in silence, without rest.

Ryan, from County Cork, who loved nothing better than a brawl or a free-for-all fight, was on his feet instantly and embraced the young Seneca in a bear hug. "I was giving odds that you were dead by now, Indian," he shouted. "You're too ugly for your luck to hold."

Ryan's partner, Ginsberg, who had learned every trick of dirty fighting in the slums of London, slapped Ghonkaba on the back and pulled his scalp lock, indignities that would not have been tolerated anywhere else. "Have you been in jail, you rascal?" he demanded. "What crimes have you committed now?"

MacDavid, who spoke with such a thick brogue that it was impossible for a stranger to understand him, punched Ghonkaba playfully in the stomach. His blows were hard enough to rock an ordinary person. "Och!" he cried. "Ye be a sight for sore eyes, lad."

Surrounding him, the quartet carted him off to their own bivouac area, where Ryan produced a bottle of Dutch gin.

"I thank you kindly," Ghonkaba told him, "but none of that is for me. I have work to do tomorrow."

"So have I," Muller said, and pushed the bottle away.

Ginsberg made a wry face. "I never take medicinals unless I'm ill, and I'd have to be mighty ill to stomach this stuff."

Ryan shrugged, took a swallow from the bottle, and passed it to MacDavid, who did the same.

The quartet was unchanged, Ghonkaba decided. Muller and Ginsberg were still abstemious, while Ryan and MacDavid never showed that their effectiveness was impaired by the copious amount of liquor they consumed. He sat down with them and answered their questions. The Seneca and other nations of the Iroquois were becoming the official allies of the British and their colonies, he told them. In turn, they revealed their optimism that France could be defeated. This was a startling development in itself; when he had last seen them, they had been in despair and had thought it probable that the cause of freedom was lost.

"Where have you been scouting?" Ghonkaba wanted to know.

The others exchanged glances. "If the truth be known," Ginsberg said sourly, "we been skulking around the foothills cooling our heels and wasting our time."

"But now that you've joined us," Muller added, "we can expand our operation once again. We can expect

54

to travel farther in search of the enemy. Almost the whole of the frontier can belong to us now!"

The comrades, all experienced in the ways of the wilderness, were so excited by the prospect of working together that they were awake long before dawn. By the time the first streaks of daylight smeared the dark sky, they were on the march.

That same morning the colonel's orderly passed along welcome news when he brought George Washington's breakfast to his bivouac area. "I reckon you know, sir," he said, "that Ghonkaba has teamed up with his old friends. They left camp before dawn, looking for trouble."

Washington smiled benignly. "You can be sure they'll find it, Corporal," he said. "Things have been quiet in our regimental sector of late, almost too quiet. But with Ghonkaba here to keep them on their toes, we're about to see renewed vigor and action again!"

The colonel proved to be an accurate prophet. By shortly after noon of that day, Ghonkaba and MacDavid captured a lone warrior of the Miami, a tribe ordinarily found in the Ohio country to the west. Returning to camp with him, they turned him over to Ryan and Ginsberg, who had effective methods of persuading a reluctant captive to speak freely.

Before they were through with him, the Miami revealed that the French high command, strained for adequate manpower, nevertheless was intending to send a number of patrols into the Virginia sector to raid towns and villages, burn crops, and kill settlers.

Taken back to headquarters, the captive repeated his story to Washington, who took precautionary measures to frustrate the French plan. Within twenty-four hours of his arrival, Ghonkaba had made his influence effectively felt.

When foes were encountered on later scouting forays in the forest, Ghonkaba and MacDavid resorted to a shrill, high-pitched bird call. This summons quickly brought Muller, Ryan, and Ginsberg. By far the best riflemen of the group, they were acknowledged to be expert shots without compare, and ordinarily they needed little time and trouble to wipe out whatever pocket of resistance their companions had uncovered.

Ghonkaba pointed out, however, sometimes a far more useful purpose was served if a foe lived than if he were killed. Only rarely did a French soldier venture into Virginia-held territory, but Indian allies of the French far more frequently scouted out the enemy region.

Europeans and North American colonials had a long tradition of keeping silent about military dispositions, and trying to reveal no information to the enemy.

As Ghonkaba made clear to his companions, the Indian nations knew no such tradition. On the contrary, a warrior was expected to talk freely when captured. If possible, he was to give false and misleading information. Therefore, the trick was to encourage a captive to speak freely and then try to trap him in contradictory stories.

All five comrades proved to be masters at the art of obtaining highly useful information, and Colonel Washington repeatedly stated that he considered them the most valuable men in his regiment.

The march north seemed endless. Ludona and his three Erie companions took care to avoid the lands of the Iroquois, so instead of going north to Lake Ontario and then eastward along the St. Lawrence River once they reached Montreal, they headed toward New England and later went in a relatively straight northward line toward Quebec.

Toshabe suffered constant degradation on the long march because of the treatment she received. Her hands were loosely bound at all times, and one end of a leather leash was looped around her neck. The other end remained firmly in Ludona's possession.

Aside from the humiliation, however, she was surprisingly well treated. She rode horseback, as did the Erie warriors, and Ludona refrained from ordering her to engage in any chores. She was not required to cook meals or build fires or clean up the camp area.

Similarly, the braves made no advances to her and went out of their way to avoid possible intimacies. This, she knew, was Ludona's doing, because one day the youngest of the warriors spoke in a friendly fashion to her and afterward she heard him receiving a tongue-lashing.

Gradually the realization dawned on her that he was being neither considerate nor kind. He was taking her to Quebec for a specific purpose, and if she was in good physical condition she would fetch him a far higher price than if she was marred by mistreatment.

Weary, disheartened, and helpless, she lost count of the number of days that they spent in the wilderness. At last they came to the south bank of the great St. Lawrence, and looking across toward the north shore, she recognized Quebec, which she had not seen since she was a child.

Perched high on a steep cliff at the river's edge stood the Citadel, the great stone fortress. It was considered even more impregnable than Louisburg, which Jeffrey Amherst had finally captured. Behind the fort stood the barracks and other buildings of the military complex that gave France a foothold in the New World.

Below the Citadel were the civilian town's narrow, twisting lanes and alleys that ran all the way down to the river's edge. Here lived those who served the military garrison, and here, too, was centered France's fur trade—heart and soul of the country's commerce. Half a dozen large schooners and barks rode at anchor in the river, all waiting to carry furs and lumber to France. Also present were several warships of the mightiest French fleet ever assembled in the New World.

Toshabe was unfamiliar with the types of warships commonly seen on the high seas, but she recognized the differences between the mighty ships of the line, the frigates, the swift sloops of war, and the cumbersome bomb ketches.

While she gazed across the river at a scene reviving memories of her childhood, Ludona busied himself at her side and then tugged at her leash, drawing her back into the woods.

He handed her an abbreviated skirt such as the one she had worn as a captive of the Seneca, and laughed unpleasantly at her expression of distaste, then gave her a container of berry stain and another of black soot. "Prepare yourself just as you did when you were a Seneca concubine," he instructed. "I want you to make the best possible impression on your new masters in Quebec."

She hesitated, feeling so ill that she doubted she could go through with his scheme.

Ludona grasped her wrist, twisted her arm behind her back, and produced a sharp, pointed knife that he held to her throat. "I haven't brought you all this distance to be thwarted at the last minute," he declared. "Do as you're told, or I'll slit your throat from ear to ear. Expect no compassion because you once meant something to me. All you mean now is the best price I can possibly get for you." He tugged her arm upward painfully by way of emphasis, then pricked her throat with the tip of the knife so that she knew that he had cut her and drawn blood.

Toshabe capitulated because she had no choice. She stepped into the skirt that she hated, loosened her hair so it would hang freely, and after applying a rim of soot to her eyes, dabbed berry juice on her lips, cheeks, earlobes, and nipples.

Ludona inspected her carefully. "I can see why you were popular with the Seneca," he said. "I could almost take you myself." Callously, he flung her a cape to cover her nearly naked body.

They approached a ferry landing, where Ludona's effort to pay was rebuffed; he was told that free transport for Indians was the policy. The ferry carried them a mile across the swiftly moving waters of the St. Lawrence to the Quebec waterfront, and they made their way up the steep incline, following first one narrow, twisting street, and then another. The town was vaguely familiar, but she had left it at too early an age to remember it clearly. Besides, it had grown to three times its previous population.

Ludona knew precisely where he was going, and just before he reached the Plains of Abraham, a tableland at the crest of Quebec, he stopped before a large yellow brick house. Surrounded by a high wall, the establishment looked as though it could be part of the actual battlements of the Citadel.

Leaving his prisoner with his fellow Erie, Ludona rapped at the front door, and a serving maid in a black-and-white uniform answered the summons. In the background Toshabe caught a glimpse of a husky French-Canadian, apparently a strong-arm man.

The wait seemed endless, and Toshabe would have fled had it not been for the leash around her neck. At last the door opened, and Ludona curtly beckoned her.

Entering the house hesitantly, Toshabe was conducted down a corridor to a parlor. She was stunned by its magnificence. A crystal chandelier that held at least a hundred smokeless French tapers provided the light. Rich tapestries decorated the walls, a heavy Turkish rug was spread underfoot, and chairs in the style of Louis XIV and Louis XV were magnificently embroidered. Seated near glowing logs in a marble fireplace was a stout woman of perhaps fifty, expensively gowned in a dress that dripped with lace. She wore a powdered wig, a velvet beauty patch was pasted to one cheek, and her fingers were covered with sparkling rings.

After dismissing Ludona and instructing him to wait in an anteroom, she greeted Toshabe with a smile, but her eyes remained cold and calculating. "I am told," she said in flawless French, "that you speak the language of France. Is that true?" When Toshabe unhesitatingly replied that it was indeed true, the woman clearly was pleased. "You may call me Madame," she said.

"Very good, Madame."

Suddenly switching to the tongue of the Huron, the woman asked if Toshabe also spoke the language of the various Indian tribes fluently.

As it happened, the tongue of the Huron was identical with that of the Seneca, and since Toshabe had spent years speaking only the language of the Seneca, she found it easy to reply.

Madame was elated. "You can easily become a much-sought-after girl here," she said. "Remove your cloak and step closer, please."

Deeply embarrassed, Toshabe cast aside the cloak, revealing her almost nude body.

Madame rose and circled her slowly, examining her in infinite detail.

Toshabe felt like a prize animal on exhibit, particularly when a forefinger poked and probed, testing the firmness of her breasts and buttocks, running across her stomach, and up and down her thighs.

"You will more than fill the bill for those who want a savage Indian girl," Madame proclaimed. "Now let's see how you'll do as a young lady of France." She tugged a bell rope and two provocatively attired young blond women entered.

"Take this new arrival, who hasn't yet been given a name," she said, "and dress her as you are accustomed to dressing. Then return her here to me."

They took Toshabe to a large bedchamber, and sitting her down at a dressing table, scrubbed the primitive makeup from her face and applied more sophisticated cosmetics from France. She marveled at her transformation, particularly when they settled a blond wig on her head and attached a velvet beauty patch to one cheekbone and another to a place on her chest that would call attention to her breasts.

As they draped her so lavishly, she was impressed at first by the silks and satins, but it dawned on her that these were almost as revealing as her crude Indian attire. The neckline was cut so low that her breasts were almost totally exposed, and her nipples were plainly visible through a thin layer of gauze. A slit in the long skirt revealed her long legs, and the gown was cleverly devised to emphasize a tiny waist and rounded buttocks.

The young women looked at her, and then at each other. "You will do well here, mademoiselle," one of them murmured. "I must admit that you will at least rival both of us in attracting the most advantageous clientele. But we bear you no ill will."

"Indeed you will rival us," the other added. "Your figure cannot be equaled, and you will soon find yourself one of the most popular girls in the house."

"But come," the first young woman said. "We dare not keep Madame waiting, or she'll be angry, and then we shall all suffer for it."

They returned with her to the drawing room, where Madame awaited them, a jewel-handled riding crop of white leather in one hand. She waved the two young women out of the room, then again subjected Toshabe to a careful scrutiny with a gaze so intense and penetrating that once more she was greatly embarrassed.

"You have all the physical qualifications necessary to achieve a great success in this business, my little one," she announced. "Now your future will depend on the enthusiasm with which you make love. But also on your ability to obey orders promptly and cheerfully. Do you expect to do what you're told?"

"I—I suppose so," the startled Toshabe replied.

Madame smiled humorlessly. "I have a very rare and refined clientele," she said. "Our guests include the finest gentlemen in all of New France. In fact, it is no secret that even the general who commands the armies visits this establishment. So for your sake I hope you are pliant and agreeable and obedient. If you are, you will benefit a great deal. If you are not, I regret to say that your body will feel this riding crop, which I will not hesitate to use." The leather swished as she gestured menacingly.

Toshabe was frightened, but her training enabled her to conceal her fear, and she showed no reaction, even though the riding crop passed within inches of her face.

Madame was impressed. "You have courage, little one," she said approvingly. "I like that! Now we will get rid of the Erie who brought you here, and then you shall be put to the supreme test." She went to the door, opened it, and called. A moment later Ludona came into the room. He stared at Toshabe admiringly, but moments passed before he recognized her, and then he gaped.

"I didn't know you!" he said in wonder. "Madame, what do you charge for her services?" He could not tear his eyes away. "She is so different now I can forget her past—for this one time. Bring her to me!"

Madame smiled thinly and handed him a small silk bag in which several coins clinked. "Here is the price that we agreed you would receive for bringing her to me," she told him coldly. "But I must inform you she no longer is available to you. Our clientele is restricted, and we do not open the doors to outsiders." Bluntly, she was telling him that he was not welcome as a patron because he was an Indian who might cause her better class of patron to stay away.

Ludona appeared to be losing his temper, but before he could react violently, the door opened again and the burly French-Canadian came into the room. He held a short, ugly iron club, and a pistol was prominently displayed in his belt.

Toshabe knew that Madame had summoned the strong-arm man, but she had no idea how. She felt certain that she was about to witness an eruption of violence.

The French-Canadian was a giant, a tall man with a massive torso, a barrel chest, and long, sinewy arms. He towered over Ludona, and it was plain that he was spoiling for a fight. Taking a firm grip on his iron bar, he took two steps toward the Erie.

Ludona hesitated. As much as he wanted the provocatively attired Toshabe, he knew he had no chance of getting her without a fight in which he would risk injury and also risk losing the money he had been paid. Perhaps, he quickly decided, he would be wise to take his profits and put the wench out of his mind. Bowing to Madame and not even glancing at Toshabe again, he took his leave. In any event, he was telling himself, the coins from Madame were sufficient to enable him to enjoy many months of relative comfort and leisure in other bordellos and in taverns without the need to lift a finger. He would remain in Quebec indefinitely, he decided.

In the house, the French-Canadian was laughing coarsely.

"You did well, Pierre," Madame said, and turned to Toshabe. "Don't you agree?"

Toshabe smiled. "I am pleased when anyone puts Ludona in his place. It gives me great joy to see him lose face."

Madame exchanged a significant glance with Pierre. "Then I'm sure you will find a way to express your gratitude." She gestured with the crop. "Take her, Pierre, but be careful not to tear her costume. It is far too expensive to be wasted. And don't mark her up, either!"

The giant bared his teeth and beckoned. The development was so unexpected that Toshabe was stunned. It seemed she was to make love with the French-Canadian as casually as she might converse with a stranger. When she hesitated momentarily, Pierre reached out, caught her wrist, and pulled her, almost knocking her off her feet as he dragged her out of the room and down a corridor.

He firmly closed a bedchamber door behind them,

flung her from him so hard that she staggered and had to sit down abruptly on a four-poster bed. Then, facing her, his face expressionless, he demanded, "Remove your clothes at once. That will be better than having me tear them off you as I would like to. I don't wish to needlessly arouse the wrath of Madame."

Toshabe was still in shock. She had thought of the French as being cultured and civilized, yet she was being treated like a mere piece of property, however her captors wished. Even as a prisoner of the Seneca she always received a certain measure of dignity, and her own feelings were taken into consideration. Here, they would count for nothing.

"Well?" the giant demanded. "Are you going to do as I have ordered, or must I teach you manners? I'm a patient man, but I don't have all day."

Toshabe swiftly reviewed her situation. She could count on no one but herself, and she was helpless, in the grip of ruthless people who intended to have their own way with her. She knew some tricks of Indian free-for-all fighting that probably were unfamiliar to the French-Canadian and might stave him off for a time. But her knife had been taken from her by the women who had dressed her, and she knew that without it she would soon be subdued. Not only would she be punished by him, but she already had been threatened by Madame, and she had no reason to doubt that the Frenchwoman would keep her word.

Viewing her dilemma practically, she knew that she had much to lose and nothing to gain by putting up a fight. After all, she had already served the Seneca as a prostitute, and it was a matter of changing masters. So she could only bide her time, watch for a break, and hope for something to happen enabling her to improve her lot.

She realized, too, that Pierre would report to Madame on her expertise and proclivities and that his comments would be the basis for determining the clientele she would serve. Believing that the higher-ranking French officers would be more genteel and probably more considerate, she reasoned that she would be wise to act now in her own interest. Accordingly, she disrobed slowly, flirting blatantly with the giant and hiding her loathing of him.

But subtleties were wasted on Pierre. No sooner was she naked than he threw himself at her as though attacking her. He displayed no finesse, no consideration for her feelings, only his animal desires. She found him far cruder, more primitive, and more barbaric than the Seneca warriors whose lovemaking she had been forced to endure.

Never had she encountered any man so demanding, so selfish. His behavior made her want to retch, but she retained enough presence of mind to know that she would gain nothing by showing her intense disdain. So she concealed her violent hatred and managed to pretend that she relished his lovemaking.

Pierre did not linger, but dressed hastily and departed to report to Madame on the newest girl in the stable.

Toshabe took her time recovering. She bathed in a tub provided by a serving maid, scrubbing herself with a pungent soap. Then she lavished perfume to rid her body of Pierre's lingering scent. She carefully repaired her makeup, then dressed again in the lewdly provocative attire.

Only when she was satisfied with her appearance did she saunter back down the corridor to the reception room. Madame, waiting for her, greeted her jovially and offered a glass of wine.

Toshabe, like so many Indians, disliked the taste of alcoholic beverages, but nevertheless accepted the glass and pretended to sip.

"I have never heard Pierre so enthusiastic about any new girl here," Madame told her. "You're going to go very far, little one."

Accepting the remark as an intended compliment, Toshabe bowed her head slightly.

"I believe in being fair in my dealings with those who are fair with me," Madame said. "Rest assured that I shall obtain the highest possible fees for your services, and my practice is to divide the proceeds fairly as I see fit from time to time."

Pretending to be grateful, Toshabe murmured, "That's very kind of you."

"I promise you," Madame said, becoming enthusiastic, "that General Montcalm himself will be your regular client. So will every other leader of consequence in the Citadel and in the town. You're unique, and it's a fortunate day for this house that you have come to us."

A prostitute of such great value would be closely watched, and she could expect to have an almost impossible task in trying to escape, Toshabe thought unhappily.

Madame drained her glass of wine, rose from her chair, and went to Toshabe's side. To her astonishment, the woman fondled her breasts for several moments, then kissed her full on the mouth.

"I think it unlikely that you shall need disciplining," Madame assured her. "If there's something you need at any time, just let me know." Smiling, she left the room.

Toshabe raised her fingers to her lips as if to brush away the recollection of Madame's kiss, and looked after her in appalled surprise. It began to appear that life in the bordello was going to be even more complex than she could have imagined.

Madame proved to be a remarkably accurate prophet. Toshabe soon achieved unprecedented popularity. General Montcalm visited her frequently, always specifying that she should receive him in French attire, rather than Indian. They often talked together at length, and she found him considerate and highly intelligent. He plainly was homesick, but she could see that he was determined to do his duty for his country, scrupulously refraining from remarks that might reveal any military secrets.

His favoring her won her the attention of his subordinate generals and colonels, and some wealthy Indian chiefs began to clamor for her services, offering to pay with choice peltry or even gold they had acquired fighting for the French. Toshabe rejected all the chiefs as lovers, and though they pleaded for her favors, she was adamant.

Madame granted Toshabe the unusual privilege of selecting her own clients, rejecting any who did not appeal to her. Pierre was provided as a personal bodyguard to make sure that her wishes were carried out, and though he leered at her and sought ways to touch her intimately, Madame made sure that he never tried to repeat their lovemaking.

Toshabe was pampered and began to acquire a considerable nest egg. But she was miserable, feeling at least as degraded as when she was a captive of the Seneca.

With servants to prepare her meals, clean her clothes, and wait on her, her living conditions were relatively luxurious. But she was still a captive, forced to earn her living by surrendering her body to men, and if she rebelled she would face severe punishment, even possible death.

Renno had granted her freedom without qualification, but she had been tricked into renewed slavery by one of her own people. She wondered whether Ghonkaba would come to her aid if he knew of her predicament; she concluded that she knew him well enough to believe that he would move heaven and earth to assist her. Because Ghonkaba was a Seneca, he therefore was an enemy of France. She could think of no way in which she could possibly summon his help.

But once the kernel of an idea was planted in her mind, it grew, and she could do nothing to stop it. Finally, she thought of a scheme that, though risky, seemed to promise at least a faint hope of success. She would find an Indian who would help her get word to Ghonkaba. Thus, she kept her ears open, and sometimes subtly questioned a French officer about various Indians.

The Huron and Algonquian chieftains did not interest her, but her curiosity was piqued by what she heard of Ordonay of the Ottawa, who was reputed to be displeased with the treatment he felt he had unjustly received at the hands of the French for many years.

Somewhat older and vastly more experienced in battle than any of his confreres, he had expected a position comparable to a general's. Instead, the French high command had kept him as the leader only of his own Ottawa, and gave him no control over other tribes. Consequently, Ordonay was badly disgruntled and was complaining so loudly that high-ranking French staff officers entertained serious doubts about his loyalty to them.

On the strength of these references to him, Toshabe let it be known that she would be willing to receive Ordonay. The Ottawa sachem responded even more rapidly than she had thought he would. The very next evening, he appeared at the bordello. He was a great bear of a man, with dark copper-colored skin like that of all Ottawa. He was gruff, blunt, and direct, precisely as she had anticipated.

She received him in her abbreviated skirt and spoke to him in the language of the Seneca or Huron.

Emptying her mind in order to anesthetize herself, she allowed him to do as he pleased, ignoring his crudeness. After he had made love to her, she astonished him by refusing to accept payment.

Ordonay tried to remain wooden faced but did not succeed and blinked in amazement.

"It is the wish of Toshabe," she told him, "to honor and to pay homage to the greatest of sachems."

Had another man flattered him so blatantly, Ordonay would have been suspicious. But he was far more ready to accept at face value these words from an exceptionally attractive woman.

"A mighty chief like Ordonay," she continued, "can achieve what lesser warriors cannot accomplish."

He had no idea what she meant but was ready to agree with her. "That is true," he conceded.

"If the French were wise," Toshabe said, "they would help to make Ordonay the great sachem of all the nations allied with them. But they did not do this because they feared him. He does what he pleases and what he believes to be right. He docs not cringe and bow his head before them, and he does not acknowledge them as his masters."

It was astonishing, the Ottawa thought, that a squaw—and a very pretty one at that—could be so sensible.

"And only a mighty sachem like Ordonay," she said

lightly, "would have the courage to deliver a message from Toshabe to a warrior of the Seneca."

The Ottawa's eyes widened as he weighed her extraordinary suggestion. "What is the nature of this message?" he asked at last.

She smiled disarmingly. "Toshabe," she said, "spent two years as a captive of the Seneca, and there she came to know Ghonkaba, a senior warrior. She promised that she would keep in touch with him, and she has here a brief message in which she tells him where she is. Other allies of the French would not have the courage to deliver such a message because the Seneca are the enemies of the French. But Ordonay is as bold as the lion, as steadfast and courageous as the bear. He knows that the delivery of such a message can do no harm to the cause of France, and that a simple letter from a girl to a brave can do no harm to anyone." She unfolded a small piece of paper and showed him a few simple words. Their message was not quite as innocent as it appeared, saying,

I have been sold into bondage by the Erie to a bordello in Quebec.

Ordonay looked at the paper, and not wanting to admit his inability to read the message, he said agreeably, "The words Toshabe has written have nothing to do with the conduct of the war."

With movements that were slow and deliberate, Toshabe folded the paper and then went up to him and gave him a kiss. She promised she would be waiting for him after he carried out the mission and returned to Quebec.

A gleam appeared briefly in the Ottawa's eyes, and although his expression remained unchanged, Toshabe knew that he was rising to the bait and was sorely tempted. She had appealed successfully to his vanity, and he preened himself at the mere thought of what he might gain in return for an act that would cause no harm to his own nation or to the French. If his worth had been recognized appropriately by General Montcalm and his staff, Ordonay might have felt differently and would have been unswervingly loyal to his allies. But he could see pleasant rewards for himself by living up to her high opinion of him and doing this small favor for her.

The Ottawa reached out a massive hand and took the paper. No further words were exchanged, but none were necessary. An understanding had been reached that would benefit both of them.

No Indian nation had devised a foolproof security system that prevented intruders from entering their lands. The Seneca, however, were proud of the network of sentries around their principal towns. On only rare occasions had outsiders been able to work their way into the nation's communities without being first recognized, and, if necessary, apprehended. But in his stealthy approach, Ordonay was able to determine the sentries' locations so well that he could slip between them and approach the principal town of the Seneca.

It was a great surprise, therefore, when his arrow soared over the town's palisade before dawn one morning and landed directly in front of the council lodge. Ordinarily the arrows used by various nations were easily distinguishable, but this particular shaft bore no identifying marks of any kind.

Tied to the tail of the arrow was a folded sheet of paper that seemed to have some bearing on the situation, and the senior warrior who found the arrow was unable to read the symbols written on it. He went straight to the hut of Ja-gonh and Ah-wen-ga, who were eating a breakfast of fish and cornmeal at the open pit fire outside their dwelling.

Badly worried, the warrior explained that the arrow had soared over the palisade, and that whoever had shot it had vanished into the forest. He could not explain how the sentries could have failed to become aware of the intruder's presence.

Ja-gonh listened in silence, then took the mysterious paper. Opening it, he promptly lost interest in his breakfast. Ah-wen-ga knew her husband well enough to realize he was deeply perturbed. But she did not presume to interfere and asked no questions.

A few minutes later Ja-gonh silently handed her the paper. Ah-wen-ga caught her breath as she read Toshabe's message. "This is frightful!" she exclaimed.

"She must have been betrayed by members of her own nation after Ghonkaba returned her to her people," Ja-gonh observed. A note of harsh contempt crept into his voice. "The Erie can be trusted by no one. If they are untrue to their own people, how can their allies rely on them? They deserve to have no brothers."

His wife was thinking in far more personal terms. "It will be necessary," she said, "to show this letter to Renno."

He sighed. "My father is not well," he replied. "His years are well advanced, and his ancestors beckon to him from the hunting grounds on the far side of the great river. His days are numbered, and an upset of this kind will not prolong his stay with us."

Ah-wen-ga was adamant. "It was Renno," she pointed out, "who granted freedom to Toshabe of the Erie. It was Renno who ordered Ghonkaba to escort her to the land of her people. He was responsible for her return there, and only he can decide what must be done."

Ja-gonh fought with himself, but it was a losing battle. Ever since the time of the great Ghonka, Renno's father, duty had been the first consideration of every member of the family. One did what was needed, what was expected of him, regardless of the personal cost. It was impermissible to deviate from this mandate.

Ja-gonh rose, his back straight, his jaw set, and taking the letter from her, he left the house. Most of his breakfast was uneaten and forgotten.

The deeds performed by Renno throughout his long life were legendary, celebrated in song and story by the Seneca and by the other nations of the Iroquois. His leadership in war and in peace had been extraordinary, his skills in combat unique, and his courage unrivaled. Few people looking at the white-haired man, his skin a sickly gray, could have believed that this was the son of Ghonka, the Great Sachem obeyed by the Iroquois without question.

With both hands, he held his gourd of hot herb tea, brewed for him by his sister-in-law, Deborah, and he sipped slowly, without relish for the taste.

Ja-gonh paused at the entrance of the hut and raised a hand in formal greeting.

Renno immediately sensed that something was amiss, but he continued to drink calmly. He had surmounted so many crises that he rarely became excited. His son sat down opposite him, cross-legged like his father, and waited for the right to speak. Ja-gonh was sachem of the Seneca, but nevertheless was conscious of his subordinate place to his father in the hierarchy.

"You and Ah-wen-ga are well?" Renno asked.

Ja-gonh inclined his head slightly toward his father.

74

"You've had no disturbing news from my grandson?"

"None."

"What is wrong, then?"

Ja-gonh handed his father Toshabe's message and explained how it had been found.

"Summon your war chiefs to a council," Renno ordered severely, "and let them understand that a slip in security is inexcusable. Let each of the war chiefs be responsible for the sentries in his own sector and deprive the negligent sentry of his rank until he mends his ways."

"It will be done as you command, my father." Ja-gonh knew the reprimand was well deserved.

Only after he had satisfied himself regarding the security of the Seneca nation did Renno concern himself with the paper he was holding. He unfolded it, then read it carefully. Gradually the years seemed to fall away. His back straightened, his jaw jutted forward, and his blue eyes flashed angrily. "This," he said in a deep, resonant voice, "is a disgrace. Dirt has been smeared on the honor of the Seneca!"

Ja-gonh agreed but said nothing.

Quieting himself with great effort, Renno sipped his tea, placed his gourd on the ground beside him, and folded his arms. "When I was young," he said, "this deliberate insult to the honor of the Seneca would have caused a war with the Erie. But today far greater issues are at stake. Great Britain is at war with France, and if she loses, the liberties of all men, including those of the Iroquois League, will be doomed."

Again Ja-gonh agreed. "You are right, my father," he said. "For the sake of our children and of all the generations as yet unborn, the needs of our allies must be given priority above all else. The French must be defeated, and with them, the Indian nations."

"In my heart," Renno said, "I feel a strong yearning to humiliate the Erie. I am tempted to declare a special war against them and to send our warriors on the march against them. But if I do this, I will not be faithful to the trust imposed on me by my people and by our friends. I have pledged my word to follow the orders of General Amherst and faithfully obey his instructions. For more than seventy summers the word of Renno has been sacred. It must be sacred still, and I cannot do what I wish at the cost of damaging the cause to which I am pledged."

Ja-gonh recognized and honored his father's great strength—refusal to compromise with principle.

Renno's fingers curled into a fist that struck the ground hard. "Nevertheless," he said in a deep, authoritative voice, "my personal honor and that of my family are at stake. In good faith, I granted freedom to Toshabe and sent her off to the land of the Erie, with my grandson as her escort. I have been mocked by my enemies, and I will not tolerate this insult!"

His son was pleased by this prompt decision, which would make it possible for them to respond forthwith.

"Send a letter to my grandson at the headquarters of Colonel Washington," Renno went on. "Be careful to tell him nothing about the fate that Toshabe has suffered. Ghonkaba is still too impulsive for his own good, and I want to be able to tell him my own views of the matter.

"Leaves are falling from the trees and the season is changing," Renno continued. "Soon the regiment of Colonel Washington will go into winter quarters, as will their French foes. Tell Ghonkaba that he is to stay with Colonel Washington only until he is no longer needed as a scout. When that day comes, he is to return here as rapidly as he can travel. When he arrives, I will instruct him on what to do."

"What instructions will my father give to Ghonkaba?" As Ja-gonh knew, the word of the patriarch was absolute law, and never could be questioned.

"First," the old man said, "I wish to see for myself whether Ghonkaba feels as you and I do about this outrage. Does he share our anger at the perfidy of the Erie toward a woman who has been granted her freedom? If he does, my instructions to him will be different than if he should happen to appear indifferent toward the behavior of the Erie."

"If I know Ghonkaba," Ja-gonh said, "he will fully share our anger."

A trace of humor appeared in Renno's eyes. "You're probably right, my son," he said. "But the ways of those of us who have lived for many tens of moons are not always the ways of the young. Our thoughts are not their thoughts. And Ghonkaba, especially, hears the manitous with ears that are not necessarily attuned as our ears are."

Chapter IV

G honkaba was bewildered when he received his father's message asking him to come home as soon as Colonel Washington's regiment went into winter quarters.

Washington, although puzzled by the unusual request, realized that Ja-gonh undoubtedly had a valid reason, and sympathetically offered to release Ghonkaba immediately.

The offer was declined. "If the crisis the Seneca face was urgent," Ghonkaba said, "my father would have said so. In the tradition of my family, we do our duty first and always, regardless of personal matters. I am serving you out of a sense of duty. I will return to my

78

people only when that obligation is properly discharged."

It turned out that he remained for an additional six weeks with the Virginia regiment. Then the scouts brought in reports that the Indian allies of the French were disappearing from the wilderness.

Muller and Ginsberg told the regional commander in a written report,

We cannot yet be certain, but it appears that the French and their Indians have gone into winter quarters. We now seem to be alone in the field.

With Ryan and MacDavid, Ghonkaba now ventured deep into what was regarded as enemy-held territory and returned with word that corroborated the other scouts' findings.

So the regiment, thankful for the impending respite, went into winter quarters, and Ghonkaba was released. Before he left, Washington instructed him not to return until whatever mission awaited him at home was satisfactorily disposed of.

The Seneca were renowned above all Indian tribes for their ability to cover great distances swiftly and scarcely tire. The secret lay in their training from early boyhood on. Ghonkaba's stamina was extraordinary. As he made his way through the wilderness, he kept a sharp watch for potential enemies, both human and animal. No sign of the recent presence of others in the forest was too small to escape his attention.

Even though the shortest route led through the heart of country controlled by the Erie, he chose it. He was intent on saving several days' travel. He could have continued his journey without rest. But because his presence at home apparently was not urgently required, late each night he climbed into the upper branches of a big tree to sleep for a few hours. He drank from rivers and brooks along his trail, and his only meals consisted of parched corn and jerked venison, emergency rations for every Seneca warrior.

At last the echo of drums announcing his approach assured Ghonkaba that he had arrived in the land of the Seneca. A surprise awaited him when he was half a day's journey from the principal town. A middle-aged brave, wearing the distinctive feathered headgear of a war chief, appeared beside the trail. As they exchanged greetings, simultaneously raising their left arms, Ghonkaba recognized his uncle, No-da-vo.

Instead of stopping to talk, he motioned for No-da-vo to fall in beside him. "I bring you greetings from your father and your mother," No-da-vo said. "They rejoice that you have arrived at home, and they are especially pleased that their prayers to the manitous are answered."

Ghonkaba realized that if his parents were praying to the manitous something must be seriously amiss. In addition, his uncle's traveling for several hours to greet him was significant, suggesting some crisis of grave proportions.

"When your father wrote to you," No-da-vo went on, "he sent you orders at the direction of the Great Sachem. Those orders were given for a good reason, and Renno will explain to you why he sent for you.

"But when your father wrote to you," No-da-vo continued, "he did not know that the need for your presence would be as urgent as it has now become. The ways of the manitous are mysterious to behold, and we who are but humans cannot fathom them."

Glancing quizzically at his uncle, Ghonkaba waited for him to explain.

Aware of his nephew's gaze, No-da-vo turned to face him. "The time each of us is allowed to spend in this world before being called by the gods to the land of our ancestors varies according to the individual and his deeds. Your family has been favored by the gods because they have contributed so much to the Seneca and to our brothers of the Iroquois. Ghonka, whose name you bear, lived a long and useful life. Renno, his son, has also lived beyond the span that the manitous ordinarily allow to men."

Now Ghonkaba understood, and a spasm of fear gripped him. "My grandfather," he said, "lies ill."

"That is so," No-da-vo replied. "If Renno were an ordinary man, he would have died many days ago. But as all men know, Renno is no ordinary mortal. He determined that he would live until you arrive to say farewell and to heed his last instruction. You will go to him at once and hear his words."

Having undergone rigorous training all his life to avoid showing emotion, Ghonkaba still had to exert supreme willpower to prevent tears from rolling down his cheeks. Only through extreme self-discipline was he able to speak calmly. "Is there no hope that he will continue to live among us?"

Trotting beside him, No-da-vo shook his head. "Renno has already said that the manitous have summoned him. At his instructions, the senior warriors are already at work in the grove, building the funeral pyre where he will depart from this world."

Renno's formal announcement that he was preparing soon to join his ancestors meant that no Seneca dared question his will or his word. "So be it," Ghonkaba said bleakly.

In silence, they ran on for a time.

"I have been called before Renno," No-da-vo said at last.

The young warrior knew he was being given this information for some reason, and waited for the full story to unfold.

"It is his wish," No-da-vo explained now, "that I succeed your father as sachem of the Seneca."

"If that is the wish of my grandfather, I pledge you my full support and offer you my fealty for all time," Ghonkaba replied promptly. His mind raced; he could not ask, but it seemed certain that if his father was being replaced as sachem that must mean that Ja-gonh would move up to the place held by his father as Great Sachem of the Iroquois. That tradition, in turn, placed a great burden on Ghonkaba, for he, too, could expect to be called upon ultimately to rise to the highest post in the Iroquois League.

Realizing what must be going through his mind, No-da-vo remained expressionless but said gently, "When one is a Seneca, one does what is ordered by the manitous. I was satisfied with my life the way that it used to be. As a war chief I had achieved enough honor and glory to assure me that a place would be reserved for me in the afterworld beyond the great river. But I now am to be called to a higher duty as sachem of our nation, and I must respond to that call. I must do what is best for the Seneca, regardless of my own feelings."

Ghonkaba understood what was ahead in the conversation.

"So it is also with you," No-da-vo told him. "Your grandfather and your great-grandfather have been Great Sachems of the Iroquois League, and now your father is to join them in that exalted status. Not only will our people expect you to follow in their footsteps, but this feeling will be shared by the other Iroquois tribes."

Ghonkaba could not entertain the slightest doubt as to the significance of his uncle's words. No-da-vo, as new leader of the Seneca, was reminding him bluntly that no longer was he free to do as he pleased, to live as he wished, to accept or reject responsibility at will. His grandfather's death was indeed placing a new burden on him, and he would be required to live up to it. That was a penalty he would pay for being the grandson of Renno and the son of Ja-gonh.

The sachems, war chiefs, and principal medicine men of the nations of the Iroquois League wore no identifying national war paint, or the feathered headdresses and other symbols of their high rank. Singly and in pairs, they filed through the hut of their dying chieftain, pausing just long enough to bid him farewell. Because they were Iroquois, no signs of their lamentation occurred—no weeping, no wailing, no beating of breasts. Their dignity was intact, and above all, they were making certain that the dignity that had surrounded Renno all of his long life also remained intact.

Standing guard over Renno were his brother, El-i-chi, the aged Seneca war chief, and his wife, Deborah, who, though originally a Massachusetts colonist, was as devoted to the Great Sachem as was her husband. They kept him under close observation as he intoned the name of each visitor and accepted each gesture of farewell.

Deborah had objected to what she regarded as a primitive, barbarous ceremony, and had consented only on condition that Renno not be allowed to become unduly tired by the ordeal.

He seemed to be bearing it well, however. She could not penetrate his façade and had no idea what he was really feeling. But if she were to judge only by external signs, she was reassured that his voice was strong, and she noted that although he closed his eyes frequently, they were clear and steady when open.

As the last of the Iroquois leaders was saying his farewells, a messenger entered to say that No-da-vo—running at a full sprint—had arrived to report that Ghonkaba would soon be at hand.

Renno sighed faintly and seemed very much relieved. "I must bid farewell to others who are my relatives," he said wearily. "And it is only fitting that I begin with you, El-i-chi. My brother, you have fought at my side in more battles than I can count. I will await your coming to the land of our ancestors on the far side of the great river. We shall be together again, side by side for all time."

Emotion threatened to overcome El-i-chi, but his lifelong training in self-control prevailed now. "Give to Ghonka, our father, and to Ena, our mother, my respect and my love for them. Tell them I will not be long in following you, my brother, and that I look forward to seeing them, as well."

Leaving reluctantly, El-i-chi went to summon Googa-ro-no, Renno's only daughter, and her husband, No-da-vo, who were to say their farewells next. When they appeared, looking distraught, Renno promptly tried in his noble way to put their minds at rest. "This is a time for a temporary parting only," he assured them in the strongest voice he could muster. "We have not experienced this before, you and I, so we naturally feel the sadness of parting, rather than remembering the joy that soon is to be mine. And we must remember, too, that all of us will eventually be together. The days will pass quickly until that time. Believe me, my beloved children, and rejoice."

Goo-ga-ro-no and No-da-vo were buoyed by his words, and determined to bravely assist him in the kind of farewell that he obviously sought. They assured him of their everlasting love for him and told him that they, too, looked forward to their ultimate reunion. Finally, No-da-vo adopted a warrior's resolute stance beside Goo-ga-ro-no as she bent over her father to give him a last embrace and kiss. They left, feeling more able to accept his demise than they had upon arriving.

Renno asked No-da-vo to summon his sister, Ba-lin-ta, and her husband, Walter, a onetime colonist who had served the Seneca long and faithfully as a war chief. Before they arrived, Renno turned to Deborah, who had stayed behind when El-i-chi left.

"The manitous," he said, "have written in the sky that the brave who finds the love of one woman in his lifetime is among the most fortunate of all warriors. I am doubly fortunate. Not only did I enjoy the love and companionship of Betsy, my wife, for many years, but before I knew her I loved and was loved in return by Deborah."

Color rose to the old lady's face. She and Renno, although they saw each other daily, had only once referred to their romance of many years earlier.

"I have wondered on occasion," he said, "what life would have been like, Deborah, if you and I had married when we were young. I do understand that the manitous were looking out for us because at that time we were too young. And do you remember when I was so sick many moons ago and you came to help nurse me? I told you then that I believed we ultimately would have been happy despite all the problems of a warrior marrying a woman of the colonies. But you were destined to find happiness with the Reverend Jenkins, and after he went off to join his ancestors, you then were permitted to enjoy a new happiness with El-i-chi, my brother. I rejoice for you, and your happiness has been mine."

He closed his eyes for a few moments before Ba-lin-ta and Walter entered and stood beside Renno, waiting for him to speak and to recognize them.

He smiled up at them. "It would grieve me, Ba-lin-ta, my sister, and Walter, my brother," he said, "if I thought that we were to be long parted. But I know in my inner heart that you will follow me to the land of our ancestors across the great river and there we will be reunited. I will give to Ghonka and to Ena your love and respect."

"And tell them," Walter said, "that we look forward with joy to the day when we, too, will be with them."

"I will tell them," Renno said, and again closed his eyes. Without opening them, he spoke again. A note of urgency had crept into his voice. "My time grows shorter. Tell Ja-gonh and Ah-wen-ga that I await them."

His son and daughter-in-law replaced Ba-lin-ta and Walter beside his pallet.

"Among the first whom I will seek in the land of our ancestors," he said, "are Sun-ai-yee and Talking Quail, the parents of Ah-wen-ga. I will assure them that their training was not in vain and that their daughter has done them great credit throughout her life. She has fulfilled her duties well as the squaw of the sachem of his people, and has been a splendid mother. Now a greater responsibility awaits her."

The old man moistened his lips, and his eyes seemed

to bore into Ja-gonh. "My son," he said feebly, "it is my wish, as you know, that you succeed me, as I succeeded my father, as the Great Sachem of the Iroquois League."

"I hear the voice of my father, and I will do as he commands me," Ja-gonh responded.

"I selected you not because you are my son and the grandson of Ghonka," Renno told him. "But because of all the warriors in the land of the Seneca, of all in the lands of our allies of the Iroquois, you understand best those things that we have striven and fought and made sacrifices for."

Ja-gonh bowed his head.

"Our future as Seneca, our future as Iroquois," Renno continued, now rather haltingly, "is bound up with that of the settlers from England who have landed on the shores of this continent and have made their homes here. Only through an alliance with them will we stay free, able to keep the ancient customs that our people have passed from one generation to the next, and able to keep our hunting grounds and forests, our lakes and our rivers. If the French triumph over the English, we will perish with our allies and lose our liberties. We must remain vigilant and strong and free at all costs, and we can do so only through the alliance."

"Just as you, my father—and my grandfather before you—devoted your life to the alliance with the English settlers, so will I devote my life to it," his son promised. "I swear to you, in the names of all the holy manitous that dwell in invisibility around us; nothing will ever alter my determination to keep that alliance."

Renno was satisfied. "On a wall peg on the far side of the hut," he instructed, "are the feathered bonnet and the embroidered cloak of buffalo skin that only the

Great Sachem of the Iroquois can wear. Get them now and put them on."

Ja-gonh demurred. "While my father yet lives," he said, "there can be but one Great Sachem."

Renno raised his voice, surprisingly full and resonant. "Do as I command you," he ordered. "This is no mere whim on my part. I want our brothers of the Iroquois who are gathered here to see you in the regalia of the Great Sachem and to be assured that I have approved you for this post. That is important. Otherwise, some among them may say that the Seneca have held this position for enough years and that the time has come for a leader from another nation. The Mohawk and the Oneida are ambitious and would bicker, and the alliance itself would be in danger. I command you to do as I bid, not out of vanity, but only for the sake of solidifying the Iroquois League, the cornerstone of our security."

Without another word, Ja-gonh took down the feathered headdress and the buffalo cape embroidered with dyed porcupine quills that symbolized his father's exalted rank.

Ah-wen-ga took pleasure in helping him put them on. He stood self-consciously as his father scrutinized him.

"It is done," Renno murmured. "Soon I can cross the great river."

Ah-wen-ga, who had received a signal from Deborah, said hastily, "Ghonkaba has returned home at last."

"Let him come to me without delay. My time grows short."

Ja-gonh raised his left arm in a gesture of farewell, and Ah-wen-ga bowed her head.

Renno feebly returned his son's gesture. They had

said all that they deemed necessary, so they needed no further words. In a heavy silence, Ja-gonh and Ah-wen-ga withdrew.

When Ghonkaba came into the dwelling a few moments later, his war paint had been carefully removed from his face and torso. It seemed to him that his grandfather already had expired. Renno's eyes were closed, his arms folded, and he looked as pale as the light of a waning moon.

To the young warrior's infinite relief, he suddenly spoke. "You have answered my summons, Ghonkaba."

"You called, my grandfather, and I am here," Ghonkaba said in a barely controlled voice.

When Renno spoke again, his own voice was so low that Ghonkaba had to lean close. He learned of the word that had come from Toshabe of her betrayal by the Erie and of her captivity in Quebec.

Ghonkaba was horrified, furiously angry, but he made no attempt to interrupt his grandfather, whose breathing was labored.

"It was I who set Toshabe free," Renno whispered. "I sent her back to her people in the land of the Erie. So I alone am responsible for her plight."

His grandson started to protest, but Renno would have none of it and silenced him with a feeble but firm gesture. "The gods who rule this world and the manitous who serve them," he said, "have dealt fairly and generously with me always, in part because I have accepted full responsibility for my errors, as well as for my triumphs. In this case, I alone am responsible. Because of my advanced years, I am unable to rescue Toshabe and set her free, and I cannot ask my son to do it because of his duties to all the people of the Seneca. Now I am about to cross the great river, and my son will have even more demands on him from all the people of the Iroquois. That leaves only you, Ghonkaba, my grandson, not merely to seek revenge against those who have soiled my good name, but chiefly to obtain freedom for Toshabe. My soul will not rest easy in the land of our ancestors until you have accomplished this mission for me."

"I hear you, my grandfather," Ghonkaba assured him, "and I will do as you bid."

"Good," Renno replied with satisfaction. Making a great effort, he opened his eyes and looked up at his grandson. "Heed these final words of mine to you, Ghonkaba, and remember them always. If you would serve your people—and your descendants—as you have been served by your ancestors, be true to yourself. No matter how great the temptation may be, do not give in to laziness or corruption or a love of the white man's luxury. And if you are true to the principles that guide the Seneca now, as we have been guided in past generations, you will be true to yourself. When you cannot decide which course is right and which would be wrong, look to the manitous for signs. They will guide you always."

To show any emotion was a violation of custom, but Ghonkaba was no ordinary Seneca warrior. Impulsively, he bent down and kissed his grandfather's forehead. When he raised his head again, Renno was smiling.

For a few moments, Ghonkaba was unable to realize that the Great Sachem was no longer present. His spirit had left his body.

Renno felt a deep-rooted joy, an exhilaration that he had not experienced in many years. His body was young and sound again, his energies were boundless, and he was filled with the spirit of comradeship and goodwill. He ran swiftly, effortlessly through the forest, his step light.

This was a wilderness strange to him, one that he had never before seen. But he experienced no uneasiness, and felt perfectly safe as he was guided by a hawk flying directly overhead and leading him to his destination. On numerous occasions in his lifetime he had willingly submitted to the guidance of hawks, and they had never led him astray. So he knew that he now was doing what was right.

At last he came to the bank of a river wider by far than the St. Lawrence. As he stood on the bank he barely could see the far shore in the distance. It was smudged and indistinct, but he knew it was the land to which he was headed, the home he would occupy for all eternity.

He had no idea how he would cross that vast, silently moving body of water, but he was not concerned. When his funeral was ended, he felt certain, he would be transported to the other side. He sat down, folded his arms, and waited for those who mourned him to conduct the ritual of their final farewell. He could hear drums in the distance and was content.

The sound of the drums became louder, reverberating until it seemed to fill the entire being of those who heard it.

The body of Renno, in full war paint, with the three feathers of a hawk denoting the rank of war chief attached to his scalp lock—the highest rank recognized in death—was carried by his brother, son, grandson, brother-in-law, and son-in-law. Like all other warriors who attended the funeral, they had smeared ashes on their foreheads, faces, arms, and torsos. Out of respect for the departed, they wore no war paint.

The drums throbbed unceasingly as the pallbearers laid their burden atop the funeral pyre that had been made ready. Then, after they moved off to the places allotted to the principal mourners, the medicine men of the Seneca and the other Iroquois nations came forward and began to dance. Completely surrounding the pyre, they moved slowly at first, more or less in unison. Gradually, as the rhythm took possession of them, they began to gyrate wildly, their movements totally abandoned.

On such occasions, squaws who had been close to the deceased were permitted to show emotion. Deborah wept openly, and Ah-wen-ga and Goo-ga-ro-no covered their faces with their hands.

Sweat glistened on the bodies of the medicine men, but they did not cease their efforts. Instead, their dancing became more frenzied as they hurled themselves around the pyre to the rhythm of the drums that seemed to creep into the very souls of all those present. The Seneca warriors remained unemotional, but some of those of other tribes in the Iroquois League, lacking Seneca discipline, began to weep openly. The funeral of a man as great as Renno was truly an occasion that caused men to show their emotions.

Only when the medicine men began to falter and fell to the ground in total exhaustion did the drums desist. Silent for a moment, then they began to beat again, throbbing slowly, their rhythm stately and measured.

Tradition called on Renno's son to perform the act that he had dreaded for years. Wearing the Great Sachem's feathered bonnet and buffalo robe, Ja-gonh came forward slowly and prostrated himself before the pyre. Ghonkaba, his face ashen, approached and handed his father a flaming torch. Ja-gonh rose and stood alone for a moment, then with a final word to his father and supreme effort, hurled the torch high onto the pyre.

The wood soon burned and began to smoke; flames appeared, flickering, and they spread quickly, rising higher and higher. Soon the entire pyre was enveloped in an inferno, and a plume of black smoke rose toward the heavens.

Surely it was no accident that a hawk circled overhead, rising higher as the smoke became thicker.

On the bank of the great river, Renno watched in fascination as a hawk circled overhead, flying in and out of a thick cloud. The nature of that cloud was evident to him. It was wood smoke, so he knew that his funeral was nearing its completion.

As he had anticipated, he found himself transported across the river. He was not carried there in a canoe, nor did he swim, but suddenly, inexplicably, he found himself on the far bank.

The forest here was seemingly impenetrable, with oaks and maples, birches and evergreens crowding one another, with bushes of every description making the ground almost impassable.

Renno needed all his skill to penetrate this wilderness, but he plunged ahead without hesitation. He came to a clearing, and as he emerged into it, he saw a huge, brown animal appear at the far end and also enter the clearing. He reached first for his bow and arrows, then for his tomahawk, but quickly smiled at his error. In the land of his ancestors, he knew, no one had weapons, and his hand fell to his side again.

The bear lumbered to the center of the clearing and stood facing him, blinking in the sunlight.

A chill crept slowly up Renno's spine. "Ja-gonh!" He mouthed the name of the bear who had been his boyhood friend, the beast after whom he had named his son.

They regarded each other silently, in a serenity unblemished and complete.

Overjoyed, Renno wanted to shout and whoop like a boy. The manitous indeed were showing him a sign of their highest favor by permitting this reunion with the bear that he had loved as though the animal were human.

They continued to look at each other, communicating silently, just as on countless occasions in the other world. They did not touch or speak, but Renno felt a perfect sense of kinship binding them together, now and always.

After a time, the bear turned and lumbered off into the forest. Renno made no attempt to call him back. He knew that they would see each other frequently throughout eternity.

It was time to renew his journey. Renno began to run with the familiar Seneca pace that he had not used in years. He was elated to discover that his stamina and strength were miraculously restored. He had no idea how long he ran, but in his heart he believed he must be headed in the right direction.

He came at last to a small lake and, feeling thirsty, stooped to drink from its water. A shock awaited him as he saw his own reflection in the smooth waters. No longer was he white-haired. His skin had become smooth, and he looked as he had many years earlier—young, vigorous, and alert.

Resuming his run, he felt the first pangs of hunger, but told himself it would be wrong to eat any of the emergency rations from the pouch at his waist. His wife and mother, he had no doubt, had prepared a welcoming feast for him.

Directly ahead, the forest ended abruptly, and he saw fields under cultivation. Instantly he recognized the plants that were the staples of Seneca fare: corn and squash and beans. He could see the many huts of a town and was puzzled until he realized that no palisade surrounded the community. That was as it should be, because no enemies were in the land of his ancestors.

Three figures emerged from the town and stood at its edge in the fields awaiting him. As he moved toward them, a bulky figure came forward alone to greet him.

Renno's heart leaped for joy when he recognized his father. This was the Ghonka he had known as a boy. Like Renno, his youth had been restored, and he was in the prime of life, his strength bull-like, the aura of authority that surrounded him all-encompassing. He raised his left arm in greeting.

Renno halted and returned the gesture.

"Welcome, my son," Ghonka called. "We have long awaited you."

"I, too, have longed for this day," Renno replied huskily.

Ghonka moved aside, and a woman stepped forward slowly, a smile creasing her lips, her eyes sparkling with pleasure.

She was the Ena that Renno remembered so vividly from his boyhood, warm and lively, loving and tender. He went to her, intending to embrace her, but made an astonishing discovery. Direct physical contact was unnecessary in this land of his ancestors. He and his mother embraced without touching, and her maternal love flooded him and covered him like a warm blanket.

Then Ena gave her place to Betsy, his wife, who awaited him with her arms outstretched in greeting. She looked as she had when they were young and first married. She was even lovelier than he had remembered in his most vivid daydreams.

Tears of happiness filled her eyes as she walked toward him.

Not until now had Renno known how very greatly he had missed her, how lonely he had been without her. Suddenly he was whole again, and he knew that they would be content forever.

The hawk that had led Renno to this place circled higher overhead and vanished.

The presence of a hawk in the sky, hovering above the council lodge in the town of the Seneca, was regarded as a favorable omen by Renno's son and grandson, as well as every other male in the family. Reared in the tradition of the benevolent wisdom of the hawk, they could not feel otherwise.

While the women prepared the funeral feast at which venison, fish, and buffalo would be served, the Council of the Iroquois League met.

As Renno had prophesied, the confirmation of Jagonh as Great Sachem was carried out swiftly and without significant discussion. Renno's understanding of his fellow Iroquois had been so acute that the vote was by a rousing shout of acclamation, and Ja-gonh was installed as Great Sachem.

Next to meet in the lodge were the senior members of the Seneca nation, the war chiefs, medicine men, and other elders. No-da-vo was quickly chosen as the new sachem. Then they turned to other business, as Ghonkaba discovered to his surprise when a senior warrior appeared and summoned him to the council chamber.

Not knowing what to expect, he went, and received a further surprise when No-da-vo informed him, in his typically blunt way, but also with a smile, that he had been promoted to the rank of war chief.

The ceremonies that were customary at such a time were held to a minimum because everyone was emotionally exhausted. The three hawk feathers of a war chief were affixed to Ghonkaba's scalp lock, and No-da-vo made a brief speech, extolling the new war chief's virtues in battle.

Ghonkaba was embarrassed because he had not actually fought in enough battles to have earned his rank, but he had no way to protest.

Only when the council meeting was adjourned did No-da-vo beckon to him after all the others had left. Ghonkaba finally learned the reason for his promotion.

"I want you to begin accepting the responsibilities that have fallen on your shoulders," No-da-vo told him. "You are henceforth a marked man. You are more than a member of the family of the great Ghonka in a direct line of succession. You are marked now as a certain leader in that succession."

Ghonkaba lowered his head to show his acceptance of the responsibility. His youth, he knew, was ended.

"Before you are given duties fitting for your new rank," No-da-vo told him, "I believe you have another mission to perform."

"You know that my grandfather charged me with making a journey to Quebec and setting Toshabe free?" Ghonkaba asked.

"Your father ordinarily would have ordered me to prepare to send a rescue expedition to Quebec," No-da-vo said. "But because he understood Renno's wish that you perform this rescue, you alone must carry it out."

"I will leave at once," Ghonkaba declared, "for the land of New France and the city of Quebec."

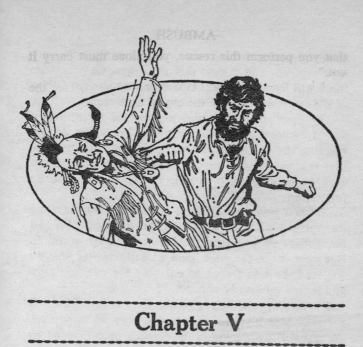

AMBUSH

that you perform this rescue, but someone must carry it
out.

Chapter V

Ghonkaba made his way rapidly through the dense forests en route to Quebec. He had accepted the mission from his grandfather without question, but now that he was launched on it, he became aware of the many difficulties he faced.

One aspect caused him no concern: how best to disguise himself. That was an almost absurdly simple matter. When his grandfather and father had gone to Quebec on wartime missions, they had transformed themselves into Huron—the principal Indian allies of the French—by simply washing off their Seneca paint and applying Huron war paint to their faces and torsos. The two tribes were virtually identical: they spoke the same language; looked similar, being tall, relatively light-skinned, and rangy; and they even ate the same foods and had innumerable similar customs. So it was as a Huron that Ghonkaba traveled northward.

The most immediate and pressing of his problems would be locating Toshabe. All he knew for certain was that she was incarcerated in a brothel, and he realized that many such places must exist. He could not even begin to think of arranging her escape until he found her.

Autumn was the best time of the year for traveling through the wilderness, when game was bountiful and fat, berries abounded, and edible roots were plentiful. But now, since the cold hand of early winter was on the land, he was forced to eat only the parched corn and jerked venison he carried.

Ghonkaba nonetheless would have enjoyed himself thoroughly if his mission had not been so important. He traveled swiftly, using the running pace favored by the Seneca, but rather than press too hard, he rested often. Because of the unknown difficulties ahead, he wanted to be fresh, ready for any eventuality.

He crossed into French Canada without incident and carefully avoided contact with other Indians, wanting nothing to do with the Huron, Algonquian, or Ottawa. At last he came to the St. Lawrence and followed its banks northeastward until he saw the Citadel of Quebec looming in the distance on the high cliff that opened onto the Plains of Abraham far above the river. Now, he warned himself, he would have to exercise extreme caution.

Just before he arrived he plunged into the forest on the south bank to study the city. Several large barges were being operated as ferries by buckskin-clad settlers who looked remarkably like settlers in the English colonies.

As he watched them, he saw various Indians at the landing site. All were carried across. They appeared to be paying no fee, so he made up his mind to risk appearing at the barges to seek passage.

Assuming an air of confidence far greater than he felt, he emerged from the forest and went down to the barge that was waiting. Several Indians and two trappers were already on board the vessel, each trapper with a large bundle of furs. He recognized the Indians as Micmac.

A waiting bargeman in buckskins accosted him. "I suppose you're looking for a ride, Huron," he said in French.

Ghonkaba looked at him, his face impassive. "It is better to be transported," he replied in heavily accented French, "than to swim at this season of the year."

The Frenchman found his remark humorous and roared with laughter. "I also assume," he said, "that you have no money to pay for your voyage."

Here was a dangerous moment, but Ghonkaba faced it without faltering. "It is true that I have no French gold," he replied.

A second bargeman grimaced, smiling sourly. "What did you expect from a Huron?" he asked his companion. "I've never yet seen one with as much as a *sou* he could pay us."

"General Montcalm has ordered that we give the red devils transportation when they need it, so what else can we do?" He turned to Ghonkaba peevishly and said, "Don't just stand there! Come on board if you don't want to get your feet wet."

Rejoicing, Ghonkaba hastily boarded. The bargeman pushed off. Maneuvering the ungainly craft was a delicate operation, as the current was strong. Their progress was slow, and Ghonkaba had ample time to study Quebec.

The Citadel itself, Ghonkaba knew, was the greatest and most impregnable fortress in the New World. In its walls were cannon capable of destroying even the strongest enemy fleet and preventing the landing of an invader's army. Taking the place by surprise would be almost impossible because any foe approaching, whether by land or by sea, could be seen from the Citadel's watchtowers. He remembered having heard General Strong say, "The Citadel is a nut too hard for an ordinary army to crack!"

Below the Citadel's massive walls Ghonkaba could see the narrow, twisting streets of the frontier city that had grown up not only to service the garrison, but also to take care of the flourishing fur and lumber trade with France. Somewhere, between the riverfront below and the Citadel at the peak, stood the bordello in which Toshabe was held captive.

Two war frigates, both flying the official insignia of the French Navy, rode at anchor some distance from a dock. Nearby stood several sloops or barks, also flying the French flag. Maneuvering dexterously, the bargemen worked their craft between two of the merchantmen and brought her alongside a pier. After she was made fast, other passengers promptly departed, but Ghonkaba took his time in leaving, unsure of which way to go or what to expect. His arrival in Quebec, however, proved completely anticlimactic. No one paid the slightest heed to him. Half a dozen soldiers in their distinctive white and gold uniforms were loitering in the dock area, but none even glanced in the direction of the warrior who appeared to be just another Huron.

Ghonkaba began his scouting mission while at the

same time looking for a band of Huron with whom he could temporarily ally himself. He soon realized the immensity of the task awaiting him. In the waterfront area alone, he noted half a dozen brothels with sturdy French country girls loitering in nearby doorways waiting to accost seamen and soldiers who frequented the district. He knew he might have to search every bordello in Quebec before actually encountering Toshabe. Instead of searching blindly and taking countless risks, he needed reliable information.

At last he found what he was seeking. Behind a tailor shop and adjacent to a tavern was an open area that the authorities provided as a camp for the Indians. A cooking fire burned from early in the morning until well after dark every night, with middle-aged squaws from nearby communities in charge. There, any lone warrior who came to Quebec could always get a meal. Blankets, though somewhat more difficult to come by, were available, too, for those who needed a place to sleep.

Ghonkaba wandered into the yard and, taking in the whole situation at a glance, went to a squaw who was ladling out bowls of what smelled like elk or moose stew. He accepted a gourd with a grunt of thanks, then went off and squatted beside two senior warriors of the Huron, who were resting on their haunches as they ate.

He did not greet them, nor did they acknowledge his presence. It was enough that a fellow Huron had decided to join them.

He ate quickly, realizing that criticisms he had often heard of Huron cooking were valid: they used too few herbs, so their dishes were inclined to be tasteless. At last making conversation, he casually addressed the two warriors. "I come from a village far from this place," he said, "and have spent many days and nights

103

in the wilderness. Now that my belly is being filled, my greatest need is for a woman. Where are there any in Quebec who are available?"

The elder warrior grinned at him. "Women in Quebec?" he replied. "Women of every size and shape and color! All you need is money, and if you have the wallet of a French officer or fur trader, they are all available to you. If you have no funds, I advise you to go back to your village."

Ghonkaba continued to play the role of a naive brave, unfamiliar with city ways. "I have the money, if the woman meets my needs. But she cannot be just an ordinary woman."

The second Huron glanced at him, his manner superior. "What do you regard as a special woman who meets your needs?" he asked loftily.

The ingenuousness that Ghonkaba was simulating was working extremely effectively, so he carried his ruse one final step. "I have heard," he said, "of a woman in Quebec who is like no other. She is a squaw of the Erie, and in her veins also runs French blood."

The older Huron snorted derisively. "That sounds like Toshabe."

Ghonkaba's pulse throbbed, and his heart hammered against his ribs, but his face remained expressionless. His voice was completely calm as he remarked, "It might be that she has such a name."

The two Huron looked at each other and burst into prolonged laughter.

Ghonkaba pretended great indignation. "If my brothers will tell me what amuses them, perhaps I, too, will laugh."

Wiping tears of amusement from his eyes, one of them told him, "Toshabe is the most renowned girl in all of Quebec. She is what the French call a courtesan.

You don't have enough money to pay her fee, and neither does any other brave."

Ghonkaba slipped back into the role of the credulous bumpkin. "If I had the funds," he asked, "where would I find this marvelous creature?"

"She lives in a yellow brick house directly below the Citadel," the older Huron told him, "and if you're wise, you'll stay as far from it as you can. A man who works in that place—a Frenchman—likes nothing better than battering warriors. This is French territory, so he has the protection of the government, and if you raise a hand against him, the general would take you into the Citadel and hang you from the flagpole on their parade ground. So stay away from Toshabe if you value your health."

Ghonkaba thanked him, belched politely, and went off for another portion of stew. He had learned precisely what he wanted to know, and he was relieved that he had achieved this first step so easily.

Not until he began to climb the steep, narrow paths that led to the top of the cliff did he realize that his troubles might be just starting. He had located Toshabe quickly, but she was as remote as if they were separated by hundreds of miles of wilderness. He would have access to her only if he paid her outrageous fee. Not only was he penniless, but he had no doubt that whoever now protected her would not allow an ordinary Huron warrior to go near her, and in this he was of course entirely correct.

As he climbed, he pondered and made his plans with great care. The scheme he devised was far from perfect, but he had to take the risk. He could see no choice, and his plan seemed the only possible course of action.

At last he came to the place the two Huron had

described. It resembled the home of a well-to-do merchant—a three-story building of substantial yellow brick. The shutters on the windows of the upper floors were tightly closed. Surrounding the property, a brick wall about eight feet high was topped with metal spikes.

Only the front entrance opened onto the street. He could see no other means of entering.

Taking a deep breath, Ghonkaba went to the door, picked up the knocker, and rapped smartly. After an interminable wait, a smartly dressed young French maid opened the door. She registered surprise to see a roughly clad warrior, smeared with Huron paint, on the threshold.

"What do you want here?" she demanded curtly.

"I want Toshabe," he replied, deliberately thickening his accent. Before she could stop him, he nimbly slid past her into the entrance hall. His whole scheme depended on his ability to get into the house.

She looked at him with surprised indignation. "Toshabe would not deign to speak or look at such as you," she informed him. "Leave at once, or I'll have you thrown out."

He had to act quickly, as well as decisively. Feigning intoxication, he staggered toward the central marble staircase that led to the upper floors. He cupped his hands and shouted in the language of the Seneca. "Come quickly, Toshabe! Ghonkaba of the Seneca is here!"

He barely had time to repeat his words when a door burst open and a red-haired giant with massive shoulders came into the first-floor hall with a rolling gait. He flexed his hamlike hands and, lunging at the Indian, punched at him with all his strength.

Ghonkaba, thoroughly familiar with European styles

106

of fighting, had become an expert boxer. Now, stalling desperately for time in order to prolong his stay in the house, he had to absorb a measure of punishment. So instead of sidestepping and evading the blow, he took the Frenchman's punch on his chin. It was even harder than he had anticipated, and it sent him sprawling into the wall. Again he raised his voice to a shout. "Hurry, Toshabe!" he called. "My time is limited!"

The giant advanced toward him, intending to finish him off with another blow. Ghonkaba could see that the oaf was slow-moving, and he knew that in a real combat he would have no trouble in subduing and even killing him. But he had no wish to have the authorities searching for the Indian killer of a Frenchman.

Footsteps sounded on the staircase, and Ghonkaba looked up to see Toshabe, though he scarcely recognized her. Her head was covered by blond hair that was probably a wig, and her cosmetics were heavily applied. She had a velvet beauty patch on one cheekbone and another to accent the cleavage between her breasts. She wore a shimmering cloth of gold peignoir. She looked at him in amazement; that he could penetrate this place was astounding, for Madame boasted it was as unavailable to unwanted visitors as the Citadel itself.

Now that Ghonkaba knew Toshabe had recognized him and was aware that he had responded to her message, he needed nothing more on this visit. He bounded to his feet, tripped the red-haired giant, and dashed through the doorway and into the street. Pierre started to follow but was stopped by Madame, who, having put in a startled and belated appearance, now wanted no public disturbance, and the door slammed shut behind him.

Ghonkaba stood on the cobblestones outside the

house, rubbing his bruised chin and smiling quietly. He had won this round of his strange adventure. The next move had to be with Toshabe's help.

Darkness would not come for another two hours. Until then, he could not remain near the house. The woman and the Frenchman would be sure to notice him. Any further altercation would be possibly followed by even a jailing. So he wandered off down the hill, killing time until the mantle of night settled over Quebec.

It was essential that he remain as inconspicuous as possible. But that would not be easy in a Europeanized city where he was a complete stranger, knowing no one and carrying not a *sou* in French money. The one place that seemed a refuge was the Indians' outdoor gathering place, so he wandered back toward it.

On one street a French sergeant was having a loud argument with an Ottawa brave, who appeared to have drunk too much liquor. Ghonkaba hurried past them so as to make sure he wasn't on hand if violence broke out.

When he came to the Indians' area, the odors on the breeze told him that the Huron squaws no longer were in charge. Several women of the Algonquian nation were stirring the contents of a large pot, and Ghonkaba's nose told him they were preparing a seafood chowder, using various shellfish and vegetables.

Although the Seneca, an inland people, were familiar with fish, they rarely had the occasion to experiment with clams, oysters, and lobsters, and so had never developed a taste for them. Having no choice, Ghonkaba accepted a large bowl of the chowder. He went to a far corner and squatted on his heels. If he had to eat shellfish, he would have preferred it in some form other than such an aromatic dish. He let the soup cool until it became more palatable. Then, when he raised the bowl to his lips, he nearly gagged.

He smiled to himself at the thought of what his grandfather would say if he was watching from the land of their ancestors. Having already overcome great hardships and difficulties on his mission, he must not allow an unfamiliar dish to endanger it. He steeled himself to drink the chowder. As he drank, he had a strong sensation that someone was staring at him. Slowly he raised his head and found himself returning the gaze of an Erie warrior, older than himself, who stood some distance away. The man looked familiar, but Ghonkaba could not place him. Rather than arouse a greater interest in himself, he looked away casually. He began to pick bits of vegetables from the chowder with his fingers. In this way, at least, he could avoid most of the shellfish.

Only later did he realize that his failure to recognize Ludona of the Erie was the worst error that he could have made and he would long regret it.

The captain who had night duty in the Office of Military Security at the Citadel was annoyed. Having planned to go with several comrades to Jacques's Restaurant for supper, he had been looking forward to a delicious meal. He would select *petite marmite,* roast lamb in mustard sauce with new potatoes, a salad of watercress, and then savor a dessert that Mme. Jacques herself would make.

The place was unique in Quebec, and though it could not compare with numerous restaurants the captain knew in Paris, it was by far the best here. Its popularity was so great that reservations had to be made weeks in advance.

The illness of a subordinate lieutenant had forced

the captain to change his plans. Instead of going to Jacques's for the anticipated feast—with wines imported directly from Paris—he was obliged to be in charge at the office. Consequently, he would have to wait at least six weeks before he would have another chance to obtain a table at Jacques's.

So he was short-tempered and in a particularly foul mood as he listened to the Erie warrior who sat babbling beside his desk.

"I recognized Ghonkaba of the Seneca, even though he was wearing Huron war paint. He did not choose a very effective disguise," Ludona was saying. "I know he noticed me, so I went off into the background and waited. After darkness came, he went up the high hill again and paused outside the house where Madame and her girls live. I stayed in the shadows and watched, and at last my vigilance was rewarded. Lights were turned on and off in one of the upper chambers. Eventually a window opened and a woman appeared. Then a long string of sheets and blankets was lowered. The Seneca climbed over the wall, then started to pull himself up the ladder toward what I believe is the woman's room. I did not wait longer, but hurried here."

"It strikes me," the captain answered with a yawn, "that this warrior, whoever he might be, was having a private rendezvous with one of the girls in the stable. I daresay this sort of thing happens all the time. Personally, I can't afford to patronize the place, but if I became fond of one of the whores, I wouldn't hesitate to sneak in, too."

"Your Excellency fails to understand," Ludona argued urgently. "I didn't see the woman clearly, but I suspect she was Toshabe."

The officer thought that the Indian stank of bear

grease, and his one desire was to get rid of him. "I cannot see the significance," he replied stubbornly.

"It was I," Ludona told him proudly, "who brought Toshabe to Quebec and sold her to Madame. I chose to remain in the city ever since. At one time in years past I was betrothed to her, but she was spoiled for me as a future wife because she was captured by Seneca, and worked for two years for them as she works now for Madame. The Seneca I saw tonight is the very warrior who had brought her back to the land of the Erie."

"That's logical," the captain declared shortly. "They naturally came to know each other well when she was a captive. I can't see anything sinister in what you're telling me."

White men were the most stupid, arrogant creatures on earth, Ludona thought now, wishing that the gods would consign all of them to the nether regions. "The Seneca," he explained patiently, "are not like the Indians you know. They are the principal Indian allies of the British and the leaders of the Iroquois League. They have fought hard and well in previous wars against the French. The warrior who is in Quebec at this moment, disguised as a Huron, is a descendant of the Great Sachems of all the Iroquois. He is no ordinary brave."

The captain's attention and interest were at last aroused. "Why should such a Seneca come to Quebec?" he demanded. "And why should he sneak into that house to see Toshabe?"

Ludona's eyes glittered. "You may well ask why," he almost shouted. "To me it is plain. Toshabe has clients who hold high places in your government and in the armed forces. Perhaps she learns military secrets

111

that she passes to the Seneca spy, who will carry them back to his people and to the British."

The captain was becoming thoroughly concerned at last, but he saw complications to be considered. "Toshabe," he muttered uneasily, "is no ordinary courtesan. General Montcalm himself enjoys her favors from time to time. So do a number of high officers on his staff. I can make no accusations against her unless I have concrete proof of her guilt."

"She's nothing but a stupid woman," Ludona replied. "Remove the threat of the Seneca, and she becomes harmless. Forgive me if I offer advice as to what to do next, but it is plain that Your Excellency does not understand Indians and their ways."

"That may be so," the officer replied a trifle stiffly.

Ludona smiled tightly and leaned forward in his chair. "Go to the yellow house," he said, "and let your men surround it. The Seneca cannot remain there forever. When he emerges, capture him, and you can go to General Montcalm with your prisoner, an enemy caught in the heart of the general's capital only yards from the entrance to the Citadel itself."

The captain sucked in his breath. "You're right," he said as resolution formed within him and quickly took shape. "By God, I'll do it!"

Chapter VI

In the shadows of night, Ghonkaba had stolidly watched the windows on the upper stories of the house where Toshabe was held captive. Wilderness training helped make certain that he could remain motionless for hours on end. No flickering of shadows, no motion whatsoever, could possibly be detected by anyone peering out through the shutters. Only his eyes, which roamed across the second and third stories, were in motion.

The bordello was a popular place. Several high-ranking officers, including two colonels and four majors, arrived, spent half an hour to an hour, and then took their leave. The place was also a mecca for prosperous civilians. A number of middle-aged gentlemen, most of them portly and wearing wigs, also came and departed.

At last Ghonkaba's patience had been rewarded. In a third-floor room with floor-to-ceiling French windows, a light flickered on, then off, on, then off. Several moments passed before he realized that a deliberate signal was being sent. Someone apparently was placing a cloth over a lamp, removing it, then replacing it. The signal could be coming from only one person.

A few minutes later, the shutters and window were pushed open, and he caught a glimpse of Toshabe's cloth of gold peignoir. She seemed to be searching for him in the gloom beyond the wall. She ducked back into the chamber, and within several moments Ghonkaba saw an object slowly being lowered from the window. As it snaked its way to the ground, he recognized it as a ladder made out of knotted sheets and blankets. He hoped that she had remembered to fasten the end securely to some solid object in the room.

He waited until the neighborhood seemed quiet, meanwhile growing increasingly impatient but maintaining his motionless vigil. Finally, he decided the time had come.

He hastily scaled the high wall around the property by gaining a foothold in cracks between the bricks, then hoisted himself up by clinging to those overhead. The climb was not easy, but his training as a brave had involved much more difficult challenges such as surmounting smooth palisades in order to force his way into an enemy's town. At the top he carefully avoided the sharp spikes there, and then dropped noiselessly into the garden.

The makeshift ladder was directly ahead, its loose end trailing in a flower bed. He tugged to make sure it was secure and began the slow ascent hand over hand to the third floor, where he discovered that the French window opened onto a small balcony. Toshabe, looking glamorously beautiful but very frightened, awaited him inside.

Ghonkaba quickly hauled up the ladder before he turned to greet her. The room, he noted, was the sitting room of what clearly was a suite.

"I had given up hope that you would ever come for me," Toshabe told him, after explaining the impulse that caused her to take the risk of sending a signal into the night and dropping the "ladder" out the window.

"I'm here now," he replied simply.

"I'm so relieved," she said, "that the Ottawa chieftain delivered my message. But it occurred to me—too late to do any good—that you would have great difficulty in finding me once you arrived in Quebec. How did you ever locate me?"

Ghonkaba gestured curtly. "We should have ample time to talk about all that when we have put Quebec behind us," he said. "What we have to do immediately is to leave without delay."

She was perplexed and frightened. "I don't see how we can possibly leave," she whispered. "Pierre—who fought with you this afternoon—keeps guard here day and night, and as you know he is like a bull."

Ghonkaba tapped the handle of the knife in his belt. "I am prepared to do what I must," he assured her.

About to reply, she suddenly caught her breath. "I hear Madame coming up the stairs," she told him. "Go out to the terrace and stay there! Quickly!" Not waiting for him to obey, she hastily rolled the ladder's sheets and blankets into a ball and shoved them into a closet.

Ghonkaba stepped outside to the tiny terrace, pulling the tall French window behind him, but leaving it ajar sufficiently so he could hear what was being said inside.

Peering through its thin silk curtains, he saw the woman he had seen briefly on the first floor.

"My dear," she said to Toshabe, "I am reluctant to ask this of you, but you will have another customer tonight."

"No, Madame!" A hint of alarm as well as petulance entered Toshabe's voice. "I've already had more visitors than usual this evening, and the hour is very late."

"I wouldn't ask you if it weren't important," the woman said soothingly. "You remember Colonel Vante?"

"Vaguely," Toshabe replied, pouting.

"I know of no more important officer in the Citadel, other than the general himself," Madame told her. "He's director of operations on General Montcalm's staff, you know, and so he's a man of great power and prestige. He asked specifically for you, so you are obliged to accept a visit from him, no matter how you feel about it."

Toshabe sighed and seemed to refrain from glancing toward the terrace only with an effort.

"You won't be sorry," Madame assured her, patting her cheek and then letting her hand fall to Toshabe's breasts, which she expertly caressed. "He's very generous, and then, too, I shall devise some little treat to make up for the inconvenience."

Toshabe let Madame do what she pleased. From experience, she knew that the "little treat" would be a strenuous session of Madame's own lovemaking instead of that of a client. But deliverance was at last at hand, and the knowledge of it gave Toshabe strength to go on.

After Madame left the room, Toshabe hurried to the

terrace window. "I'm sorry," she murmured through the slight opening, "but I have no choice. Stay where you are, and you can be sure that I'll get rid of this colonel as fast as I can." She moved away again, disappearing into another room of the suite.

With no alternative, Ghonkaba remained on the tiny balcony, feeling foolish and impotent. The thought of hiding while a stranger made love to Toshabe infuriated him. But now, of all times, he needed to keep his wits about him. With a superhuman effort, he dismissed from his mind what she was experiencing. He waited what seemed to be a long time. Toshabe's intent to send the colonel on his way promptly was not working out as she had anticipated.

Noise in the street below caused Ghonkaba to stiffen, all his senses suddenly more alert. The street had been very quiet except for Madame's visitors, but now it was coming to life. He could hear the rhythmic tramp of booted feet, and peering down into the dark, he was astonished to see a full company of French troops, each armed with a musket and a bayonet, approach the building and surround it.

He estimated a strength of fifty men, and with their leader was an Indian wearing Erie war paint. He knew it was the man who had stared at him at his evening meal.

Suddenly he recognized the man! This was Ludona, one of the warriors to whom he had returned Toshabe in the land of the Erie. Understanding flooded him: Ludona undoubtedly was responsible for her present troubles, and it was equally plain that he had recognized Ghonkaba. Furthermore, the Erie must have kept him under observation and had followed him here. The troops were there for only one reason: taking Ghonkaba into custody.

If taken captive, he would be tortured and then hanged. They would see no alternative, since he would be considered an enemy spy. Now a double task awaited him. His neck, as well as Toshabe's future, was in jeopardy.

His mind reeling, he watched the troops deploying into a ring around the building. Each man took up a stance a few feet from his nearest neighbor, while their captain inspected their ranks.

How could he save himself and at the same time help Toshabe escape? It seemed an insoluble problem, but at last a daring idea occurred to him. It was so cold-blooded that he almost rejected it, but after hasty though careful consideration, he decided it could offer his only chance.

He had to act swiftly while the opportunity presented itself. He opened the window a few inches and slipped into the dark sitting room. Drawing his bone-handled knife, he moved on soundless feet across the thick rug toward the adjoining bedchamber.

The door was ajar. No lights were burning there, either, but as he looked in, he could make out the figures of Toshabe and a man locked in a lovers' embrace on the bed. Both were naked, and his anger threatened to boil over. Only by supreme willpower did he control himself and creep noiselessly toward the bed.

With his arms encircling Toshabe, the Frenchman's face was buried in her neck and the curve of her shoulder. She alone could see Ghonkaba's stealthy approach. She looked up, and her eyes widened when she saw the knife in his hand. His intent was deadly, but his face was calm, and his eyes, though grim, reflected no personal anger or other feelings.

Toshabe clasped the back of the colonel's head with one hand, presumably as a gesture of loving intimacy.

But her motive was quite different. She needed to make certain that he didn't raise his head and see Ghonkaba with his poised weapon.

With Toshabe watching, her calm matching his, Ghonkaba raised his arm and swiftly brought his knife down hard. He plunged it hilt-deep into the left side of the colonel's back. The man died instantly, quietly.

Toshabe struggled to free herself from his clutch as she sought to slip from beneath him. His spattering blood had not reached her naked body.

Ghonkaba wiped the knife blade clean on the sheets. "Get dressed quickly!" he ordered. "French troops have surrounded the house, and Ludona of the Erie is with them, so you and I are in grave danger."

Her eyes widened with fear. "How can we possibly get away?"

"We're going to take a great risk," he interrupted. "The colonel was heavier than I am, but I think his clothes may fit me. I'm going to masquerade as a French officer, and we'll try to bluff our way out. But every moment counts." He crossed the room to the chair where the colonel had left his clothes and began to put them on.

Toshabe busied herself at a wardrobe, then at an elaborate dressing table. Suddenly she paused in her frenzied efforts.

"Madame is coming up the stairs again," she whispered. "I recognize her footsteps."

"Leave her to me," Ghonkaba replied softly, and snatching up a flimsy, silken chemise from the dressing table, he retreated behind the door.

Madame's brightest professional smile was fixed on her face as she minced into the room. "Well, Colonel," she trilled, "I trust you and Toshabe have enjoyed your rendezvous. I—" She broke off abruptly, her eyes bulging with horror as she saw his blood-smeared body sprawled on the bed.

While she gaped, too paralyzed to move, Ghonkaba approached her from the rear, encircled her with one arm, and with the other jammed the chemise into her mouth.

She struggled, but her efforts availed her nothing. The match was unequal, and Ghonkaba swiftly subdued her. Meanwhile, Toshabe seized the knife and cut several strips from a silken coverlet.

With these, Ghonkaba bound Madame's hands and feet securely, and doubled the size of the gag in her mouth.

As Toshabe looked down at the woman who had caused her so much misery and degradation, ironic amusement entered her eyes.

Madame writhed in growing alarm when she saw the knife in her hand. "Don't fret," Toshabe said. "I have no intention of killing you. I don't want to deprive you of the pleasure you're going to have when the authorities question you, as they will when we're through with you. I do hope you have a convincing explanation for them." She slashed away the front of Madame's gown, deliberately tearing it open. Then, with the knife blade, she scooped up some of Vante's blood and smeared it on her breasts.

"General Montcalm and his officers know how perverted you are," she said with vicious sweetness, "so you're going to have a terrible time convincing them of your innocence in his death—particularly looking the way you do." She laughed, wiped the blade on Madame's skirt, and then returned to getting ready for departure.

With Madame immobilized, Ghonkaba was able to return to his own preparations. Colonel Vante's gaudy uniform, boots, and helmet, though slightly large for him, fitted him reasonably well. A glance at his reflection in a pier glass assured him that his scalp lock was hidden beneath the burnished bronze helmet.

He buckled on Vante's sword and took his pistol, making certain it was loaded and primed. He found room in the colonel's belt for his own tomahawk and knife. Unfortunately, he had no way to carry the clothes he was discarding. Then he turned to Toshabe and forgot his own appearance.

She had freshened the almost bizarre makeup and pulled on a striking, low-necked gown of black velvet and matching velvet slippers with absurdly high heels. Her blond wig was gone, and her glossy black tresses were piled high on her head.

Before he could speak, she anticipated his objection. "I know how inappropriate these clothes are," she said, taking a silk cloak from the cupboard and throwing it over her shoulders, "but I have no choice. All the clothes that Madame buys for me are of this style."

"We'll have to make do as best we can," he replied grimly. "Let's be on our way."

She paused for an instant to look down at the helpless, frightened Madame. "Good-bye, little dear," she said, her voice saccharine. "I shall think of you often, looking as you do at this moment."

At her words and a meaningful look at Ghonkaba, he raised a heavy candlestick and brought it down hard on the woman's skull. As soon as he was sure that she was unconscious, he set about removing the gag and then the bindings on her arms and legs. While he worked, Toshabe quickly stripped off all of Madame's clothes, exposing her gross nakedness. She tossed the garments onto the bed with a satisfied smile. When the

121

authorities found Madame, they would wonder why she was in a room with a murdered man.

But before they could leave the suite, they heard footsteps pounding heavily up the stairs, and Pierre burst into the room. He took in the scene in a glance, and having heard the unusual sounds from above, he was prepared for hostile action. Toshabe was closer to him, and he caught her by the wrist, hauling her roughly to him, using her as a shield. Meanwhile, he fumbled with his free hand in his belt for a pistol.

Toshabe struggled in his grasp, making his task more difficult, and the Frenchman required several seconds to loosen the belt and draw the pistol.

Those seconds were all that Ghonkaba required. He snatched his tomahawk from his belt, took careful aim, and let fly with a decisive snap of his wrist.

Not even the most experienced Seneca warrior would have dared throw a tomahawk at a man who held a hostage in front of him. But Ghonkaba was a fourth-generation marksman, an expert beyond compare in the use of the tomahawk. The sharp, heavy weapon cut into Pierre's arm, penetrating to the bone; he loosened his grip as an agonizing pain shot through him.

Toshabe, too, was equal to the emergency. Even though she resembled a French courtesan, she was an Erie half-breed capable of utter ruthlessness. Reaching inside the neckline of her gown, her hand emerged with a knife. Unhesitatingly, she plunged it into Pierre's throat. He staggered backward, then collapsed on the floor, his blood spilling as he died.

Ghonkaba retrieved his tomahawk, noting that the knife that killed Pierre was one issued by the French Army. Toshabe had taken it from Vante's possessions, but now she did not glance again in Pierre's direction and made no attempt to retrieve the knife.

If it had been a wilderness fight, Ghonkaba would have been certain to present her with Pierre's scalp. But their troubles almost surely were far from over, and he decided they must not lose the time that would be involved.

"Should we go out the front door?" Toshabe asked breathlessly.

"That is dangerous, I am sure, but it seems the best route out," he told her. Alert to anything that might move, he followed her swiftly out of the room and down the stairs.

When they reached the door, she unbolted it. "Wait here for me," he instructed. "Leave the door open a crack and watch and listen. When I signal, you'll know it's safe to come out."

She had no way of telling what he intended to do next, but she nodded obediently as he gave her his Seneca knife.

Ghonkaba opened the door, slipped out, and stood on the broad stone at the top of the steps. He could see easily the troops but could not discern the captain. Hoping that his command of the French language would be good enough, and would not give him away, he concealed his tomahawk, and called, "Capitaine!"

The security officer approached and was dismayed, first recognizing the uniform of a senior officer, and then the broad sash of yellow watered silk across his chest marking him additionally as a member of the commanding general's staff. He hadn't realized that such an officer was in the bordello.

He saluted and stood rigidly at attention. "Yes, sir?"

Ghonkaba braced himself, his face hidden beneath

the helmet's visor. "Who authorized the posting of these troops here?" he demanded gruffly.

"I deployed them on my own authority, Colonel. I've had information that a Seneca spy is hiding in that house."

"Nonsense!" Ghonkaba said. "I've just come from inside, and I assure you that no such person is there. Return to quarters with your men immediately!"

The captain swallowed hard as he accepted the rebuke. "Very good, sir," he responded, and saluted.

Ghonkaba returned the salute, and then went inside. From a window, he watched gleefully as the company of soldiers marched off.

"That was brilliant!" Toshabe exclaimed.

"We'll see if it really gets rid of them. And most of all, whether we are now able to get away." He opened the door wider, bowed her out and then, closing it firmly, offered her his arm.

They looked like an elegant French couple as they came down the outside steps, went down the walk, and emerged onto the street. The incongruity of their situation and appearance struck Toshabe forcibly, and she giggled.

The laughter died in her throat, ending in a gasp when she saw a dark figure in the shadows ahead and quickly recognized Ludona. She was uncertain whether Ghonkaba would instantly understand the significance, but she mouthed Ludona's name and with a slight nod pointed out his location.

Ghonkaba's grim expression showed he understood only too well. Instantly taut, he gripped the handle of his tomahawk. His disguise might be sufficient for him to escape detection, but Toshabe's beauty was so brazenly displayed that anyone who knew her must unfailingly recognize her. He was loath to attack Ludona.

Any noise would call attention to them, and Ghonkaba's French uniform would make him doubly conspicuous.

The more time that passed, the more difficult would become their escape. They had left behind the bodies of Colonel Vante and Pierre, as well as the unconscious Madame. At the very least, when morning came the normal flow of people through the establishment would disclose the bodies, and Madame would be sure to do a great deal of talking, apart from the explanations she would be called upon to give of her own role.

They should put Quebec behind them by dawn. They would be fortunate, indeed, if they were not apprehended before then.

Hoping to evade Ludona, or preferably shake him off, Ghonkaba turned away from the town that stretched out below and, grasping Toshabe by the elbow, went in the opposite direction. In silence they climbed the short distance to the summit of the hill and saw the high walls and gate of the Citadel looming before them.

Unaware of why Ghonkaba had brought them to higher ground, rather than seeking the St. Lawrence and escape, Toshabe peered at him in the dark. He smiled at her reassuringly, and she was calmed. Her confidence in him was complete.

As they approached the Citadel's gate, a surprised sentry saw the colonel's uniform and jumped to attention, his musket held at a "Present Arms" salute.

Ghonkaba barely remembered to return the salute as, without slowing his pace, he kept walking with Toshabe's arm in his. They strode rapidly outside the forbidding wall, and followed its circuitous route not far from the cliff that rose up almost to its base.

Let the sentinel wonder where he was headed with

this lovely courtesan; that should be strictly the colonel's own business.

"We can't possibly go down through the city to the river," Ghonkaba explained to her in a low voice, as they made their way between the cliff and the wall. "Though it's late, soldiers and seamen and civilians are sure to be wandering about. Prostitutes from the brothels will see you and be jealous, and may want to start a cat-fight quarrel. Drunks will want to fight me for you. We couldn't be more conspicuous if we were carrying lanterns."

Toshabe quietly absorbed his reasoning.

"What's equally important," he went on in the same low tone, "is that Ludona is still following us and seems to have picked up two other Erie braves. Three of them are stalking us."

"Three of them! Then we have no hope of getting away!" Toshabe exclaimed. "If Ludona were alone, you could fight him, but three braves against one makes the odds too great."

"We can't risk a fight with them. There's no time, and any noise would give us away. We need to escape quickly and silently. I wonder if there's a path of any kind leading down to the water?"

"If there is," Toshabe replied, "I've never heard of it. I'm sure the only way to reach the St. Lawrence from the Citadel is through the town."

Ghonkaba's instinct told him that she might be wrong. It seemed that the Citadel's builders would have provided for some way to obtain reinforcements in case they were needed. He felt sure that some means of reaching the fortress from the river must exist without the need to go through the settlement.

As he pondered the problem, they reached the far end of the Citadel's high wall and left it behind, finding themselves on a spreading, windswept plateau. Known as the Plains of Abraham, it seemed to extend for a considerable distance. Almost no trees were to be seen, a strange phenomenon in a land where the forest was everywhere.

Ghonkaba slowed their pace, then halted in order to take his bearing, and looked around slowly in the dark.

"Remove your shoes and carry them," he murmured to Toshabe. She understood his instructions and obeyed instantly. She had encountered difficulty in walking over the rough terrain wearing her high-heeled slippers.

The three Erie were still following, but their respect for his prowess kept them some distance away. Dismissing them from his mind, Ghonkaba instead prayed, asking the manitous to arouse his grandfather. Renno had escaped miraculously from situations as delicate as this; perhaps he could send word now to his grandson that would show him a way out.

As Ghonkaba heard a strange but familiar sound, the flapping of wings overhead, he looked up, peering into the dark sky. His blood ran cold when he saw the dark shape of a hawk hovering in the air almost directly above.

He knew what he could never explain to anyone on earth other than another Seneca: his prayers had been answered by the manitou.

The hawk was rising higher and higher overhead, flying in lazy circles until it blended with the night, making it scarcely visible, even to someone with Ghonkaba's superb vision.

Quickly, it became apparent to Ghonkaba that the hawk had a specific destination in mind. Still flying in looping circles, it descended enough to be visible, then moved off toward the north.

127

Ghonkaba followed without hesitation, with Toshabe close beside him. He had every confidence in the manitous who had sent the hawk as their messenger in this hour of great need.

To the uninitiated, the hawk's moves would have seemed erratic and pointless. After edging toward the north, it veered toward the east, and occasionally doubled back toward the south. Wherever it went, Ghonkaba followed.

Gradually the realization dawned on Toshabe that Ghonkaba was being led by a bird. Ordinarily she would have wondered if he had lost his reason, but in her time with the Seneca she had come to know some of the legends about the family of Ghonka and Renno. She had heard numerous tales of how, when in precarious circumstances, they had been saved by the intervention of hawks sent by the manitous. Ghonkaba himself had been helped by hawks. Her own training was such that she could accept the tales unreservedly. Now she, too, followed willingly.

In spite of their gaudy attire, she and Ghonkaba were still Indians and suitably responded to the challenge of making their way as silently as they could across the plain.

Because so few trees, bushes, and boulders could be used for concealment, it should have been relatively simple for Ludona and his companions to maintain a close surveillance. But beneath the hawk's meandering flight, Toshabe and Ghonkaba's path was totally unpredictable. In the murky darkness, their maneuvering helped make them able to elude their pursuers.

Evergreens and maples now began to appear, and soon they found themselves in a heavily wooded area. They slowed their pace, but the hawk, continuing to circle overhead, still guided them. Toshabe was astonished to realize that they were slowly making their way down a rather steep grade.

As they walked, Ghonkaba was committing to memory the location of this hidden path. His grandfather had so often preached to him: in enemy territory, note everything about the terrain that might prove useful—and remember it.

Their descent was circuitous and slow, but finally they could hear and, through the trees, catch glimpses of the St. Lawrence directly ahead. They had performed the seemingly impossible feat of leaving the immediate area of the Citadel and reaching the river without going through the city of Quebec!

The hawk swooped low in a gesture of farewell, then rose swiftly and disappeared from view, its mission accomplished.

For some moments Ghonkaba stood in silence, his head raised and eyes closed as he expressed fervent thanks to the manitous.

Now he was faced with the problem of crossing the river and leading Toshabe southward as rapidly as they could travel. The night was well advanced, and not many hours remained for them to make good their escape. They could expect an immediate and vigorous manhunt once the bodies of the colonel and Pierre were found.

For the time being, it seemed best to remain in hiding. The first rays of dawn were lighting the sky as he realized that the hawk had not guided them aimlessly. Now they could hear distinctly a paddle being dipped into the river. Peering through the trees, they saw a canoe approaching the shore. Seated in it were a warrior and his squaw.

The brave's war paint identified the couple as

Micmac. They could provide the badly needed clothes and transportation!

Ghonkaba put his lips close to Toshabe's ear. "You still have my knife? I hope you will not need to use it—but be prepared," he whispered. When the canoe came up onto the north bank he stepped boldly into the open, gesturing for Toshabe to follow.

The Micmac gaped in astonishment at the lighter-skinned strangers, who appeared to be a French officer and his lady of high fashion.

Ghonkaba raised his left hand, and in the language of the Algonquian, universal tongue of the northern tribes, he extended cordial greetings.

Amazed to hear a French officer speaking in an Indian language, the Micmac could only stare.

Ghonkaba was quick to take advantage of their bewilderment. Such a meeting, he told them, was providential. He and his wife were preparing to start a trip into the wilderness and required both clothing and transportation. Therefore, he proposed a simple trade. He and his wife would exchange garments with the Micmac and would take possession of the canoe, as well.

The dark-skinned warrior's eyes gleamed when he heard Ghonkaba suggest that they also exchange weapons. In return for the Micmac's bow and arrows, he would get the colonel's handsome sword.

The Micmac squaw greedily eyed Toshabe's crystal earrings and necklace. Toshabe responded immediately. Removing the necklace, she placed it around the overjoyed squaw's throat, and put the earrings on her ears.

Ghonkaba pressed this new advantage. Unbuckling the sword of shining steel with its silver scabbard, he handed it to the Micmac. The brave fingered it lovingly, his eyes huge and round. Struck by good fortune when he least expected it, he was overwhelmed.

So the bargain was speedily consummated. Shedding their elegant attire immediately, Toshabe and Ghonkaba put on the simple clothing of the Indian couple, a knee-length skirt and breastband of doeskin for Toshabe and a breechclout and trousers and fringed shirt of buckskin for Ghonkaba. Fortunately, the Micmacs' moccasins were of sizes that would fit. Later, Ghonkaba would add Seneca war paint after finding some roots or other substance that he could boil as dyes. At the moment, simply escaping was infinitely more important.

Ghonkaba felt sorry for the Micmac pair and knew from Toshabe's look that she felt as he did. The couple surely would be apprehended when they appeared in Quebec in the dead colonel's stolen uniform and in a gown belonging to the courtesan who must have had a hand in two murders.

No permanent harm would come to them, Ghonkaba felt reasonably certain, but until questions of their identity were straightened out they would create considerable confusion for the authorities. He could only hope that by that time he and Toshabe would be well on their way home. Unfortunately, that was not to prove the case, as luck would have it.

By Seneca standards, the bow and arrows of the Micmac were crafted less than perfectly, Ghonkaba thought as he slung the bow and quiver over one shoulder. But he felt infinitely better able now to protect Toshabe and himself.

At his signal, Toshabe climbed into the canoe, seating herself in the center. Ghonkaba took his place in the stern, and waving farewell to the happy Micmac

131

couple, he set out for the south shore of the St. Lawrence.

Navigating the great river was far more difficult than it appeared. Not one current, but several, prevailed in the waters that flowed from the interior of North America toward the Atlantic. Here the current was swift, there it changed without warning to a slow crawl, and then, before the paddler was aware, a baffling crosscurrent arose. Because the Seneca were accustomed only to small rivers and lakes, Ghonkaba's experience as a canoeist was severely limited, though he had crossed the Hudson and other major streams in his travels. He had to struggle constantly to prevent the frail craft from capsizing as he sought to move the canoe forward, seeking to reach the far shore as soon as possible. He was aware that his awkward attempts were slowing the canoe's progress, and they were losing more time. Sweat dripped down his forehead, but he persisted, performing the unfamiliar, laborious task with dogged determination.

Toshabe seemed to sense when he most needed encouragement, and at that moment called softly, "We are drawing nearer to the bank by the moment. There is only a short distance still to go."

Ghonkaba redoubled his efforts at this, and soon the prow shot up onto dry land. They hastily disembarked and dragged the craft into the deep forest that extended southward from the shore. After several dozen paces, they came to a nest of brambles, and there they deposited the canoe, covering it with layers of dead autumn leaves. Though it was only a crude job of concealment, he hoped that pursuers would waste time in locating the canoe. By then, the quarry would be gone.

Their journey together from the land of the Seneca

to the town of the Erie had given them experience that was useful now. It often was unnecessary to exchange words. Ghonkaba merely signaled, and Toshabe knew instantly what he meant and followed without question.

Again and again, she proved herself agile as well as courageous, and her stamina was considerably greater than Ghonkaba had dared hope. So they made far greater progress than he had planned. Only when he saw her stumble or drag her feet did he call a halt. Then they rested very briefly until, at her insistence, they resumed their flight.

A watery sun rose higher, filtering into the forest through the treetops, and by the time it stood almost directly overhead, Ghonkaba knew that he would have to call a prolonged halt soon. As they came to a stream, about ten yards wide, he motioned to Toshabe to sit on a thick, hollow log while he took stock of their situation.

Toshabe sank gratefully onto the log and, removing her moccasins, plunged her feet into the icy cold water of the stream, happily wriggling her toes.

Meantime, Ghonkaba put an ear close to the ground and listened intently. When he raised his head, his manner was grave. "It is as I feared," he reported. "The French already are in pursuit. The bodies must have been found even sooner than we expected. Ludona probably is with them, and they most likely also have some Huron warriors acting as advance scouts. I'm sure the French care very little about the death of the guard at the bordello, or what has happened to the woman. But General Montcalm must be greatly distressed by the death of the colonel, and he cannot permit it to go unpunished."

"They've undoubtedly decided that I'm actually an enemy agent," Toshabe acknowledged. "Because of my involvement with you, they'll go to great lengths to find and kill us. Now you should leave me behind and save yourself. You can make far better time traveling alone than while shepherding me. I'm already tired out, so I must either rest or I shall walk slower and slower until they overtake us."

"Under no circumstances will I abandon you," Ghonkaba informed her, "and leave you to face such a fate."

"Then I can only do my best to be worthy of your regard," she said, "and try to face without flinching whatever comes."

He smiled wryly. "It is not my intention that we die," he told her before drifting into a deep silence as he pondered the problem. The fact that the enemy seemed to be drawing closer with each passing moment, plainly traveling very rapidly and having no difficulty in following their trail so far, did not seem to upset him.

Toshabe knew better than to interrupt his thoughts, and sat quietly, her feet resting in the water, as she awaited his decision. In thinking about their plight, and the proximity of the pursuit, she concluded that the Micmac couple must have been questioned very quickly and revealed the direction of the "spies'" flight.

At last Ghonkaba stirred. "This is an extraordinary situation," he said. "So whatever measures we take also must be extraordinary. I would like you to climb into that log and conceal yourself there. Do you think you can do it?"

Startled, she could say only, "I don't know."

"Try it. Quickly!"

She dropped to the ground and gingerly inched into

the log feet first as chunks of rotted wood showered over her.

"When you're completely out of sight," Ghonkaba told her, "stay there and make no sound. They'll approach shortly and should come past this very spot. I will be trying to lead them away from you, but as soon as I can I'll return for you."

"How can you lead them away?" she wanted to know.

He picked up her moccasins and held them at eye level, but offered no explanation. "Trust me," he said.

"I place my complete trust in you," Toshabe told him solemnly, and then her face and head also disappeared into the log.

"That's perfect," Ghonkaba called softly. "Stay where you are, keep silent until I return, and no harm will come to you."

She made no reply, and silence reigned in the forest.

He slipped his hands into her moccasins. Then, on all fours, he followed the course of the stream, staying close to the bank. Here, his footsteps and those his moccasin-shod hands were making would be more easily seen.

With surprising speed and agility, he covered several hundred yards, and only when the ground became harder did he abandon his ploy.

Stepping into ankle-deep water, where he would leave no footprints, he moved at a rapid trot, emerging occasionally to leave a print either with his own moccasin on one foot or with Toshabe's moccasin in his hand. A single print could be sufficient to draw pursuers farther and farther on a false trail.

When, at last, he came to terrain of the kind he was seeking, he could see a high hill on one side heading toward the St. Lawrence into which this smaller stream presumably emptied, and he deliberately made two of his own footprints and two of Toshabe's heading toward the top of the slope. The pursuers, he hoped, would think that the fugitives were moving back toward the St. Lawrence.

Inspecting the footprints carefully and finding them apparently good enough for his purpose, Ghonkaba carefully doubled back, leaving no prints or other traces underfoot, then plunged into the river. Wading to its center, which was waist deep, he walked for a short distance, then swam toward the far bank. Heading south, away from the river, he began to double back toward where he had left Toshabe.

Partway toward his destination, he heard the sound of men approaching through the forest, and he burrowed deep into a bush, which concealed him completely. Looking out from it, he could examine the enemy.

Precisely as he had anticipated, Ludona was leading the group, accompanied by two senior Huron warriors. Behind them ranged a dozen Frenchmen carrying muskets. These men apparently were not Regulars in the French Army; instead of the conspicuous white uniforms they wore the buckskin shirts and trousers such as English colonists would wear. To Ghonkaba, that identified them as settlers similar to the militiamen of the English colonies, men thoroughly familiar with the forest, and therefore extremely dangerous.

But he was not overly concerned about them. Having succeeded in the main stroke of his attempt to outwit them, his battle was more than half won.

Waiting until the men moved beyond hearing range, he left his hiding place, then sped through the wilderness as rapidly as he could travel toward where Toshabe was concealed. With an unerring sense of direction, he crossed the small river at a point just beyond where he recalled the hollow log would be, and doubled back, taking care to leave no footprints. The spot was deserted and looked as though no human had come near.

He halted, rapped lightly on the log, and called softly to Toshabe.

After a brief pause and a rustling sound within, she emerged slowly, disheveled, with bits of rotting wood clinging to her hair and skin. But her expression was calm, and when he pointed to show that they were to cross the stream, she immediately understood. Instinctively, she raised a hand to brush off the bits of wood. Ghonkaba caught hold of her wrist to prevent her from shedding it. Now she comprehended; no telltale signs should be left in case their pursuers returned to the spot.

They crossed together, but on the far side, Ghonkaba picked her up, placed her over his shoulder, and started southward at the Seneca jogging pace. For the next hour, he maintained that speed.

Only after he had covered many miles and reasoned that he had provided a safe cushion of distance from their pursuers, did he finally halt and lower Toshabe to the ground.

"You must let me use my own feet," she told him firmly now. "You'll collapse if you try to carry me any farther." As he jogged, they had exchanged no words.

Ghonkaba shook off her objections. "I've carried a deer on many occasions back to the main town of my people after I shot it. You can be sure you weigh less than a large deer."

He had made up his mind, and she knew it would be a waste of breath to argue. Instead, she told him her impressions of the enemy troop that had passed within a few feet of the log.

Ghonkaba cut her short, telling her that he had actually seen their pursuers. He was impatient to be moving again. Abruptly throwing Toshabe across a shoulder as he would have carried a wounded warrior, he started off once more through the forest. Now was the time that he had to put more and more distance between them and the enemy. Later they would have ample opportunity to talk, provided they really were able to escape while the pursuit was being pressed.

Resuming his run, he traveled once again at the grueling pace that would have soon exhausted anyone else.

Impressed by his stamina, but concerned for his welfare, Toshabe murmured a protest from time to time, trying to insist that she could walk or run through the forest. Ghonkaba continued to refuse to be distracted.

With nothing better to occupy her, Toshabe began to note the life abounding nearby in the wilderness. She heard a chipmunk chattering, and the sound made her smile. She caught a glimpse of squirrels scurrying around in the underbrush near a pair of towering oaks, searching for nuts to hide away for the winter. In the distance, barely discernible in the underbrush, she saw a fox that halted and froze as it heard the unfamiliar sounds made by humans; in its mouth dangled a rabbit. Only the fit and the strong survived in the forest, and the rabbit's fate was a reminder of what could happen unless she and Ghonkaba were clever enough to outwit their foes.

Daylight faded and gave way to night, but Ghonkaba's feet continued to pound rhythmically, and he showed no sign of tiring. Toshabe marveled at his strength, but she kept quiet in order to avoid unduly diverting him. Not until at least half the night had passed did he finally draw to a halt beside a small stream, where he suggested they drink.

Stooping on its bank, she drank her fill, and as Ghonkaba kneaded his leg muscles, she busied herself nearby. He paid no attention until he motioned to her to climb onto his shoulder again. Then she showed him what she was holding in both hands.

Astonished, he saw that she had dug up several roots, which she had washed off in the stream.

"I understand," she told him, "why you do not want to take the time to hunt or fish or light a fire. But surely these cannot hurt you, and they may even succeed in warding off hunger until we can get a real meal."

Her thoughtfulness made him smile sheepishly and accept some of the roots. They tasted good, far better than he had anticipated, and he realized now that he was hungrier than he had known. But he could not allow himself to dwell on the idea of food for many hours yet, and again he swung Toshabe across a shoulder and started forward. His effort was still in its early stages.

To her astonishment, he continued to run all through the night and far into the morning, pausing only infrequently for sips of water. Because Seneca made no complaint when their stomachs were empty, Toshabe did not dare complain. Sometimes she dozed, sleeping an hour or two at a time. But Ghonkaba neither slept nor rested and managed to maintain his incredible pace, giving no sign of tiring. Toshabe was afraid he would drop.

In the afternoon she heard a muffled roar in the distance but could not identify it, hard as she tried.

They had traveled much farther to the east than she had realized, and the Atlantic coast lay directly ahead. Ghonkaba was intending to enter the English colonies by way of the Maine District of the Massachusetts Bay Colony. They would be far from their final destination, but at least they would be relatively safe after passing through the lands held by the Algonquian, who lived on both sides of the border between French Canada and the English colonies.

They came at last to the coast, and Ghonkaba lowered her one last time to the ground. They were on a high bluff that seemed to jut out over ocean waters pounding against the rocks below. Ghonkaba raised a hand and scanned the horizon, paying particular attention to the area to the north and west. Finally he turned and smiled broadly.

"We have outwitted the enemy and have won the battle," he said. "We have completely escaped from the French."

She felt infinite relief. "You're sure we are not being followed?"

"I'm certain of it," he replied flatly. "I thought several hours ago that we probably had shaken them off, but now I am truly sure. The location of the border in this area is a mystery to me, so I am uncertain whether we are still in New France. But I know for sure that we have cut across the top of the Maine District, and I am willing to stake our lives that this water is what I believe the English call the Bay of Fundy. That would mean we are out of French territory. We have lost our pursuers, and with them, Ludona."

"You think we're safe, then?" she demanded.

"We're as safe as we shall ever be, I believe," he assured her. "The only nation in this region is the Algonquian, and although they are numerous, one Seneca can stand up to a hundred Algonquian with ease." He laughed boastfully, as only a young warrior filled with the pride of nationhood could laugh.

Chapter VII

Gazing down from the heights of the cliff along the coastline that stretched toward the south, Ghonkaba could scarcely restrain his excitement. He had spotted something of real interest along the inner edge of a broadening stretch of beach that provided a dry footing. He offered no explanation, but Toshabe followed him down a trail along a ledge leading to the beach, and at last she could see the reason for his interest. Directly ahead in the side of the cliff, with its entrance concealed by boulders, was a cave.

Eagerly they explored it together. It consisted of a single chamber with a high ceiling and walls that were surprisingly dry.

"We have earned a rest, I think," Ghonkaba said.

"We'll stay here for a time and gather our strength for the remainder of our journey."

They made their way back up the cliff, gathered dead branches and other firewood in the forest, and brought it down, placing it just outside the cave entrance.

Ghonkaba had been staring at the sea. "I am sure," he told Toshabe, "that the waters of the Great Sea are very cold at this time of year. But surely they are not too cold for a Seneca." He began to peel off his buckskin shirt.

"If you go swimming," Toshabe said, "I, too, go."

They both removed their clothes and ran toward the breakers.

The water of the Atlantic proved to be even chillier than expected, but they nevertheless were invigorated and swam energetically for a short time. Feeling refreshed, they then dashed laughing into the shallows. The tide had washed in large numbers of clams and oysters, and Ghonkaba plucked two large sea crabs that were trying to burrow into the soft sand where the tide had dropped them. Despite his distaste for unfamiliar seafood, he resolved to overcome it and make the best of the situation. Baked, the crabs might be more palatable than in a stew. They returned with their booty to the cave, and while Ghonkaba built and started a fire, Toshabe vanished for a time. She returned bearing an armload of edible roots with which she could brew a tea.

While the shellfish and the roots cooked in the coals, Ghonkaba departed to fill two large conch shells at a small, nearby inland lake. After a prolonged time without food, they were at last able to feast.

The fire dried and warmed them, as well, which pleased Toshabe, since she was starting to shiver, but tried to curb this desire. Ghonkaba, she noted, displayed no such tendency, and she wondered if all Seneca warriors were as resilient as this remarkable young brave.

The crabs proved to be so delicious that they hurried down to the shore to find more. They ate until their hunger pangs were dissipated, and drank enough tea to quiet the thirst that the food brought on.

Completely relaxed, they sat cross-legged before the fire, facing each other. As they looked into the flames, Toshabe was the first to speak.

"My debt to Ghonkaba is so great," she said, "that I can never repay it, not if I live until I am ten times the age of the oldest of my ancestors. At great risk to yourself, you have rescued me from a life of slavery and shame. I wish I could properly thank you for what you have done for me."

"You owe me nothing," Ghonkaba replied. "I acted at the bidding of my grandfather. It was the last request he made on this earth."

She sucked in her breath sharply. "He is gone?"

Ghonkaba bowed his head. "He has departed to the land of his ancestors."

Tears came to her eyes, but because they were unseemly in an Indian, she immediately blinked them away.

"My grandfather," he said, "granted you freedom while you were in the land of the Seneca. The perfidy of your fellow Erie robbed you of that freedom. So his honor was at stake. He told me he would not be able to rest with a pure heart among his ancestors unless I could rescue you."

Overwhelmed, Toshabe could not speak, and Ghonkaba misunderstood her silence. "I am not returning you to the land of the Seneca as a captive," he assured her. "You cannot return to your own people because they will most likely abuse your freedom again. Therefore, you will stay with us as an honored guest, and you will be under the protection of Jagonh, the Great Sachem of the Iroquois. He will give his personal pledge for your safety and security."

"What have I done to deserve so happy a fate?" she asked.

His reply encompassed all that he knew. "I can tell you only that you won the favor of my grandfather and my father."

"But why was it that you were sent to rescue me?" she persisted.

"I am their seed, and in my veins flows their blood," he replied. "They carried the burden of many responsibilities that made such a mission impossible. I am young, and so it was my duty to perform this task for the honor of my family."

She pondered for a time, and when she spoke again she seemed miffed. "You sound," she said, "as though you would have come to Quebec for me even if you had not known me well in the past."

"That is true," he agreed. "My grandfather gave me an order on his deathbed, and I obeyed it. I would have sought you out in Quebec and done all that was necessary if I never had set eyes on you."

Toshabe drew in a deep breath, and then sighed. Curiously, Ghonkaba looked sharply at her, unable to understand why she seemed to be unhappy. Though the whims of women always were mysterious to him, he hoped that he would be able soon to understand whatever was on her mind. And now she spoke clearly enough.

"It was my hope," she said, "that perhaps you were

taking such terrible risks for my sake because you had formed an attachment to me."

"I suppose that is true," he conceded at last, after reflecting on it. "It may be that I took extra risks because I know you and am very fond of you."

He wasn't responding as she had hoped, and in frustration she dug her fingernails into her palms. She needed to speak even more bluntly than she had intended.

"We have been alone," she reminded him, "sharing each other's company for days and nights on end. In all this time, you have not made one gesture that indicates any desire for me. Is it possible that the occupation I have been forced to follow in Quebec, as in your own land, cooled your interest in me?"

Ghonkaba laughed aloud. "The Frenchmen in Quebec," he said, "paid large sums of money for your favors, and I am sure that none paid overly much for them. You are unique and extraordinary, and I know of no other woman like you."

Toshabe was completely exasperated. "But for some private reasons of your own," she exclaimed, "you no longer want me."

"That is untrue," he replied hotly. "I have never failed to want you for a single moment when we have been separated!"

"Then why haven't you demonstrated such a feeling to me?" she demanded, her patience exhausted.

He blinked in surprise. "I carry no purse heavy with gold, such as the wealthy French traders and the generals and colonels carry. How do I know how you would regard a poor Seneca after that kind of experience? Even though," he could not help adding, "I have been promoted to the rank of war chief."

She was pleased for him, and so his digression did

not irritate her greatly. "I'm sure you deserved the promotion," she told him.

"I must earn it in the days that lie ahead. When we go into battle, then I must prove my worth."

Toshabe now knew how to end the impasse that was keeping them apart. Rising slowly to her feet, she said softly, "You have earned my gratitude, which will not diminish through the years, and you have earned a great deal more, as well." With slow deliberateness and without coyness, she unwound her breastband and slipped out of her skirt. "Take me whenever it pleases you, and do with me as you wish," she whispered.

Though trained never to reveal his feelings, Ghonkaba realized that the veins that pounded at his temples bulged and throbbed. "If I lie with you," he said, "it can no longer be as a brave who beds a captive from another nation. You are now a free woman. When a warrior lies with such a woman, she becomes his lifelong squaw."

Toshabe was stunned. She hadn't expected that this heir to the proudest name in all of the Indian nations would respond with what seemed to be an implicit proposal of marriage. She could think of nothing to say other than to murmur, "So be it."

Ghonkaba looked at her proud nudity for a long moment, then quickly removed his shirt, buckskin pants, and breechclout and tossed them aside. Stepping around the fire, he picked Toshabe up, this time cradling her instead of throwing her over his shoulder, and carried her into their cave.

The fire cast a dim light into the naturally protective room, and enough warmth had seeped in, too, to make it eminently comfortable. But Ghonkaba and Toshabe were no longer aware of their surroundings. They embraced, and as their lips met and their bodies touched, their tribulations and hardships were swept away. They were together again, and now nothing else could matter.

As their lovemaking became more intense, Toshabe vividly remembered what she had almost forgotten: he was the only man who could truly arouse her and give her the total satisfaction that she craved but had to pretend with any other man.

Ghonkaba knew only that he wanted her now as he never had before with her or any woman. It did not really matter that they had made love numerous times previously. His yearning was so intense, so deep, that this seemed to be the first time he had taken her. As always, he was as concerned for her gratification as for his own, as she gave herself to him freely, unstintingly. The trials they had undergone seemed to sharpen their desire, and their lovemaking was explosive, its climax shattering.

Their appetites seemingly insatiable, they began to make love again, almost as soon as they had achieved a mutual satisfaction. This time their love play was slower, more deliberate.

In the morning, Ghonkaba scarcely remembered having placed his weapons close at hand before he and Toshabe drifted off into a long and dreamless sleep.

A series of surprises awaited him when the sun, streaming in through the cave's entrance, awakened him. Outside, a fire was crackling merrily, providing needed warmth. Shellfish and roots were cooking in the coals, and in two large clam shells some other substance bubbled. Looking bright and rested, Toshabe promptly explained these. "In these shells," she told him proudly, "there is green dye and yellow dye, which I made from the entrails of the fish we've been eating. As it may be that we have now entered territory claimed by the British colonies, I knew you would be eager to proclaim your identity by wearing your own war paint once again. Soon the liquid will cool, and you can use it."

He was amazed by her industry and thoughtfulness, and greeted her with a prolonged kiss. "You not only prepared dyes," he said at last, "but you also built up the fire and you gathered more food for our morning meal. You could have awakened me so that I could share the work."

"You carried me for many miles through the wilderness," she told him firmly. "Let me, in return, do a few simple chores that can make the burden of travel easier for you."

Never had he encountered such generosity of spirit, and he was deeply impressed. One aspect of their relationship troubled him, however, and as they ate he decided the time had come to speak candidly. "Never have I known there could be such tenderness in lovemaking as we shared last night," he said. "But I am troubled. I'm not sure I can reciprocate the open generosity of Toshabe. The Iroquois are engaged in the most bitter war we ever have fought, and now is not the time for me to enter into marriage, particularly as I must justify my new status as war chief."

"I have not asked for marriage or for any other reward," Toshabe protested with great dignity.

Her attitude upset and confused him. In the Seneca nation, a young woman who allowed a warrior to make love to her would expect marriage. But Toshabe's seeming indifference left him bewildered. Perhaps he would be wise to take the problem to his father. Jagonh was more experienced than he in the ways of women and the world.

For forty-eight hours, they rested at the cave, renewing their energy and returning to their rude couch time after time. The second night, she persuaded him to relate the thrilling story of how he had found her in Quebec and had prevailed against all odds to reach her.

When they resumed their long journey, Ghonkaba soon solved their food problem by bringing down a deer. Toshabe expertly butchered the carcass, plunging into the task eagerly. That night they ate their fill of meat, and they smoked enough of the venison over their campfire to assure a supply that would last for several days.

Grateful to Toshabe for having found the means to make his green and yellow war paint that marked him as a Seneca, Ghonkaba wore it proudly. Because they were uncertain whose territory they were in, however, they avoided other Indians, and several times they detoured around towns, presumably of the Algonquian.

With no pursuers dogging them, they were able to travel at a more leisurely pace, and Toshabe walked along behind Ghonkaba, or occasionally beside him when the countryside opened up into fields. Her stamina determined the speed of their travel, and they moved at no faster a rate than she could easily manage. Considering her feelings, safety, and strength, he never called on her for anything that would prove injurious or too difficult. He could hardly believe that a young woman who had been the most glittering courtesan in Quebec could be so at home in the wilderness. Their earlier travels hadn't prepared him for her gallantry. But Toshabe's helpful attitude continued despite the daily hardships. She kindled the fires, cooked their meals, collected edible roots and berries, caught fish in the lakes and streams—and proved equally adept at choosing campsites that would be comfortable and safe.

Winter came swiftly and unexpectedly. With it, a new problem arose. They both were unsuitably clad for snow and severe cold. But they had no opportunity to pause anywhere long enough to make cloaks from the hides of animals that Ghonkaba shot.

Improvising ingeniously, Toshabe nevertheless hit upon a solution that Ghonkaba readily approved.

"I suggest," she said, "that we anoint ourselves with animal fat. We will then smell very bad, but we'll become immune to the odor. At least we will be warm."

The grease, easy enough to apply, made them far warmer and better able to tolerate bone-chilling winds.

From a hilltop one afternoon they saw in the distance a small group of log cabins surrounded by a palisade. It was a community of colonists from either England or France, Ghonkaba concluded immediately. Surprisingly, the gate of the palisade was wide open, though no one was guarding it.

They walked cautiously closer to the community, and as they approached it, Toshabe remained hidden in the woods while Ghonkaba went forward to investigate.

He entered the town easily, annoyed by the inhabitants' lack of security, and concealed himself behind a large woodpile.

He did not have long to wait. A door opened and two boys carrying buckets left the house. From inside a woman called instructions not to loiter but to return at once with the water she was sending them to fetch. She spoke in English, and Ghonkaba was greatly relieved. The assurance that they were out of territory controlled by the French was enough to speed them on their way, able to discard the precautions that had been advisable at the cost of slowing them down. Returning to the forest, he told Toshabe, "All is well. We are in New

England now." She was overjoyed, and responded by putting her arms around him as an expression of thankfulness that they actually had made their way to relative safety.

Ghonkaba had friends in both Boston and Springfield, but he decided to avoid both cities as well as all other communities because that would delay their arrival in the land of the Seneca. So they cut through the Berkshire Hills—no mean feat in winter—and reached the upper valleys of New York Colony. They could have found warmer clothing in one of the towns, but both wanted to end the journey as rapidly as they could.

At last, without incident, they reached the main town of the Seneca, still inadequately clothed and covered with grease. Their arrival created a sensation. Men, women, and children poured out of the lodges and dwellings to gape. Despite their strange appearance, no one laughed aloud, largely due to the respect that the Seneca had for Ghonkaba's temper. No one, surely, wanted to be challenged if the warrior felt that he and Toshabe were being mocked.

As for Toshabe, who had been a prostitute in the town, everyone knew Renno had granted her freedom and that Ghonkaba had been sent to rescue her in Quebec. Despite her onetime status, she was treated respectfully.

Immediately after greeting Ja-gonh and Ah-wen-ga, Ghonkaba searched out some dull knives with which he and Toshabe could scrape off the thick layer of grease that had so effectively protected them from the worst effects of winter during their long adventure. Their clothes from the Micmac couple were so worn they could only be discarded.

Then he dived into the icy Seneca Lake, promptly followed by Toshabe, in order to finish scrubbing away the remaining evil smell of the animal fat. This they did as briefly as possible because large chunks of ice floating in the lake made the water quickly unbearable.

Shivering and feeling half frozen when they emerged, they ran immediately to the house of the Great Sachem.

Even before providing clothing to replace the discarded rags, Ah-wen-ga gave them gourds of scalding Seneca broth. The broth, in which vegetables and animal bones had been cooked for many hours, traditionally was drunk as hot as human mouths and gullets could stand.

Toshabe now was bundled into a huge robe of Ah-wen-ga's, one made of fox skins. For the first time since fleeing Quebec, she felt comfortable.

Ghonkaba put on only the buckskin shirt, trousers, and leggings that were the warrior's customary winter attire. He would lose stature with his comrades if he seemed to indulge himself. He was proud to place three hawk feathers, symbols of his new rank, in his scalp lock.

No-da-vo, now the sachem of the Seneca, came to supper that evening with his wife, Goo-ga-ro-no, sister of Ja-gonh.

Mindful of her previous status as a captive and prostitute, Toshabe had been nervous at the prospect of meeting the Seneca hierarchy as an equal instead of an inferior being. But Ja-gonh and Ah-wen-ga, setting the tone, treated her with great cordiality.

After the meal, the Great Sachem and the sachem of the Seneca listened attentively to Ghonkaba's recounting of his rescue of Toshabe. She herself heard the story again with delight. Whenever he paused, his father and uncle interrupted with searching questions. No mention was made of the life Toshabe had led in Quebec.

"The most important development in all this adventure," Ghonkaba concluded, "is even greater than the fact that Toshabe is able to be among us tonight and to share with us this meal. She is also sharing with us her freedom from oppression, which was the heartfelt desire of my grandfather, Renno, when with his dying words he laid upon me the responsibility for finding her in Quebec and bringing her safely away from there. This has been done. And now I am able to repeat to you for the first time the words that my grandfather spoke to me just before he crossed the river to join his ancestors. What Renno spoke to me was this: 'My soul will not rest easy in the land of our ancestors until you have accomplished this mission for me.' "

When he had finished speaking, Ja-gonh, who had been sitting with bowed head, raised it and gazed with great pride at his son. "Now the soul of my father and your grandfather is able to rest," he told Ghonkaba, "and this is possible because of the brave actions of you, my son, and your steadfast behavior in doing exactly what he bid you to do. The manitous know all this and will be especially aware of your comings and your goings in the future. As I am sure you heard from your grandfather many times, they will be faithful guides for you always, as they were in your time of great need in this successful adventure."

"Let us not only be thankful to the manitous," Ahwen-ga added now, "but be thankful that the soul of our great father, the revered Renno, can be completely at peace. We must be very happy tonight for that reason, and happy that the way in which our son followed his grandfather's final instructions has made this possible."

Before Ghonkaba bowed his head in response to the words of his mother and his father, he could see the shining eyes of Toshabe on him, full of the thankfulness that she, too, felt and also full of awareness of the heroic deeds that had brought about her freedom. All present could see the love that she directed toward him.

"One thing is certain," Ja-gonh remarked later to No-da-vo, "Ghonkaba undoubtedly knows Quebec better than does any other warrior. But now we must be very prudent in giving him an assignment that would take him back there as either an espionage agent or an advance scout."

"That is true," No-da-vo agreed. "The French undoubtedly have put a price on his head. He would be obvious there, and would have to be extraordinarily careful in order to avoid being parted from his scalp."

Ghonkaba found another matter far more interesting. "There will be an attack on Quebec, do you think?"

"That has yet to be decided," Ja-gonh told him. "I have been asked to accompany General Strong to Louisburg to confer with General Amherst and his deputy, a General Wolfe. But it seems logical that there will be a major attack. I know that some of the officers who lead troops into combat are in favor of it. Townsend Whiting, who I understand now holds the rank of brigadier, favors it, and from Virginia Colonel Washington has written urging such a course, too."

"You've heard from Washington?" Ghonkaba inquired eagerly.

"I received a communication from him about a

quarter-moon ago. I read between the lines, and it seems to me that he is unhappy because the future action in the war is passing out of his theater of operations."

"That cannot be helped," No-da-vo added. "The British and their colonials grow ever stronger, and by now they greatly outnumber the French and their Indian allies in the wilderness. They must concentrate on using this strength to go after the enemy, boldly fighting him where he is strongest."

"So it makes sense," Ja-gonh declared, "to end the campaign as rapidly and as decisively as possible by attacking the very heart of the French empire. I am curious as to the opinion of Ghonkaba on its strength and the feasibility of an attack there."

Ghonkaba weighed the question. "I can see why some leaders would think in such terms, I grant you, my father," he said, "but conquest of Quebec will not be easy. The city is well protected by nature, and the location of the Citadel makes her almost incapable of being taken by assault."

No-da-vo laughed derisively. "Do not speak to General Amherst about French bastions being unconquerable. Louisburg was supposed to be the strongest fortress in the New World, but Amherst has captured it. It was a masterpiece of strategy and tactics."

"I have little doubt," Ja-gonh said, "that the meeting to which General Amherst has summoned me will determine the war goal of our allied forces. In the meantime, my son, work awaits you. Colonel Washington requests that you be sent to join him."

Ghonkaba was surprised. "Surely he does not intend to begin an operation in the field in this season?"

The Great Sachem smiled faintly. "Hardly. I think he's eager to join in a campaign elsewhere, and he wants to make certain that everything is in order within Virginia's borders. Then he can apply to the governor of Virginia and to General Strong for permission to join their armies where the action appears most likely to occur."

"Colonel Washington, no doubt, will explain his reasons to me, as he always does," Ghonkaba said. "It is enough that he is summoning me. I must go at once. I will leave early tomorrow."

His mother was startled. "You have just completed a very trying mission," she objected. "You deserve time to yourself at home."

Toshabe was even more dismayed. "Yes," she agreed immediately. "You need to rest."

Ghonkaba waved aside their protests. "You know that what you ask cannot be, my mother." Deliberately, he refrained from speaking reproachfully. "As for you, Toshabe, learn this rule of the Seneca: when a warrior is called to duty, he obeys no matter what the cost. When the campaign ends and the war is won, I will have ample opportunity to rest and to be with my people. Until then, I must do what is required of me."

Ja-gonh was pleased to hear his son's words. Ghonkaba, he could see, had matured since he had tried to rebel against the authority of his elders.

Toshabe, however, was unsatisfied, and clearly upset. Ah-wen-ga seemed to understand.

"Toshabe," she said flatly, her tone indicating that she would tolerate no dissension, "will live under this roof and will be under the direct protection of the Great Sachem. She suffered once because we were careless. We shall not make that same mistake again, and Toshabe will be safe dwelling here with Ja-gonh and me."

No-da-vo and Goo-ga-ro-no enthusiastically approved the plan.

Toshabe was stunned to find herself being treated as a member of the family, actually as a daughter-in-law would be.

Ghonkaba, too, was uncertain how to interpret his mother's generous gesture. It was not his place to question her; whatever her motives, they would be explained to him only when she was ready. Until then, he was obliged to keep silent. He was greatly relieved because he knew that no place on earth would be safer for Toshabe than in the home of his parents under the wing of the Great Sachem. No enemy would dare approach her there.

That same night, however, a price for such protection became apparent. For the first time since they were in the cave, Ghonkaba and Toshabe did not sleep together. To Ja-gonh and Ah-wen-ga, official upholders of the old morality of the Seneca, it would have been unthinkable for her to share her room with Ghonkaba. So they slept at opposite ends of the house, and although Toshabe knew why she was restless all night, Ghonkaba failed to understand his own feelings and attributed them to his desire to be on his way to Virginia.

Ah-wen-ga rose at dawn, as she always did, to prepare breakfast, and Toshabe silently joined her in the area that served as both kitchen and living room. She built up the cooking fire without being asked, and then cleaned the fish that would be broiled. Working swiftly and surely, she took a pestle and mortar and began to grind corn into tiny crumbs for making bread.

Ah-wen-ga smiled from across the room. "You will spoil me if you do all of my work for me," she warned.

"You honor me by allowing me to stay here," Toshabe told her. "I must repay your kindness as best I can."

"I have been more than repaid," Ah-wen-ga said, "by the satisfaction that you bring into the life of my son."

The pestle was frozen in midair as Toshabe gaped.

"It is plain to me," Ah-wen-ga continued, "that you have won the love of Ghonkaba."

"At moments, I have shared that thought," Toshabe said, "but I believe you are mistaken. Sometimes he is very gentle and loving with me, but most of the time his thoughts are of war, and he forgets I am alive. He does not love me, I'm afraid."

"Ena, the wife of Ghonka," Ah-wen-ga said softly, "often complained that he did not know she existed. Betsy, the wife of Renno, who sometimes boasted she enjoyed a perfect marriage, was in despair on other occasions, and felt certain that her husband had forgotten her. I have been the wife of Ja-gonh for more than twenty-five returns of the spring, but on occasion—like last night when he was talking about the war against the French—I would swear that he scarcely remembers my name. So it is also with Ghonkaba. The glory of the Seneca and the honor of our traditions mean much to him. Victory for warriors of the Seneca in battle can seem to overshadow all else in his thinking. But I knew the very moment the two of you appeared out of the forest yesterday that you love Ghonkaba and that he returns your love."

"I wish I could be sure of that," Toshabe replied with a gentle sigh.

"You may be very sure," Ah-wen-ga replied. "Why do you think I offered you a home with us? I want to preserve you from all possible harm until Ghonkaba returns for you. Take my word for it; he will!"

Further conversation was impossible because at that moment Ja-gonh and his son entered the room, earnestly discussing the military situation of the English colonists versus the French.

Ah-wen-ga raised an eyebrow and rolled her eyes, and Toshabe busied herself putting the fish on the fire to broil.

"When I attend the meeting of General Amherst," the Great Sachem was saying, "I will tell him we should move with speed and strike with as much force as we can muster. And I will propose that we do it as early in the spring as possible."

"Why do you see speed as so essential?" Ghonkaba wanted to know.

"It's the only way," his father explained, "that I know to minimize the losses to our side, particularly in the English frontier settlements. When the weather becomes warm, the Indian allies of the French are certain to take to the warpath again, and they'll be attacking isolated farms and small communities. They cannot be prevented from crossing the border because bands of armed men can sneak across at too many places. So it strikes me that the only way to prevent these raids is to strike at the heart of the French defenses."

"And of course that means Quebec," Ghonkaba observed.

"Correct. As I said before, if Quebec can be taken, the entire French effort will collapse, and we can force the enemy to surrender."

"It's easier to say than to accomplish," Ghonkaba replied thoughtfully. "I have just come from Quebec, remember, and as I said last night I find it a formidable target. We are likely to suffer severe losses in any attempt to capture the Citadel."

"In my experience in war," Ja-gonh told him, "I

have found no such place as an impenetrable barrier. I have fought at the side of the English colonists in many campaigns. The French always boast that they have at last built a totally secure fortress that cannot be captured. That is the way they think. But in practice they are mistaken."

"You are right, my father, though I have never thought in those terms. They claimed that of Fort Duquesne but it fell to the English, who have now renamed it Fort Pitt. Louisburg fell to Amherst after a relatively easy struggle. Perhaps some way will be found to take Quebec."

Toshabe exchanged quick, subtle glances with Ah-wen-ga, who seemed to be amused. But the younger woman contained her indignation only with difficulty. Neither Ghonkaba nor his father seemed to be aware that the women were present and also ready to eat.

Toshabe served father and son their food, and they began to eat absently. Neither seemed conscious of her presence or Ah-wen-ga's.

The vision of impending battles hardly impaired the appetites of the men, and they ate heartily. Later, as they renewed their analytical discussion, both were completely engrossed.

Ah-wen-ga, whose attitude suggested that she had tolerated such scenes on countless occasions, finally decided to call a halt. "The sun is rising," she said, "and it will soon be broad daylight. If Ghonkaba is intending to leave this morning, he should be on the trail very soon."

Her son looked up at the sky, then, rising, faced his father. "I do not presume," he said, "to tell the Great Sachem how to conduct the affairs of state for which he is responsible. But I hope that if circumstances warrant, he will send for me so that I may participate actively in the combat that lies ahead. I have great admiration for Colonel Washington, and am pleased to serve under his command. But even more, I yearn for the opportunity to lead warriors into battle and to fulfill my duties as a war chief."

"Your attitude is most commendable," Ja-gonh told him, "and I will keep your words in mind."

They clasped left wrists in a gesture of family closeness, then turned from each other, neither speaking.

Ghonkaba faced Ah-wen-ga, bowing his head slightly toward her. "I bid you farewell, my mother," he said.

Ah-wen-ga, having played such a role many times, knew what was expected of her. She inclined her head in return and, folding her arms, made no reply. This was a Seneca mother's way of saying good-bye to a son going to war.

At last Ghonkaba turned toward Toshabe and looked long at her. She could feel his eyes penetrating her very being, and wondered in vain what he might be thinking.

"I bid you farewell, Toshabe," he said stolidly, his voice betraying no emotion.

He made no mention of his feeling for her, of their future together—if any—or of any other personal matter.

So Toshabe had no choice. Folding her arms over her breasts as Ah-wen-ga had done, she bowed her head a fraction of an inch. "Farewell, Ghonkaba," she said, grateful to the manitous that she was able to speak in a steady voice.

A moment later the young war chief was gone. He did not tarry and added nothing to his curt good-byes. Toshabe followed him with her eyes as she saw him trot through the town, already traveling at the customary rapid Seneca pace.

Now El-i-chi and two other elders arrived to discuss matters of strategy with the Great Sachem, and Ja-gonh received them in the main room.

Ah-wen-ga approached Toshabe and put a sympathetic hand on her shoulder. "I know how you feel," she said sympathetically. "I went through much the same experience before Ja-gonh and I were married. When I was kidnapped and taken to France, he followed me there, and against great odds managed to set me free. But I hardly could have told from his apparent attitude that he cared for me and that that was the main reason why he followed me and took so many great risks. Fortunately, I was brash and forward as a girl, or I might be waiting yet for Ja-gonh to kiss me."

Toshabe forced a laugh. "The son is much like the father."

"Both are much like Renno," Ah-wen-ga said. "Their whole outlook must be affected by the fact that their skins are light, not like those of others of our nation. In their behavior, they must be more Seneca than any others. Their inner being requires them to be fiercer in war and more reserved in their relations with others. If this is any consolation to you, you'll understand Ghonkaba's feelings in due course, and you'll come to accept them."

Looking dubious, Toshabe sighed pensively. "I just hope," she said, "that I have the opportunity."

Ah-wen-ga smiled at her. "If I know my son, you shall!"

Chapter VIII

The commanding general's private quarters at Fortress Louisburg on Cape Breton Island were luxurious, as only the French can create luxuries: thick Oriental carpets, magnificent Gobelin tapestries, and decorative but comfortable furniture. It all was intended for a gentleman living far from home who nevertheless wanted dignity and comfort surrounding him.

Major General Jeffrey Amherst, supreme commander of the British and colonial forces in the New World, was enjoying his new quarters immensely. Handpicked for his position by William Pitt, the energetic leader who had taken charge of Britain's war destinies, he was still in his early forties and strikingly handsome.

Now he had the pleasure of leading distinguished guests into his sumptuously furnished dining room. They would overlook the fact that—with one exception—the fare was being served also to the troops in the garrison: fish from the waters off Cape Breton Island, bully-beef that was British Regular Army issue, and potatoes provided by opportunistic local farmers who had fed the French as well. The one exception was the splendid wine from Amherst's private stock.

All this was made possible—the luxurious quarters, the ample, delicious menu—by virtue of the fact that Amherst had only recently led the successful attack on the fortress and, to general surprise, had captured it.

To the supreme commander's right at the table sat Major General Kenneth Strong, of the Massachusetts Militia, who had just arrived at Louisburg by British warship. Next to him was the one incongruous-looking member, Ja-gonh of the Seneca.

On Amherst's left was Brigadier Townsend Whiting, commander of the colonial strike force, a new concept in colonial warfare. His unit was made up exclusively of volunteers dedicated to the cause of attack and were prepared to assault any designated bastion.

Beside Whiting was Major General James Wolfe, Amherst's brilliant thirty-one-year-old deputy. He was believed to be the youngest officer of his rank in British Army history.

The table talk, led by Amherst, concerned the political and economic affairs of the British colonies and certain concerns of their Iroquois allies.

Ja-gonh was greatly impressed by Amherst's mastery of the entire subject matter. He seemed to have genuine interest in what went on in this land so far removed from England.

Of all Englishmen whom Ja-gonh had ever known,

Amherst's interest in life in the New World seemed sharper and more intense than any other. Had the Great Sachem been able to foresee the future, he would not have been surprised when, a scant decade and a half later, Amherst, now a baron because of his successes in the current wars, was offered the supreme command of British forces at the outbreak of the American War of Independence. Only because of his sympathies with the rebels would he be forced to decline.

At the meal's end, the port wine was served and was passed to the left, as English tradition dictated. Amherst proposed a standing toast to the health of King George II, and then, settling back in his chair, got down to the business of the evening.

"Well, gentlemen," he began, "we have a decision to make. A very vital decision. We have the French where we want them now, and the big question is: do we attack Quebec?"

Wolfe and Whiting deferred to General Strong, who outranked them, and Ja-gonh was content to remain silent for the moment, too.

"Like all of us, I've been pondering that ever since you captured this fortress, General," Strong said, "and because of our victories the question becomes even more urgent. The fall of Fort Duquesne lost the West for France, and she is now hemmed into her own borders in Canada. But whether we attack Quebec becomes a very delicate problem."

Wolfe's broad smile made him seem even younger than his years. "My position in this matter is no secret," he said. "I propose now, as I have all along, that we attack the city of Quebec."

After a moment's reflective silence, Amherst said,

"I'll ask the opinions of all of you on that. General Strong?"

Kenneth Strong cleared his throat cautiously. "We now greatly outnumber the French. No longer can there be any doubt of that. Nevertheless, an attack on Quebec can mean heavy casualties—greater by far than we may be willing to sustain. Frankly, I shrink from the idea of an open assault on the city. It would mean by far the worst casualties of the war."

"Brigadier Whiting?"

Whiting also worded his reply carefully. "It seems to me," he said, "that our casualty rate well might depend on the degree of our advance planning. If we're thorough enough, then we might be able to hold casualties down to a reasonable number."

"Ja-gonh?"

The Seneca pressed his fingertips together and looked over them at the assembled officers. "My son recently returned from a personal mission to Quebec," he said, "and I was interested in all details of it."

He was not alone in his interest. The officers immediately leaned forward and listened far more carefully.

"I believe, on the basis of what Ghonkaba has told me," he went on, "the French concentration of infantry and artillery in Quebec is formidable. The cannon in the Citadel completely control the approaches to the city by way of the St. Lawrence, and any fleet that attempted to sail up the river and discharge an army at its gates would be blown out of the water. The builders of the Citadel did not do what those who constructed Louisburg did. Here, at Louisburg, they left a vast open area untended beyond the walls of the fortress. That made it possible for you to obtain a foothold and to expand it until you were able to take control and capture Louisburg itself. The Citadel, however, sits high on a bluff, and apparently in no way can it be reached by an opposing force."

"That's also my understanding," Amherst added. "It's a classic military situation, in which a limited force can exert maximum control over an area and inflict defeat on an army several times its own size."

Resuming his narrative, Ja-gonh related why Ghonkaba had gone to Quebec, and he explained in detail what had happened there. When he came to the key portion of his story, relating to the appearance of the hawk that had showed a path from the Plains of Abraham down to the river shore some distance from the city, he thought very carefully before choosing his words. The mysteries relating to the religious beliefs of the Seneca, particularly those concerning their relations with the sacred manitous, were considered secret, and never were mentioned to outsiders.

So the Great Sachem made no mention of the hawk's unexpected appearance, though he realized that the day might come when the secret would be disclosed. For now, it sufficed to say that Ghonkaba had found the head of a path on the heights behind the Citadel and had followed it with Toshabe.

The officers were intrigued, and General Wolfe was especially fascinated. "Do you think your son could find this path again?" he demanded eagerly.

Ja-gonh was quietly amused. "He wears in his scalp lock the three hawk feathers of a war chief of his people," he replied. No other explanation should be necessary. As an afterthought, he added, "Despite the unusual dangers of returning to a place where the authorities have a price on his head for espionage and murder, I am sure that he would insist on volunteering for service in Quebec if it appears that he can be of use."

James Wolfe could scarcely contain his excitement. "The success of a very bold campaign, it seems to me, may depend on the knowledge of one Seneca warrior," he said, turning to General Amherst and addressing himself exclusively to his superior. "You have promised me an independent command, and I accept the challenge with great pleasure. I suggest the following: that my corps be embarked on vessels of the Royal Navy and that we be transported up the river within striking distance of Quebec. We will disembark at night, and the warrior who is Ja-gonh's son will lead us to the Plains of Abraham behind the Citadel."

Ja-gonh approved. "That is good," he confirmed. "The great cannon of the fortress, without exception, face toward the river where they can intercept and bombard any attackers who dare to approach the city by sea. It did not occur to the men who built the Citadel that they would need guns to defend it from assault on their rear."

One of the facets of Amherst's genius was his talent for fashioning others' ideas to meet the requirements of a specific situation. "One element is missing from your scheme, Wolfe," he pointed out. "The element of surprise. You will need a diversion to attract the attention of the French in Quebec. Suppose that General Strong and I set out from Fort Albany, together with a large contingent of Ja-gonh's Iroquois. I propose that we march north through the lands of the Iroquois and up to the two fortresses that are still in the hands of the French—Crown Point and Ticonderoga. When we get there, we will attack and capture both fortresses and then march upon Quebec."

Kenneth Strong agreed. "The French maintain only medium-size garrisons at Crown Point and Ticonderoga," he said. "With our great preponderance of manpower we should anticipate no trouble in reducing both of them."

"We would continue our northward march," Amherst declared, "and time our arrival opposite Quebec on the St. Lawrence at the same time you are scaling the heights up to the Plains of Abraham." He continued: "When General Strong and I arrive at their front door and begin our operations, we will gain their full attention until it is discovered that you are attacking them from the rear. This will buy you time enough to save lives as well as to assure the success of the operation."

Ja-gonh chuckled. "You may be sure the French will be aware of all things regarding the Amherst expedition. They will know its size, the number of our armaments, and all other things of importance concerning us. If they lose Ticonderoga and Crown Point, their Indian allies will be in an unfortunate position. They will worry about the outcome of the campaign, as well they might, and fear that either the British or the Indian nations will conquer them. Each of the Indian nations on the side of the French will have its own scouts watching our progress. I would lead the contingent of Iroquois myself, and I assure you that after seeing my war group, the Micmac, Huron, Ottawa, and Algonquian would be thoroughly discouraged."

Everyone joined in his laugh, and the shaping of the campaign was well under way.

"As I see it, we will operate on a precise schedule," General Amherst said, and in an aside to his deputy, added, "The responsibility for this is mine, not yours. We will arrange to arrive on the St. Lawrence at precisely the time that your column has arrived and presumably is making its way up to the Plains of Abraham on the secret path. General Montcalm and his staff will be concerned about the foe they can see, our army lying across the river. They'll pay no heed to your column, because—we hope—they won't even know of its existence."

"What marvelous tactics!" Wolfe exclaimed, slapping his thigh. "We'll attack first, and stun the French by our assault from the rear. We'll keep them so thoroughly occupied that the larger army can cross the river unmolested and make its way up through the town to the fortress."

"That won't be easy," Townsend Whiting said soberly. "I've been in Quebec, too, and I wouldn't relish hand-to-hand combat all the way up the bluff to the gate of the Citadel."

"I don't relish the thought of such a battle myself," Amherst said, "but a double-pronged offensive is far better than the alternative. If we coordinate our moves exactly, it should work out."

"It seems to me," Wolfe said slowly, addressing Jagonh, "that the success of this plan will depend more on the accomplishments of your son than on any other element. I mean nothing wrong by this question, but I must ask: are you sure he's capable of performing the extraordinary feat we would assign to him?"

The Great Sachem nodded curtly, quietly marveling at the constant need of the English for reassurance. He had already implicitly answered Wolfe's question and saw no reason to repeat his assurance.

General Strong broke the silence that followed. "I know Ghonkaba," he said, "and I know of his distinguished service in combat. He is thoroughly competent, and you may rely on him."

"Whether he will be available to us, on the other hand, is another matter," Whiting said. "I understand that he is assigned as a scout to Colonel Washington's Virginia regiment."

"He currently holds such an assignment," Ja-gonh confirmed.

They had reached a delicate impasse, and every man present knew it. Although Jeffrey Amherst had the title of supreme commander of all forces in British North America, the title was an empty one. The militia of the individual colonies were under the control of officers who were not bound to obey orders from the "supreme commander." In the usual chain of command, Amherst would write to Washington requesting that Ghonkaba be transferred to the staff of General Wolfe, and that would be the end of the matter. Under existing circumstances, however, Colonel Washington was free to do strictly as he pleased.

"If you'll permit my interference, General Amherst," Kenneth Strong said tactfully, "I'd suggest that you send a letter to Washington, inviting him to participate in the council of war and asking him to bring Ghonkaba with him. That would solve any problems, I think. Washington is always the first officer to cooperate in the cause of freedom."

"If you wish, I would add my signature to any request, and also communicate separately with my son, if need be," Ja-gonh volunteered.

With that question presumably settled, at least to the extent that it could be arranged, they turned to other aspects.

"I don't envy you," Amherst said to Wolfe. "You have an exceptionally difficult task awaiting you, and you're going to need the best troops available for the purpose."

"I intend to employ them," Wolfe replied. "I've had one brigade of special light infantry in training ever since Louisburg fell to us, and they're capable of anything. They're trained to a razor's edge, and I'm sure they'll respond to the challenge."

"I would like to volunteer the services of my own brigade," Whiting interjected swiftly. "My men take pride in being excellent shots, incomparable in forest warfare, the best all-around soldiers in the colonies. This attack seems made to order for us."

Before Wolfe could reply, Ja-gonh also cut in. "The bulk of the Iroquois force under my command will march with General Amherst," he told them. "So be it. But as General Wolfe requires a special force, an elite force like no other, I volunteer to him the services of the warriors of my own nation, the Seneca. This will be a special force constituted for this purpose, consisting only of senior warriors who have experience in at least three battles. You will find no warriors superior to them in North America!"

The Indian allies of the French—Algonquian, Huron, Micmac, Erie, and Ottawa—were proud men, proud of their tribal heritages and accomplishments. Their heads were freshly shaved on either side of their scalp locks, in which they wore the feathers of their high rank. Their faces were smeared with their distinctive war paint, and they wrapped themselves in magnificent lambs' wool blankets given them by General Montcalm.

The Algonquian were the most heavily represented, as was fitting for the largest Indian tribe on the eastern seaboard.

The Ottawa had been closely associated with the French for the longest time. Their alliance dated back more than a hundred years. So the war chiefs of the Ottawa swaggered into the meeting with a haughty air, and although the Algonquian had seated themselves on the floor nearest the chair that General Montcalm would occupy when he arrived, the Ottawa paid no attention to them and deliberately filed into position in front of them.

The Huron, like their hated cousins, the Seneca, were the aristocrats of this Indian gathering. Their record in war was superior, their discipline was firm and impeccable, and their morale, as always, was very high. They acknowledged their colleagues by nodding distantly, but they spoke to no one, associated with no one; when they sat, they chose a far corner. Unlike the Ottawa and the Algonquian, they felt no need to sit in the front rows in order to establish their supremacy.

The Micmac, shunned as inferiors by the other nations, stayed much to themselves and eagerly awaited gestures of friendship from other tribes that were not forthcoming. It did not occur either to them or to the French that the relationship between France and her allies left much to be desired. The English colonies, on the other hand, took the lead in perfecting their ties with the Iroquois, and because they followed the principle that all men were equal, meetings of the English high command had no superiors and no inferiors. The result, chiefly a vastly improved morale and unified spirit, was among the better secret weapons that the English colonies had devised.

The last war chiefs to appear were the Erie. Ordinarily as proud as the Huron, as arrogant as the Algonquian, as sturdily self-reliant as the Ottawa, they slunk into the room. They seated themselves at the very rear, calling as little attention to themselves as possible.

The last to appear, bringing up the rear of the Erie line, was Ludona, who hated every moment of this ordeal that he was forced to endure. His eyes were downcast as he seated himself, looking at no one, and he spoke to no one. In his own opinion—which also was the attitude of other Erie war chiefs and those of other nations—he was in total disgrace.

Ludona conceded that he could blame no one but himself for his sorry state. The woman he had brought to a Quebec brothel had proved to be a perfidious Seneca spy working with Ghonkaba of the Iroquois. Thanks to her connivance, an important French colonel was dead, and the French high command continued to mourn the loss of so talented an officer, placing blame on the Erie.

Ludona had wanted to express his apologies to Madame for the trouble he had unwittingly caused, but he had stayed away after being warned that she had promised to horsewhip him if he dared set foot in her place.

In only one way could Ludona regain standing with his own people, with the chiefs of other nations, and with the French: performing a feat of such great valor that it would have outstanding, recognizable benefit to the French cause.

No useful purpose would be served, he realized, if he went to the land of the Seneca, managed to recapture Toshabe, and returned her to Quebec. Not only would the French refuse to accept her at the brothel where she had been so popular, but she undoubtedly would be placed on trial, found guilty of aiding in two murders, and then be executed. In any case, it was foolish to even think of trying to breach Seneca security. Ludona was not lacking in courage, but neither had his common sense deserted him.

The most significant gesture that the sachems of the Indian nations—and probably General Montcalm, as well—would recognize would be his capture of Ghonk-aba, dead or alive. It was Ghonkaba, after all, who had come to Quebec as an espionage agent, shamed Ludona, fooled the French, and escaped with the woman spy whom everyone had believed to be a harmless whore.

As Ludona contemplated his problem, its complex enormity threatened to overcome his reasoning. Ghonk-aba was no ordinary Indian, but was a warrior of the Seneca, which immediately set him apart and won him universal respect. Renowned as a marksman and feared as a foe, he was an enemy to be avoided, rather than faced.

Ludona realized all too well, however, that he had no real choice. If he hoped to lift up his head ever again, to win general respect, he was obliged to produce the head of Ghonkaba.

Every moment of every day would have to be devoted to such a project. Its planning and execution would require his best efforts and be foolproof. He had to succeed, or his life would not be worth living.

Two young French officers began to distribute long, curved knives of finely tempered steel; these were gifts by the high command to the war chiefs, presumably as rewards for their presence. At every such parley the French distributed some gift of considerable value, which the chiefs were eager to receive. Attendance was effectively encouraged. In bribery, the French had solved much of the problem of maintaining their allies' loyalty.

General Montcalm entered, followed by his personal entourage. His youthful appearance and slender physique belied his nearly fifty years. The French immediately stiffened to attention, and the war chiefs, knowing it was expected, rose to their feet until the major general smilingly gestured for them to sit.

Louis Joseph de Montcalm-Gozon, Marquis de Saint-Véran, was one of Europe's most distinguished soldiers. A veteran of wars in Poland and in Spain, where he had won a considerable reputation as a strategist and tactician, as well as for bravery, he had been sent to America to defend France and to save her colonial empire. He had fought long and hard against great odds to accomplish his mission. His staff, familiar with his planning and effort, were convinced he was a genius. It was an opinion in which the world later would concur.

He had begged his superiors in Paris for ultimate authority in order to centralize his command and carry out what he considered was necessary to win the war. But the entrenched bureaucracy, swollen under Louis XIV and made even larger under his grandson, Louis XV, refused to accede. Consequently, Montcalm had no voice in civilian affairs, and he even was required to submit his military plans to the marquis, who ranked him as governor of New France. The marquis would, in fact, go down in history as the official whose stupidity and greed were responsible for the loss of France's most valuable colonial possessions.

In spite of the great handicaps placed upon him, Montcalm had performed virtual miracles that had won him the respect of General Amherst, his opposite number. In capturing Fort Ontario at Oswego in upper New York Colony, he had restored to French control the whole of Lake Ontario. He then went on to capture the important British outpost, Fort William Henry, on Lake George, in the same colony. And during the past season, he had concentrated almost four thousand men at Fort Ticonderoga to hold off an assault by a much larger army of British and colonial troops and Iroquois. He was an ally to be trusted, a foe to be feared, a commander to whom every subordinate felt great loyalty. It was from a genuine sense of respect and liking that the war chiefs stood when he entered.

Exerting his customary enormous charm, Montcalm electrified the Indians by addressing them in Algonquian, the language that all of them knew.

Because he was the first high-ranking French officer who had bothered to learn their language, even though his grasp of the tongue was rudimentary, the war chiefs needed no further proof that he was their brother and true ally.

Playing to their interests with consummate skill, Montcalm pointed out that the winter would be ending within a reasonably short time. Spring was not only the season for sharpening hunting tools and preparing the ground for new crops, but was also the time to gather his allies for a supreme test that he believed was in the offing.

"We are outnumbered many times over by the British and their allies," he said. "They can put as many as five soldiers and warriors in the field for each one that we can. Their great chief, Amherst, knows the importance of this fact, and so do his generals."

An Algonquian who could contain his curiosity no longer raised his voice. "What will they do, then? Attack?"

"Of course," Montcalm replied simply. "That's what every man in this room would do. And that is precisely what they will do. We do not know exactly where they will strike. They could aim a blow at any one of a dozen targets. But if I were General Amherst, I would make my target this city, Quebec. Of course, we have agents behind their lines and in their towns, but Amherst and his officers are very cagey, and so far our people have been able to send me nothing of value. We must be prepared, in effect, for the very worst that could develop in the way of enemy attack plans. So I ask you—I beseech you in the name of our ancient friendship—to send for every warrior who can fight in battle against our common foe."

The war chiefs saw he was in earnest and none took his words lightly. Many had in mind the thought voiced by a Huron.

"When the weather grows warmer and the leaves of the trees in the wilderness begin to turn green," he said, "this is the season when the food that is lodged in our storehouses reaches its lowest point of the year. The corn and the dried vegetables that we have used through the cold months will be almost gone. The larders that contain the meat we have smoked are almost empty, too. We are looking ahead to the season when our tribes must begin to replenish their stores. But they cannot do this overnight. It takes time for corn and other vegetables to grow. Time for fish to swim freely again in the waters of the lakes and rivers, and for many animals in the forest to grow fat on new foliage.

"How," he asked, "will these warriors that our brother, Montcalm, wishes us to bring to Quebec be fed? They cannot bring their own food with them at this time of year. They will need to depend only on their brothers, the French, for food."

Montcalm had engaged that very day in a long, violent argument with the governor about supplies needed for additional warriors. Typically shortsighted, the governor had insisted that he couldn't pay for food for large numbers of hungry Indians, whom he described as of questionable value.

Montcalm had defied him, revealing that he had already written to the principal quartermaster of the French armies, asking for bread, grain, smoked meat, and pickled fish in large quantities. That food would be arriving shortly, he said, and his troops would unload it from the ships that brought it from Brest in France. The troops would stand guard at the warehouses with orders to shoot anyone who tried to get in without a permit signed personally by himself, the major general. Montcalm had made a dangerous, permanent enemy of the governor, but he no longer cared. His responsibility was to see that Quebec was made safe from any invader, and he intended to fulfill that charge.

So he now was able to tell the Indians with assurance, "You have my solemn pledge that we will have ample food in Quebec for every warrior, and he will be fed all he wishes to eat as long as he stands beside us."

His words had the desired effect. Their principal concern satisfied, the war chiefs rose, one by one, to promise that they would return to their towns without delay and bring back volunteers. The magnet of ample food supplies throughout the spring seemed likely to bring as many as even Montcalm could wish.

His eyes sweeping the ranks of the chiefs squatted before him, the general was struck by the attitude displayed by one war chief, Ludona, of the Erie. He had made a point of meeting each of them individually, although the governor ridiculed such activity as a waste of time. Because of his relatively intimate knowledge of each chief, the general realized that Ludona undoubtedly was still suffering from the humiliation of his responsibility for bringing about the death of Colonel Vante, and for placing a spy in a sensitive place.

Actually, Montcalm was not greatly concerned over what any spy could have learned. Other than the size, strength, and disposition of his forces, he had few secrets, and these were available only to a few men who worked deep in the recesses of the Citadel.

With his usual concern for the feelings of others, Montcalm took pains to ask Ludona to remain when the others were sent on their way.

Certain that the general intended to rebuke him, Ludona moved slowly toward him, shuffling his feet, his head low.

Montcalm greeted him cheerfully, then withdrew with him to an anteroom, where an aide provided glasses of wine.

"My friend is sad," Montcalm said, speaking again in the tongue of the Algonquian.

To Ludona's credit, he did not try to evade. "The great sachem who leads the armies of France knows the reason," he replied bluntly.

"What must be done to remove this sense of shame from you?" the general asked carefully.

Ludona brooded for a moment before he replied. "The new knife you gave me today," he said, "must cut deep into the heart of Ghonkaba of the Seneca. My shame will not be erased until his scalp hangs from my belt."

The personal feuds of Indians were astonishing, but as a realist Montcalm believed in dealing with situations as he found them. "Will this warrior, Ghonkaba, take part in the campaign against Quebec, do you think?" he persisted.

The Erie looked at him cynically. "He is the son of Ja-gonh and the grandson of Renno."

Even Montcalm was impressed. "Yes," he said. "He is sure to take part. Very well. I see no problem.

When the time comes, I will give one assignment—and only one—to Ludona of the Erie. In the battle for Quebec, you will search the ranks of our Seneca foes for Ghonkaba, and when you find him, you will kill him! I have every confidence that you will succeed in this mission. And now I will instruct my adjutant to publish this assignment so that all our allies will know the faith that I place in Ludona of the Erie!"

Chapter IX

A courier arrived at the headquarters of the Virginia regiment at noon, but after reading the message's contents, Colonel Washington followed his usual practice of keeping them to himself. He was thoughtful all afternoon, saying nothing to anyone. And at sundown that evening, having left word that he wanted to be notified when the scouts drifted back into camp, he sent word to Ghonkaba, inviting him to supper.

Washington's meals were prepared by his own chef, and anyone invited to sit down at his table could expect excellent food. Ghonkaba accepted the invitation with alacrity.

182

They dined sumptuously on oysters served with bread crumbs soaked in horseradish and garlic, a redolent Virginia gumbo, and a stuffed, wild young duckling that had been shot while migrating north. Ghonkaba was unaccustomed to such fancy foods but nevertheless ate his fill.

Not until they had finished their dessert, a blueberry tart that was one of the colonel's favorites, did Washington bring up the subject that was very much on his mind. "A privateer is being made available to me," he said, "for a voyage to Boston in the immediate future. I'd very much like you to accompany me."

Ghonkaba was pleased. If he traveled to Boston, he would certainly be involved in the greater action of the war.

Washington drew a sheet of folded parchment from a square black receptacle attached to his belt. "General Amherst," he said, "has asked that the militia chiefs of every colony meet in Boston as rapidly as we can assemble there, and my letter contained a postscript that I'll read to you." He unfolded the parchment, cleared his throat, then read,

Please bring Ghonkaba of the Seneca with you. His presence in Boston is urgent. If he requires authority beyond that which you exercise, his father—who sits beside me as I pen this—will be pleased to provide it. In the meantime, I'm sure that Ghonkaba will authenticate his father's signature.

Ghonkaba glanced at the sheet of parchment and instantly recognized the unmistakable signature of Jagonh. "My comrades here," he said, "will miss my services badly, but I will return to duty beside them at the first opportunity. I am delighted to be summoned to Boston!"

"The ship already is waiting for us at Norfolk," Washington replied, "and we'll start out at dawn tomorrow. We'll sail as soon as we can board it."

They set out for the seaboard shortly after an early breakfast. Changing horses frequently, they rode without pause and reached the coast in time to sail on the noon tide the following day.

Their ship was a converted brig, with additional sails for speed. Guns had been mounted on the fore- and aft decks. As always, Ghonkaba was less than completely at ease on board the vessel. He never was nervous on land, no matter what the circumstances, but travel by sea was different. The ocean was a vast, unknown, alien element, and he felt unwanted twinges of uneasiness when the brig lost sight of land and moved alone in the midst of an endless, bottomless array of water.

Nevertheless, his lifelong training as a Seneca served him well. His appetite remained good, and as far as anyone could tell he enjoyed the voyage thoroughly.

Boston was a startling, bewildering community to anyone unfamiliar with London or the other great capitals of the Old World. One of the largest cities in North America, it boasted a permanent population of almost ten thousand persons, as well as a large transient population of traders, merchants, and shipowners from other colonies, from British possessions in the Caribbean, and from the British Isles. This diverse population was entertained at evening lectures, poetry readings, and musical entertainment. But the residents and visitors were deprived of theatrical performances, which were still banned under the old Puritan regulations. Large by American standards, Boston nonetheless was not as cosmopolitan as New York, Baltimore, or Philadelphia.

Gentlemen in bicorne hats and powdered wigs, wearing silk suits and cloaks of the finest spun wool, rubbed shoulders with colonials in rough linsey-woolsey and frontiersmen in leather shirts and trousers.

Indians from various New England tribes were a common sight, too. Many were employed as messengers, and others worked in the small factories that were springing up in Boston and its environs. As the Indians wandered about with their feathers jutting from their scalp locks and their naked torsos wrapped in blankets, they seemed to find nothing incongruous in their appearance.

Ladies of fashion, powdered, bewigged, and elaborately gowned, rode out from their Beacon Hill mansions in carriages pulled by teams of matched horses. Housewives trudged to the fishmongers, butchers, greengrocers, and bakers for their daily supplies. No self-respecting homemaker would consider buying any produce more than twenty-four hours old.

On the lowest rung of the ladder were the women of the waterfront brothels, who stood in doorways or frequented taverns. They sought the trade of the sailors of the many nations who now sailed frequently to Boston, making the port the busiest in America.

An aide to General Amherst was waiting at the dock and conducted Colonel Washington and Ghonkaba to a large guest house on Beacon Hill, which the colonial government of Massachusetts was making available as headquarters for the visiting militia chiefs.

Ghonkaba was presented to the commander in chief and also met General James Wolfe, with whom he struck an immediate sense of comradeship. Something about their personalities meshed, as in his relationship with Washington.

Another guest house visitor was Brigadier Townsend Whiting, who greeted him with the cordiality that men of his class reserved for old friends. To Ghonkaba's astonishment, he unexpectedly came face-to-face with Beth Whiting. It was their first meeting since her marriage. She had volunteered to serve as a hostess during the conference, and so she had learned that Ghonkaba was coming up from Virginia with Colonel Washington.

Nevertheless, the unexpected confrontation also startled her. Taken by surprise, the young couple stared mutely at each other. Ghonkaba was very much aware of Beth's stunning beauty, and she was fully conscious of his brawny air of masculinity. Had she accepted his proposal, they would have been married for some months by this time, and that realization made them all the more uncomfortable. They lacked the sophistication to carry off the meeting with aplomb and dignity.

Stammering greetings, they shook hands hurriedly, their fingers barely touching, and then, red-faced and flustered, quickly went their separate ways. Their initial meeting was anything but successful.

Beth had been out of Ghonkaba's thoughts for months. On the other hand, he thought often of Toshabe and of the experiences they had shared in their escape from Canada. He also recalled vividly—too vividly for comfort—intimate details of their lovemaking that caused him to want her anew. Had anybody posed a direct question, he would have acknowledged that he was in love with Toshabe and that after the present campaign ended, he probably would ask her to become his wife.

Though Beth was far from his thoughts, the meeting created a sharp upheaval in his mind. He was forcibly reminded of what might have been if Townsend Whiting had not stolen Beth's affections from him. Recalling his plan to do away with his rival, and his grandfather's intervention after his wilderness encounter with the bears, he reflected that perhaps Renno had been wrong in his interpretation of that incident and had injected into it thoughts that he himself was eager to express. The Great Sachem, after all, had been an elderly man and his mind may not have functioned with his usual clarity and incisiveness.

So it was possible, certainly, that Ghonkaba had been right in wanting to do away with Townsend Whiting and to clear the blot on his good name. His present feelings for Beth were irrelevant; she now meant nothing to him, and even if she were suddenly a widow, he would have no desire to marry her. Nevertheless the family pride that was so important to him would again be unblemished if he actually disposed of Townsend Whiting.

The question obviously could not be decided quickly. Ghonkaba had not given his word lightly in promising to obey his grandfather's wish, and he could not act now without weighing all the possible consequences. Whether Whiting was to live or die needed to be considered with infinite care.

Ghonkaba's thoughts were interrupted by the arrival of a delegation of Iroquois. Each of the six nations was represented by its sachem, including No-da-vo of the Seneca. Ghonkaba was delighted to learn that his father, as Great Sachem, led the party.

The Indian leaders, together with a small band of escorts from each nation, declined quarters in the guest house. They preferred to set up their own tents on the

Boston Common. Amherst acceded to their request, and Washington immediately granted permission for Ghonkaba to join his father and uncle and his own comrades among the escorts; Ghonkaba's demeanor, however, remained grave, and his pleasure at the unexpected reunion was not evident.

Sharing a long pipe with Ja-gonh and No-da-vo outside the tent of animal skins, Ghonkaba ignored the curious stares of passing Bostonians. He was pleased to hear that his mother and other family members were in good health, but he was especially gratified that Ja-gonh mentioned Toshabe without being questioned. The Great Sachem relayed her good wishes for success.

Ghonkaba grunted in approval, then drew on the pipe before passing it to No-da-vo. "My father," he remarked, "knows the reason that I have been summoned to this meeting of colonial and allied leaders."

Ja-gonh remained unperturbed. "That is true," he admitted cheerfully, but said nothing more.

Ghonkaba knew he should not persist, but his curiosity was too great. "What has been decided," he asked, "at the conclave of the great chieftains at Louisburg?"

No-da-vo frowned. A traditionalist, he regarded such prying as unworthy of the dignity of one who wore the three hawk feathers of a Seneca war chief.

Ja-gonh knew his son better, and his smile was almost jovial as he said, "My son should know that he'll be asked to perform no deed that is beyond his capacity to perform. The manitous have shown him their favors, and they continue to be partial toward him."

Ja-gonh took the pipe from No-da-vo, puffed on it, and handed it to his son.

Ghonkaba knew he had been outsmarted and reflected that he should have known better than to try to pry information from his father. Now he would simply have to wait until the appropriate time to learn what was in store for him.

Shortly before sundown, the leaders gathered in what had been the ballroom of the mansion. The British wore their uniforms of scarlet and gold, and the colonials were in blue and buff, so for once the Indians were relatively inconspicuous in their feathers and war paint. They sat in orderly rows, with Ja-gonh in the front, and the sachems of the six nations lined up behind.

A full company of Massachusetts infantrymen, doing sentry duty, searched through the house and the surrounding yard before the meeting began. After they reported no unauthorized persons present General Amherst opened the session.

The commander in chief then explained in full that a two-pronged offensive against Quebec would be launched in the immediate future. Troops from the New England colonies and New York and warriors of the Iroquois League would participate. All other militia units, he said, would be assigned to guard the borders of their respective colonies against hostile infiltration. Some enemy Indians might hope to take advantage of the absence of so many fighting men.

A rear admiral and two commodores of the Royal Navy then proceeded to assign the various ships that would be used as troop transports and as supply convoys. It gradually became clear that one of the expeditions that would participate in the attack was destined to see more action, and its men would be the first to take part in the assault.

When the Navy officers finished speaking, General Amherst took charge again, introducing Major General Wolfe, who would lead the direct assault on Quebec.

The atmosphere became supercharged, picking up

Wolfe's personality as he spoke. With great enthusiasm, he explained how he and his men would move ashore east of Quebec and be out of sight of the city's sentries. They would march along the shore for a time and then head inland, climb to the Plains of Abraham, and attack the Citadel from the rear. He emphasized that the defenses of the fortress were all keyed to an attack from the river side. The rear, largely undefended, had no cannon to repel a foe.

Colonel Washington rose to his feet. "I don't mean to punch holes in your plans, General Wolfe," he said, "but don't I see a discrepancy that could lead to great problems? For many years, we have heard the French boast of the impregnability of the fortress of Quebec. They claim that it can be attacked only from the side facing the St. Lawrence. Yet you propose to lead your force in an assault on the rear. May I ask how such an attack can possibly be conducted?"

The colonels and generals leaned forward in their chairs, eager to hear the reply, and General Wolfe laughed aloud. "It so happens," he said, "that our forces are endowed with a secret means of breaching the enemy's so-called impregnable line. But I must ask that you, Colonel Washington, temporarily release the services of Ghonkaba, your Seneca scout."

"He's the best scout the Virginia regiment has ever employed," Washington replied, "but I'm willing to relinquish his services for a greater cause."

"Thank you, Colonel," Wolfe said briskly. "Will Ghonkaba of the Seneca stand up, please."

Somewhat confused at finding himself the unexpected center of attention, Ghonkaba obeyed.

"If you don't mind," Wolfe said, "please tell these officers how you once managed to make good your escape from Quebec."

Ghonkaba had no objection to telling his story again and quickly repeated the high points of the incident, omitting the key portion that concerned the appearance of a hawk that he had followed on a path that led to safety.

Ja-gonh interrupted to address his son in the language of the Seneca. "Those who listen to Ghonkaba's tale," he said, "do not understand. The manitous will not object or vent their anger upon you if you explain the role they played in sending the hawk to you."

Ghonkaba was startled. "You are sure, my father?" he asked.

"On this one occasion only," Ja-gonh said firmly, "you may lift the veil of mystery that separates the ways of the manitous from the ways of ordinary men."

Certain subjects, by long tradition, never were mentioned outside the immediate family circle, and the influence of the hawk as a messenger of the manitous was paramount among them. "My father is sure?" Ghonkaba asked again uncertainly.

Ja-gonh replied firmly once more without hesitation, showing no impatience. "I am sure, my son," he said. "These are times that put the very souls of men on trial. We have no right to hold back from those who are our allies and friends, from those who stand beside us in battle, the truth of the powers we are capable of exerting."

Ghonkaba now launched into a full, detailed account of his family's long association with hawks acting as messengers from the all-powerful manitous, the personal representatives of the gods. In typical Indian fashion, he recounted incident after incident in which the life of Ghonka, his great-grandfather; Renno, his grandfather; and Ja-gonh, his father, had been saved by the timely appearance of a hawk. Even the most skeptical of his listeners refrained from scoffing. Instead, they gave him their full attention as they listened in rapt silence. Finally, Ghonkaba related previous experiences of his own.

At last he launched into an account of the desperate plight in which he and Toshabe had found themselves on the Plains of Abraham behind the Citadel above Quebec.

Omitting no detail, he related how a hawk had mysteriously appeared overhead in the dead of night and had succeeded in leading him and Toshabe down to the edge of the St. Lawrence by a long and circuitous route that took them several miles away from the city of Quebec. In the process of making good their escape, he emphasized, they lost the three Erie warriors who were following them; they did not consciously try to evade the Erie, but when they were well on the path to safety, they had realized that the enemy warriors had vanished.

When Ghonkaba finished, absolute silence reigned. No one moved or spoke. The high-ranking British officers, other than Generals Amherst and Wolfe, could not help but react skeptically, and their faces silently revealed their lack of belief in the young Seneca's story. Observing this, Wolfe's face was as inscrutable as that of a veteran Indian warrior. It was impossible, looking at him, to know what he was thinking.

The colonial militia chiefs had no difficulty in accepting the truth of what they had heard. Almost without exception American-born, they had grown up in the vicinity of various Indian tribes and had spent their entire lives associating with them. Therefore, they were not only more accustomed to tales of the supernatural that Indians told, but many had, with their own eyes, seen the results of supernatural intervention by the

192

manitous on behalf of warriors whom they favored. So they were far more inclined to accept Ghonkaba's story at face value.

Townsend Whiting, with a hint of skepticism in his voice, asked, "Are you sure, Ghonkaba, that you could find this same path another time, without the intervention of a hawk as your guide?"

Ghonkaba thought he was being mocked, and a black fury rose within him. Concealing his anger, however, he replied with quiet dignity. "I have traveled on that path one time. I am a Seneca! Therefore, I remember every step I took and everywhere that it led." Ja-gonh and No-da-vo were proud of his reply.

General Wolfe came to the edge of the platform. "You will march with me, Ghonkaba!" he said. "You will lead my troops and me to the Plains of Abraham so we can launch a surprise attack."

Ghonkaba stole a hesitant glance at his father and uncle, who sat wooden-faced. He looked next at Washington, whose expression was equally unrevealing. They were refraining from encouraging him in undertaking to perform a mission hazardous in the extreme, but neither would they suggest that he compromise his honor by failing to carry out a responsibility that belonged on his shoulders.

Ghonkaba was not afraid to die in battle, knowing that such a death would guarantee his reunion with his grandfather in the land of his ancestors beyond the great river. Why, then, was he at all hesitant now?

It struck him forcefully that the cause was his yearning for Toshabe. He wanted to make her his squaw, to sire her children, to spend the rest of his days at her side. Now, when the question of life or death had become paramount, he realized the depth of his feelings for her.

But no Seneca could allow his love for a woman to stand in the way of his duty, and his duty was clearly defined. Only he could lead General Wolfe's troops to the Plains of Abraham. Perhaps this was a reason the manitous had sent the hawk to guide him and Toshabe to safety and to freedom. He had no right to question or deny what had already taken place.

He called up to General Wolfe in a loud, ringing voice, "I will march with you, General, and lead you and your troops up the secret path."

Ghonkaba was hoisted up to the platform by many hands, and when Wolfe clasped his hand, the entire assemblage erupted in a rousing cheer. A promise had been given and accepted, and the die was cast.

Beth Whiting's many years of training made her an excellent hostess as the head of the group providing dinner for the assembled officers. Dressed in a subdued plaid gown of silk taffeta with a square-cut neckline, she seemed to be everywhere at once, supervising her volunteers, and yet somehow finding the opportunity to exchange pleasantries with each of the forty British, colonial, and Indian leaders present.

As she moved effortlessly around the dining room, overseeing the serving of clam chowder, fillet of haddock, roast beef with potatoes and vegetables, and a green salad, Townsend Whiting plainly was proud of her, and Ghonkaba had to concede the brigadier had good cause to be proud of his lovely, charming, and efficient wife.

In spite of his preoccupation with his new and exciting mission, Ghonkaba found it impossible to put Beth out of his mind, for she seemed to be always within view, often favoring him with a warm smile. He did not realize that the smile was not intended for him alone, but was awarded equally to every man present. In contrast to her apparent warmth, he thought that Whiting's attitude was patronizing toward him, and that the officer seemed to be unduly flaunting his possession of Beth.

As he reflected on this, the resolve hardened within him that he had no real choice and would be obliged to do away with her husband in order to obliterate the slight to his honor.

He was in no rush to perform the deed, however, for Whiting would be commanding a brigade under Wolfe. Ample opportunities would exist then to sink a knife or a tomahawk into him in some suitable confrontation. What could be a more logical place for the deed to be done than among warriors, perhaps even on a battleground.

He ate heartily, surprising the officers who were his table companions by his perfect European manners and by his ability to speak flawless English no matter what subject was under discussion. Their realization that he was a descendant of the renowned Renno was helping them to feel assured about the outcome of the assignment he had accepted, considering it very likely that he could accomplish the near miracle expected of him.

After the meal, the officers gathered in small groups to chat over glasses of brandywine. Amherst considered this period important to the future of his armies, and so did General Strong. Here was a chance for Englishmen and Americans to become better acquainted. Men from the entire length of the Atlantic seaboard could come to know one another better, welding friendships that would be potentially useful in battle.

But the Iroquois did not feel at home under such convivial conditions. Ja-gonh was the first to withdraw, and within moments the leaders of the six nations followed him to the bivouac on Boston Common.

Ghonkaba, not far behind his elders, joined Ja-gonh and No-da-vo in the tent of animal skins that they shared. This was the first time they had been alone with him and able to speak freely since he had accepted his assignment.

"I hope your assignment satisfies you," his father said, and an amused light appeared in his eyes.

"I am happy, my father, and you need have no fear," Ghonkaba told him. "I will live up to the promise expected of me."

"If you need help," No-da-vo told him, "you will not be alone with General Wolfe's army. As you probably know, it has been decided that the warriors of the Iroquois nations will march with Amherst and Strong. But we Seneca insist on taking the biggest risks. Five hundred of our best warriors will accompany Wolfe's troops."

Although Ghonkaba remained expressionless, he was deeply impressed. Such a force was far larger than was usually assigned to any army commanded by the British or the colonial militia leaders.

"I will lead our Seneca into battle myself," No-da-vo continued. "So you need only ask me for such assistance as you may require, and it will be provided for you."

"Just remember this, my son," Ja-gonh said solemnly. "Do not try to shoulder the entire burden yourself. Even though you may recall the path perfectly, the French may have stationed many hidden sentinels along that route. I would like to have others join you in exploring the path in advance of the troops General Wolfe will lead."

Ghonkaba nodded solemnly. "You are right, my father," he said. "It is best, by far, to be safe, and to take no needless risks. I know how vitally important it is that the French be totally surprised."

Well satisfied with the day's events, Ghonkaba had only one regret: he would be forced to part company with Colonel Washington, for whom he had great admiration. Perhaps, he thought, it would turn out that the war would go on longer than anyone assumed, making it possible that they would serve together at some future time. He said an appropriate farewell to No-da-vo and his father, who were to return forthwith to the land of the Seneca.

Although spring was at hand, the nights in Boston were still severely cold, and Ghonkaba was glad to wrap himself in his lambs' wool blanket, a gift from Washington. Soon he dropped off to sleep, and was deeply immersed in a dream.

He first realized he was dreaming when he found himself standing in the midst of a verdant wilderness. The grass underfoot was thick, lush, and almost knee-high. Trees, among them majestic oaks, mammoth maples, and stately elms, were in full leaf, and a nearby bush was covered with pink and yellow flowers. This was the foliage of mid-summer, so Ghonkaba felt certain that he must be dreaming. A tingling sensation crept up his spine when he saw his grandfather approaching through the forest.

Renno looked years younger than when he had suffered his last illness. His flesh was firm, and he had the sinewy muscles and powerful torso that marked the men of the family. The hair of his scalp lock was blond rather than white, as were his eyebrows; wrinkles no longer were around his eyes, and as he gazed at his grandson, his expression was penetrating and impersonal.

Ghonkaba raised his left hand in greeting and wanted to bid his grandfather welcome, but the words would not come. For a reason he could not understand, he was unable to utter a sound. He suspected that Renno was displeased with him, and his heart sank within him.

The greatest of all Seneca warriors spoke in a deep, resonant voice that, nevertheless, carried only a short distance. It took on a hollow ring when he raised it.

"Betsy and Renno rejoiced," he said, "when a male child was born to them. Ja-gonh lived up to their highest hopes for him. Then as the years passed and he married Ah-wen-ga, they rejoiced again when the male succession was secured by the birth of Ghonkaba.

"But this time," he added in sepulchral tones, "their rejoicing seems to have been premature."

Ghonkaba knew beyond all doubt that he was about to be subjected to one of his grandfather's famous tongue-lashings, and although he did not understand the reason, he felt miserable.

"Ghonkaba," his grandfather said, "has shown skill as a scout and has displayed courage, as well as valor, in combat. In addition, he handled the escape of To-shabe from Quebec with great cleverness. No one doubts his standing as a warrior, and he has truly earned the three feathers of a Seneca war chief." The old man's voice dropped, becoming scarcely audible, but the contempt in it was plainly heard. "Ghonkaba," he said, "may be a war chief who will win great victories for his nation. But Ghonkaba can nevertheless be a fool."

The young warrior wanted to protest that he had done nothing to deserve such a denunciation, but when he opened his mouth to speak, he could utter no sound. The manitous were punishing him by denying him the right to rebut his grandfather's harsh charges.

"Toshabe," Renno went on, "saved Ghonkaba from catastrophe when he would have destroyed the alliance that binds the nations of the Iroquois to England and her North American colonies. Only through the good sense of Toshabe was I able to prevent Ghonkaba from putting a knife into the chest of Townsend Whiting."

Ghonkaba at last began to understand. His grandfather was annoyed because of his renewed desire to do away with Brigadier Whiting.

"I no longer dwell in the land of the living," the former Great Sachem declared, "so I am powerless to prevent my grandson from making a mistake that will not only blight his life but will change the whole course of future events for his people, the Seneca."

Huge beads of perspiration rolled down Ghonkaba's face, shoulders, and chest, drenching him in sweat. He wanted to cry out that he was willing to listen to any advice that his grandfather cared to give him and that he would gladly abide by it. But he remained speechless.

"Toshabe lives far from Boston and is in no position to intervene again," his grandfather continued. "Perhaps it is just as well. She thinks that the day will come when Ghonkaba will marry her. But once he has killed the Englishman, Whiting, he will be scorned by every warrior and every squaw and maiden of the Seneca. Only a white woman would have anything to do with him. Then what might become of Toshabe, it is impossible to foretell.

"My father, Ghonka, worked very hard for many years to establish a solid alliance with the English," Renno continued. "I followed in his footsteps and worked toward the same goal, as has my son, Ja-gonh, worked toward it since he has become Great Sachem. This was our lasting achievement, that we, who are white-skinned Indians, should make peace for all time between the English and the Seneca and our brothers of the Iroquois League. But Ghonkaba, the son of my son, will undo the work of generations in a single, rash act by plunging his knife into an English officer who has done him no harm. Ghonkaba will not only destroy an alliance, but will lose a war to the French."

Ghonkaba spread his hands in helpless appeal.

But his grandfather was not yet finished. "I cannot prevent you from doing what you will," Renno said, "but the responsibility for the consequences will rest on your hands. The gods have their own ways of punishing those who defy their edicts of justice and good sense." He stood for a long moment frowning at his grandson, and then gradually he became translucent.

Ghonkaba could see through him and could see the trees behind him. Strangely, they were stripped of their foliage now and their branches were bare.

And now it occurred to him that he no longer was asleep, but was actually looking out through the flap of his tent at trees on the Common.

Badly shaken by the eerie experience, Ghonkaba cast aside his blanket, rose, and walked out into the night. From the Common he could still see candles and oil lamps burning in the mansion where the English and colonial officers were becoming better acquainted after their day's meetings. As he looked at the flickering lights, he realized that Whiting was among those inside.

But now he knew that Whiting was safe from the attack he had envisioned. Ghonkaba never would plunge a knife into him after receiving his grandfather's warning.

Resenting Renno's interference at first, Ghonkaba gradually underwent a change of heart. Only his grandfather's intervention from beyond the grave had prevented an act that could have caused great tragedy for the Seneca and for the English colonists, he now granted. Thanks to his own blindness, the alliance that was the mainstay of freedom in America would have been destroyed.

Certainly, he realized, he was far more fortunate than most of his contemporaries. When they erred, they were required to pay the full penalty for their mistakes. But he was prevented from performing thoughtless, foolish gestures by ancestors who kept a close watch on him from the far side of the great river. Once again, the manitous were demonstrating his special place in their affections, the lofty position they had in mind for him, and the extraordinary degree of protection they offered him.

Little by little, Ghonkaba recalled the words that No-da-vo had spoken to him when Renno was dying. It was true that he no longer was the master of his own fate. The requirements and needs of the Seneca came first, and his own desires necessarily took second place.

He knew now what Ja-gonh, Renno, and Ghonka each had learned in turn before him. In return for the special favors and protection he received, he was a creature of the manitous, and the point and purpose of his life was clear: he existed to advance the cause of the Seneca, in all ways, at all times. Everything else in life was secondary to this high goal.

Toshabe was of the opinion that her experiences as a captive, first of the Seneca and then of the French, had taught her patience. But at a time when she had mistakenly thought her troubles were at an end, she was stunned to discover that her problems loomed large before her and that she had to exercise greater patience and self-control than she had imagined possible.

The new troubles had crept up on her gradually, almost imperceptibly increasing until they loomed large and threatened to destroy her equanimity.

During the winter she had lived with Ja-gonh and Ah-wen-ga, unaware of the feelings against her that she aroused elsewhere in the town of the Seneca. Those who most firmly and strongly opposed her were the younger women of approximately her own age, some of them already married, and some still single. She had no idea that they resented the fact that she— an outsider, a half-white Erie, who had lived in prostitution—had captured the affections of the most eligible of Seneca bachelors.

The young squaws and the single women had taken great care not to express their feelings openly. Ja-gonh was the most important man in the nation by far, and his power was so great that no one wanted to incur his enmity. Furthermore, Ah-wen-ga was also a strong character, and as she made obvious at every opportunity, she was very proud of her future daughter-in-law. The women of the town realized that she would become the implacable foe of anyone who dared to snub Toshabe.

Common sense forced them to behave with propriety toward the outsider at the few formal gatherings that took place during the winter months. All was serene, at least on the surface, and Toshabe was ignorant of the hatred accumulating against her.

The coming of spring created new and expanded opportunities for self-expression to the young squaws and single women. Custom required them to prepare the communal farmlands for planting, and everyone pitched in, regardless of rank or station. Ah-wen-ga spent her days in the fields, as did elderly widows and youngsters. Even the unfortunate captives who were forced to serve the braves as prostitutes were compelled to do their share of farm labor.

When Toshabe was a captive, she hated the long hours of grueling work that she was forced to endure in the fields. But now everything was changed. As a free woman, a guest of the Great Sachem and his wife and the presumed future bride of their son, she was in a far different position. Now she had a genuine interest in the fields and in nurturing and growing plants in order to produce bountiful crops.

She was one of the first to arrive in the fields beyond the town palisade every morning, and she did not stop working until the setting sun forced her to stop. Then she paused only to take a quick swim in the lake before returning home to help Ah-wen-ga prepare supper. She enjoyed the challenge of work in the fields.

The hostility of the other women completely surprised Toshabe. She became aware of their attitude early one morning when they arrived for work shortly after she had begun her day's labors and was digging up the soil with a metal spade. She greeted the other young women cheerfully, but to her astonishment they made no reply, looking at her stony-faced and beginning their work without a word.

Uncertain that she had interpreted their reaction correctly, Toshabe tried again and made an innocuous comment about the weather. Again the silence that followed was loud and clear.

The women spoke to each other in low voices, deliberately excluding Toshabe from their conversation, and they refrained from speaking to her directly. It soon became painfully clear to her that a concerted move was afoot to snub her.

This situation persisted for several days, while Toshabe kept her counsel, saying nothing to Ah-wen-ga about the mysterious behavior. Ultimately, she learned the ostensible reason for their crude and cruel actions.

One afternoon she tripped over a primitive wooden rake and went sprawling on the ground, not realizing until later that the rake had been deliberately placed in her path.

Momentarily stunned, Toshabe saw two young women standing above her.

"Whore!" one of them said bitterly.

"Foreigner!" the other declared contemptuously.

So that was it! They hated her because she had been forced to engage in prostitution and because she was part Erie and part French, rather than a full-blooded Seneca. That did not really explain their hatred, however, but it was not difficult for her to figure out the rest. They were jealous of her preferred position in the household of the Great Sachem, and they assumed that she would become Ghonkaba's bride when he returned. The fact that he had arrived at no understanding whatsoever with her made no real difference. The assumptions of the onlookers became reality.

As time went on, the feelings against Toshabe spread to others in the community, and eventually even included the town's prostitutes.

Toshabe deliberately refrained from making any mention of the problem to Ja-gonh and Ah-wen-ga. She knew they would leap to her defense and would see to it that the ringleaders were punished. But she knew, too, that any such action would merely compound the resentment. Therefore, she suffered the snubs in silence, hoping that the leaders would grow tired of their game and abandon it.

It turned out that one day they went too far. Toshabe was working on her hands and knees, twisting a sharp, pointed stick until it made a hole about six inches deep in the ground, and then dropping a seed into the opening. This was the time-tested Seneca method of planting and was observed by everyone who participated in the growth of crops.

Suddenly she felt a sharp, stinging pain in her buttocks and looked up to see a squaw grinning down at her. The woman had stabbed her with her pointed stick, using all the force she could muster, and as a consequence, Toshabe's whole body ached from the shock.

Instinct told her that she must not allow this attack to go unchallenged. If she submitted once to physical abuse, it would be heaped on her at every opportunity in the future, and her life would become unbearable.

Not hesitating for a moment, she drove the pointed end of her stick with all of her force into her tormentor's bare thigh.

The counterassault was as harsh as it was sudden, and the squaw squealed in pain before she was able to control herself and present an expressionless mien. Blood seeped from the gaping wound in her leg, for Toshabe had given far more severe treatment than she had received.

The other young women took note of what was happening, and though they remained silent, they clearly were impressed by the firm and decisive stand that Toshabe had taken. The woman who had attacked her hobbled away to the lake to bathe her wound. She was certain to be reprimanded by one of the older women for leaving her place of duty without permission.

Acting unconcerned, Toshabe placed the point of her stick in the ground and began to twist it, making another hole into which she dropped a seed. She showed no remorse and no pity. She knew that no more physical attacks would be made against her and that her enemies would give her a wide berth.

All the same, the tension was almost too great to bear, and she couldn't help wishing that the military campaign would end and that Ghonkaba would return home and claim her as his bride.

Chapter X

In all the land of the Seneca, one place was universally regarded as sacred, beyond all others. Located in the principal town of the nation was a simple log cabin, distinguished from its neighbors only by an absence of windows and of an opening in the roof to emit smoke. This was the Room of the Great Faces, and the lack of ornate decoration made it all the more impressive. On the walls were giant masks of faces that resembled those of human beings, but were not precisely those of any recognizable individual. These objects, made of wood and animal hides, had been cleverly contrived by artists who had done their best work in creating them.

Whether these faces were representations of the gods—the lords of earth and sky, water and wilderness—or were simply representations of their divine messengers, the manitous, no one except the highest-ranking medicine men knew for certain, and these individuals were forbidden to discuss the Great Faces with mere mortals.

It was enough for the people to know that in some mysterious, inexplicable way a spark of divinity had entered the Great Faces and that when one entered the room and prayed to the gods it was taken for granted that the pleas of the individual were heard by the appropriate deity.

Only on the most solemn occasions were the masks removed from their resting places on the walls of the cabin, and on these occasions they were paraded through the town in a religious ceremony of special significance. At all other times the masks reposed on the walls, and any Seneca was free to enter the Room of the Great Faces at will and to pray to the gods, making his wishes known.

Enjoying the full rights of a Seneca woman, Toshabe was privileged to visit the Room of the Great Faces if she saw fit, and late one afternoon after she had finished her labor in the fields she found herself impulsively approaching the holy place.

The young women were still unrelenting in continuing their campaign against her. Not a single word had been said to her all day in the fields, and the vicious campaign of silence was taking its toll on her nerves.

To be sure, no one dared to lift a hand against her physically. She had seen to that, and as a direct result of her prompt reaction to abuse, no further attempts had been made to harm or intimidate her. But she nonetheless was irked by the unjust silence, the deliberate snub to which she was subjected each day.

Still determined not to ask for help from Ah-wen-ga,

she found the idea of appealing to the gods and manitous gradually taking shape in her mind. She remembered how a hawk, appearing out of nowhere in the middle of the night, had led her and Ghonkaba to safety when their escape from Quebec had appeared hopeless. The gods were all-powerful, and as they were known for their strong belief in the principles of justice, she felt it was appropriate for her to go to them for assistance.

Never having visited the Room of the Great Faces, Toshabe did not know what to expect, and after opening the door, she paused timidly on the threshold for a moment and then stepped inside. The quiet was so strong it was almost a wall of silence, and she realized that she was the only person in the building. As her eyes became accustomed to the gloom, she was able to make out the features on the huge, hideous masks that covered all four walls.

Having no idea which gods or manitous should hear her appeal, Toshabe solved her problem by turning slowly in a complete circle as she spoke. In this way, she felt, her words were all-encompassing and were directed to all of the deities.

"Hear my plea, O gods and manitous of the Seneca," she said. "I am Toshabe, formerly an Erie and also French by birth. I am not a native Seneca, but I have become a Seneca by adoption, and I have accepted the beliefs and the convictions on which the Seneca nation is founded. If it is your will, I will be married one day to Ghonkaba, and together we will rear children who will continue to be faithful to the traditions of our people."

Her vivid imagination persuaded her now that the eyes peering down from the walls were regarding her with a lively interest.

"Hear my plea, O gods and manitous," she continued. "You undoubtedly know of the treatment I am being accorded by the young women of this nation, so I will not waste your time by outlining their reception of me. It is enough that I regard this as highly unfair and unjust. I have done nothing to deserve their scorn and hatred. I ask only their acceptance of me, not their friendship."

She even thought she could see one of the huge faces nod sympathetically. Her knees felt weak, and she was afraid she was going to lose consciousness. But digging her fingernails into her palms, she went on. "I do not seek vengeance against those who have tormented me," she said. "I feel no hatred toward them, but I pity them because of their ignorance and their shortsighted stupidity. So I do not ask you to punish them for their treatment of me. I ask only that you who are all-wise and all-powerful open their eyes. For this favor, I will be eternally grateful to you and will serve you faithfully for all of my days." Bowing her head, she folded her hands over her breasts and revolved slowly, bowing to the masks on each wall in turn. Then she made her exit, lost in thought.

Three young women were outside the chamber, talking together before entering. Two wore their hair in the double braids of squaws, while the third had the single braid of an unmarried maiden. They were startled when they recognized Toshabe. She did not lose her aplomb. Smiling, she bowed her head slightly and said, "I bid you a pleasant evening."

The trio were so rattled they could not reply, and by the time they recovered she had already gone on. This, in fact, was pleasing to them because they once more were at liberty to continue their slanders, and they exchanged superior, amused glances. They had no idea why she had come to speak with the gods and the manitous, but they hoped that she was sufficiently upset by their campaign that she had complained about them to the deities.

Toshabe walked on to the house of Ja-gonh and Ah-wen-ga with her head held high. When she arrived, Ah-wen-ga remarked that she smelled rain in the air, that the first rainstorm of the spring season was approaching, and that therefore they would be wise to prepare their cooking fire indoors.

Ah-wen-ga proved to be an accurate prophet, for rain began to fall before the meat was roasted in the stone pit that occupied the center of the chamber the family used for living and dining.

The downpour, which was steady, became heavier, and in the distance rumbles of thunder could be heard. After they had eaten, Ja-gonh confided some military news of primary importance. He had returned from Boston recently, but had kept in touch with the generals through messengers.

"Tomorrow," he said, "No-da-vo will leave for Boston with the Seneca warriors he is going to lead into battle."

"When will you be departing?" his wife asked quietly.

"In seven or eight days," he said, "as soon as I receive word from General Amherst. I shall join him at a rendezvous not far distant from the land of the Seneca."

Listening to the thunder that was growing louder and noting through the window opening that it was accompanied by flashes of heavy lightning, Toshabe dared to ask a question. "Will the campaign be long or short?"

Only someone ignorant of the principles of warfare

could have asked such a question, but Ja-gonh understood her thinking and took pity. "If all goes according to plan," he said, "Quebec will fall in two moons' time. My experience is that military campaigns invariably take longer than those who plan them anticipate. So it would be safer to say that Quebec will fall—if it falls—in three months. Ghonkaba is with the troops now and will sail to Canada with the fleet that is going to transport General Wolfe's army there, and if we achieve the victory we hope to win, he should be home soon afterward."

Thanking him for his information, Toshabe bowed her head. Somehow she would be forced to tolerate the rude conduct of her contemporaries for at least three more months, and although the prospect was harrowing, she dreaded the alternative that awaited her at the end of that time. What if Ghonkaba decided that he did not want to marry her after all, and so notified her when he returned home?

Ah-wen-ga understood some of what was troubling Toshabe and, reaching out, patted her hand reassuringly. Because it would not be proper to discuss Ghonkaba and his plans in the presence of his father, she said instead, "The god who brings rain is very noisy tonight."

Ja-gonh glanced out of the window. "I don't recall a time," he said, "when he has hurled more rain at us in so short a time. I'm glad that the preparation of the ground and the planting of crops has been completed. A soaking rain can be well used now."

"Perhaps we could do with a little less," Ah-wen-ga replied with a smile.

A long bolt of lightning sizzled, then cracked almost directly overhead, and was followed by an enormous clap of thunder.

Inadvertently, Toshabe flinched. Ja-gonh looked at her quietly, and when he spoke an air of finality was in his voice. "We do not need to fear the wrath of the gods," he said. "When one has lived as one should and has obeyed the dictates of the manitous, one is safe, even in weather such as this." He paused, then chuckled. "I do not advise foolhardiness, of course, and would not suggest that you go out and stand under a tree during such a thunderstorm. But only those who perform evil have cause to fear."

The words were scarcely out of his mouth when another bolt of lightning turned night into day, and a roar of thunder filled the air. These sounds were followed by some human screams. Ja-gonh and the women hurried to the door of the house to see what happened.

Some distance away, two longhouses were on fire, burning fiercely, after apparently having been struck by lightning. One was the dwelling of the young squaws of warriors who were on duty in foreign parts, and the other was the residence of the unmarried maidens. The flames were so intense that even the heavy rain pelting down did not quench them.

Ignoring the elements, Ja-gonh hurried to the scene. By the time he reached it, half a dozen war chiefs, assisted by scores of braves, had the situation under control. Toshabe quickly joined them in their efforts to save all the inhabitants. They could do nothing about putting out the fire that consumed the two buildings with the contents, but a bucket brigade was quickly formed to the shores of the lake, and the disciplined warriors managed to keep the fire from spreading.

As Ah-wen-ga came forward, she and Toshabe discovered that a near miracle had occurred. Although lightning had struck the longhouses and had burned them and their contents to the ground, not one occupant had suffered injury of any kind.

When the rain subsided, Ja-gonh found it possible to make arrangements for housing the young women made homeless. While he conferred with several subordinates, Ah-wen-ga and Toshabe continued to walk among the stricken young women, intending to reassure them that all would be well.

Toshabe's presence created a considerable stir. The two young squaws and the unmarried maiden who had seen her at the Room of the Great Faces took immediate note of her and, in low undertones, began to speak to others about her.

Toshabe had little doubt of the substance of their excited whispering and was filled with awe. She had asked the gods and the manitous of the Seneca for a favor in the name of fairness and justice, and they had complied—with a vengeance! Surely it could not be accidental that the dwellings of the young matrons and the unmarried women, the very members of the nation who had been tormenting her, had been destroyed by a bolt of lightning. Yet no one had been harmed, and the only loss suffered was the personal property of the young women.

The attitude of Toshabe's tormentors was changed instantly and sharply. The young women bowed respectfully to Ah-wen-ga, giving her the greetings due the wife of the Great Sachem. It was far more significant that they also inclined their heads in respect to Toshabe.

Her prayers had been answered; the senseless vendetta had come to an end. She returned the greetings with a warm smile for each of the young women who had made her so unhappy throughout the spring. She had no desire for revenge against them, and she did not dream of gloating over the misfortune they had suffered. It was enough that the all-powerful gods had answered her plea for help and had demonstrated their awesome strength in a way that could not be denied.

She herself possessed no magical powers, Toshabe knew, and could claim none of the credit for what had happened. The glory belonged only to the gods and to the manitous who were their intermediaries with mortals. Thanking them silently, in all humility, she knew now that she would have the strength to wait for Ghonkaba until the military campaign ended, and then to face the future with or without him. Such decisions, she realized, were not in the hands of humans, but were up to the gods to determine. With her faith in them bolstered immeasurably, she now was able to face with equanimity and confidence whatever might lie ahead.

Great Britain's North American colonies were unaccustomed to military cooperation with each other on a large scale, so before the final steps were taken and the two armies were ready to move, spring had passed and the month of August was reached. Word had been sent to Ja-gonh to bring his picked Iroquois to a rendezvous point with the British troops, and he had led them proudly into position.

General Amherst, with General Strong acting as his deputy, marched overland from his base at Albany and swung northward through the New York Colony. His army had a hard core of British Regulars supported by militiamen from New York, Connecticut, and Pennsylvania. In addition, he was accompanied by a large force of Iroquois warriors under the personal command of Ja-gonh, though his own Seneca were not included in his unit.

General Wolfe's army, which would face far greater risks, took formation slowly at a site in the remote countryside north of Boston on the coast. There a brigade of British Regulars under Townsend Whiting practiced assault tactics, as did a separate brigade of Massachusetts militiamen and another made up of colonials from other New England colonies.

Working closely with them was an elite force of five hundred Seneca warriors under the command of Noda-vo. It practiced assault tactics endlessly with the Regulars and the militia.

Ghonkaba, meanwhile, was charged with the responsibility of forming his own unit of scouts. He carefully selected fifty Seneca warriors, the best scouts in the nation, in his opinion; he was confident that they had no equal.

He and his warriors practiced working together in the wilderness, using hand signals and taking every possible precaution to make certain they glided silently across the terrain. Wolfe, who frequently observed their efforts, could find no fault with their performance.

Ghonkaba took occasion to observe preparations being made by other units, as well as his own, and was greatly impressed by what he saw. He had to admit to himself, grudgingly, that Brigadier Whiting appeared to know his business thoroughly. His troops did not wear the usual scarlet and white uniforms of Regulars that made them such conspicuous targets. Instead, like the militiamen with whom they were serving, they wore buckskins and blended into their background.

Acting on Wolfe's specific instructions, the assault brigades enjoyed an informality unique in the British Army. Stringent rules of discipline were relaxed, and

Wolfe stressed that only results in battle had any meaning. He wanted his assault troops to be flexible, prepared for any contingency that might arise.

The bulk of his strong, five-thousand-man unit was made up of more conventional troops, including both Regulars and colonials. The duty of the assault troops was to obtain a foothold from which they could not be dislodged. Then the more conventional troops would move in and press forward against the foe.

The Seneca set up patrols of unseen, silent sentinels to keep all but authorized personnel at a distance from the training site. In spite of these precautions, it was impossible to determine whether the French had learned of the expedition's presence. Wolfe, as cautious in his planning as he was almost reckless in his execution of his plans, continued to take as few chances as possible. A fleet of transports arrived one at a time at the little fishing village of Marblehead, sneaking into port only at night. Troops were embarked on them, and they put out to sea again, to be followed the next night by still more vessels. In this way, over a period of several evenings, the entire expeditionary force was embarked.

The ships put out to sea, and there they were joined by a Royal Navy fleet of warships, which included frigates, sloops, and bomb ketches, all sufficiently powerful to protect the troops if the enemy learned of their embarkation and sent the French fleet to intercept them.

At Wolfe's insistence, Ghonkaba sailed on board the flagship of the commander in chief of the army. The heads of subsidiary units also sailed on the same vessel, and Ghonkaba often found himself in Whiting's company. Noting that the brigadier went out of his way to be friendly, he was forced to concede that he was genuinely relieved that his grandfather's appearance in a dream had prevented him from carrying out his intended murder. He recognized that he would have performed a disservice had he insisted on his intentions. Whiting was endowed with an indefinable, charismatic quality of leadership. Somewhat to his own surprise, Ghonkaba now found himself actually becoming friendly with Whiting, and he could see the qualities that had won him the affections of Beth Strong.

Avoiding commercial shipping lanes, the transports and their escorts moved far out into the Atlantic in order to avoid detection by the French. They saw no French vessels, neither warships nor merchantmen, and each day that passed brought their goal closer toward realization.

After more than a week at sea, the fleet finally entered the mouth of the St. Lawrence River and ran up the French fleur-de-lis flag from the mastheads of the various ships. The thin disguise could not be expected to mislead any French Navy vessels they might encounter, but if a merchantman or travelers on either bank of the river spotted them, there would be less chance that an alarm would be sounded.

On the afternoon of the following day Wolfe issued orders from his flagship, placing the entire army on battle alert. They were drawing nearer to Quebec now, and anything might be expected. Late that evening, the captain of the sloop ordered a halt when it was possible to make out, in the distance, the city of Quebec and the powerful Citadel that crowned it. General Wolfe, examining the target through a glass, shook his head. "All that I've heard," he said, "pales when we face reality. Quebec is going to be a very hard nut to crack even with General Amherst and General Strong providing a diversionary action."

The brigadiers, one by one, looked at the city with the great fortress surmounting it, and each agreed with him. The fall of Louisburg had demonstrated conclusively that no fortress was impregnable, but without doubt Quebec was a more formidable bulwark to conquer.

To reduce to a minimum the chance that lookouts stationed in the Citadel would see them go ashore, Wolfe ordered the transfer of his entire command to longboats. Built for just this purpose, the boats had come north on the decks of the transports and warships. After they were launched one by one, the transports and their escorts turned back toward the open sea.

This maneuver had been practiced repeatedly, and as a consequence, every member of the expedition knew what was expected of him. The operation, as a result, proceeded smoothly under the cover of darkness. Each carrying forty or more fighting men, the longboats were paddled in single file up the St. Lawrence. The oarsmen had their hands full combating the powerful tide of the great river, which was running against them. Nevertheless, they performed diligently and their paddles were miraculously silent as they dipped again and again into the water.

Riding in the prow of the lead boat, which also carried Wolfe and Whiting, Ghonkaba was in temporary command of the expedition. The commander in chief had charged him with the responsibility of determining when they should turn toward the shore and proceed from that point on foot. He peered first at the forest that lined the shore, then at the lights that began to come on in Quebec, which lay ahead.

He had no way to describe the location of the bottom of the path that would lead him up to the Plains of

Abraham, but he was confident that he would recognize it when he saw it. As the paddlers continued their efforts, and the frail craft struggled against the tide, Ghonkaba began to feel somewhat less certain of himself. It would be catastrophic if he misjudged and could not find the path. Silently praying to the manitous for their help, he glanced at Townsend Whiting seated behind him, and was relieved again that he had not given in to his stupid, murderous impulse; with blood on his hands, he could not ask the manitous for their help.

In the gathering gloom he saw a patch that looked familiar. This was where he and Toshabe had emerged from the forest and met the Micmac couple with whom they had exchanged clothes.

Ghonkaba pointed toward the shore. The crew was alert, and the craft immediately turned toward the north bank. The other longboats in the long line followed, and they, too, turned toward the shore. Within minutes the entire expedition was being landed.

General Wolfe cautiously wanted to leave a potential line of retreat open in case his men needed it. He ordered the longboats hauled ashore and concealed as best they could be beneath the bushes and underbrush. Such concealment was far from perfect, but he was gambling that the enemy would not discover the crafts.

While the boats were being dragged ashore and half hidden, the fifty Seneca scouts reported to Ghonkaba and immediately set about performing the function for which they were so well suited. They spread out and slowly advanced into the wilderness.

Ghonkaba himself waited for a signal from General Wolfe ordering him to advance. Until then, he moved off a few paces into the forest, and familiarizing himself with his surroundings, made certain that this was the area he had visited previously. Sure of himself, he waited patiently, buoyed by the realization that though when last here he had been a fugitive, he was returning as a conqueror.

What Ghonkaba found most impressive was the silence in which the operation was conducted. He expected no less from the Seneca, but he was astonished that the British assault brigade and the militiamen were as quiet and as at home in the wilderness as were his fellow Seneca. Only when those Regulars and colonials who had not been trained in wilderness fighting were ordered into the line was there any noise, and that was kept to a minimum by Wolfe. He paced up and down the line like a panther, scowling, gesticulating, and demanding silence. "We are in place," he said to Ghonkaba, "and may be captured by the French if we wait any longer. We must commit ourselves to the attack." He gave Ghonkaba the signal to move forward.

The young war chief moved to the head of the column, advanced beyond it, and with the warriors of his sentry detail fanning out on either side of him, he started toward the base of the trail that would lead by a roundabout means to the heights behind the Citadel. The invasion of Quebec was under way.

General Montcalm invited his principal subordinate commanders to supper. These men included his colonels and captains, as well as the Indian leaders of the tribes allied with France. Montcalm delighted in serving them with an extravagant dish that had been one of the favorites of the late Louis XIV, and was typical of the extravagance of the Sun King. A whole pig was roasted slowly over the coals of a low fire. In the animal's cavity was a roast goose, inside of which was a roasted pigeon, which was filled with chopped goose liver mixed with olives imported from France.

At last the succulent dish was ready, and Montcalm attended to the carving himself, observing lightly, "According to legend, you know, the Sun King threw away everything but the goose liver and olives. However, we're simple military men who know a feast when we see one, so I think we'll eat everything."

His subordinates cheered, and one of them offered a toast to the general.

Montcalm accepted the tribute and then observed calmly, "This occasion may be a trifle more memorable than any of you realize. I have just been informed in a message delivered from one of our sentinel outposts of a hostile presence that seems to assure that the enemy's assault on Quebec is soon to begin."

The generals stared in astonishment.

"Our sentinels report," Montcalm continued, "that many longboats are being dropped from the frigates that had been observed approaching in the St. Lawrence. As nearly as I can estimate, the British have sent a force of five thousand against us."

His subordinates were so perturbed that their aperitifs and the feast that awaited them were forgotten. "When do you plan to start to counter this situation, sir?" one asked in great agitation.

The commanding general remained monumentally calm. "We've anticipated such an attack for many months, after all. We've done everything in our power to prepare for it," he said. "Our cannon are fully loaded and are pointed at the river and at the lower reaches. When daylight comes, we shall bombard the British with all the artillery we're capable of mustering.

"I know of no way," Montcalm went on, "that any army, regardless of whether it consists of one thousand men or ten thousand, can fight its way successfully up the cliff and into the Citadel. Such a move is impossible."

The generals nodded and again reached for their drinks.

"We may expect the enemy to lay siege to us," General Montcalm said. "Precisely as we've been predicting ever since the beginning of spring.

"As time goes on," he continued, "it might be necessary for us to give refuge to certain of the civilian population of Quebec in the Citadel. We are already prepared for this and have accumulated stocks of smoked meat, pickled fish, flour, bacon, and beans in order to meet such emergency conditions. I will go so far as to say that we are prepared, in case of need, to give refuge to the entire civilian population of the city. Then we will simply shut the gates and allow the foe to batter himself senseless against the cliffs, while our guns slowly pound him to bits."

The atmosphere became increasingly convivial as tension dissipated.

A harsh note entered Montcalm's voice when he laughed. "On the other hand," he said, "the British laid siege to us at Louisburg, and that tactic enabled them to win the fort there. The mind of the Englishman is a curious object, and they do love to repeat themselves. If instead of the assault that we expect they try a siege, they cannot win that way, either. Ultimately, the weather of French Canada would destroy them. When winter comes and the bitter cold snows arrive, no army can maintain a successful siege. Illness would decimate their ranks, and when their troops began to desert, they'd be forced to withdraw. Come, gentlemen; the repast is now ready, and I urge you to help yourselves. Enough delicacy is here for all of us to enjoy an evening to the full. And while you're about it, be good enough to try the Burgundy that was delivered to me just two weeks ago through the courtesy of His Christian Majesty's Navy. Because we are so well prepared, we cannot possibly lose! They can never dislodge us. And I await with anticipation the sight of the first redcoats trying to climb the heights that we command."

Chapter XI

Step by step, the invaders followed Ghonkaba and his Seneca scouts up the tortuous, convoluted path that led inland and rose to the Plains of Abraham behind the Citadel. At midnight, after hours of steady, slow climbing, Wolfe called a temporary halt to the advance and joined Ghonkaba at the head of the column. "Are you certain," he asked, "that you're taking us to the destination I seek?"

"I am very sure," Ghonkaba replied quietly.

The commander was reminded of what Washington had told him before they had parted company in Massachusetts. "You can trust Ghonkaba implicitly in all things and at all times," Washington had said. "He may be inclined toward personal recklessness in battle, but he'll never take unnecessary risks with the lives of others."

Wolfe would have to abide by Washington's assurance, but with so much at stake, he could not help but be apprehensive. If the young white Indian was mistaken, the entire invading force of five thousand men would be in grave jeopardy, and the campaign that had looked so promising might turn out to be a hopeless shambles. He had to give Ghonkaba a free hand, trusting completely in his judgment. Looking into the eyes that returned his glance, he felt reassured.

The quiet march was resumed, and about three o'clock in the morning, Ghonkaba and his scouts reached the wilderness at the northern end of the Plains of Abraham. They had achieved their goal.

Their troubles were far from ended, however, and they had no opportunity to rejoice. Ghonkaba and his Seneca discovered the presence of four buckskin-clad French sentries in the forest, and had to dispose of them.

This was done swiftly and mercilessly. The sentinels were killed with tomahawks, then scalped. Their bodies were concealed in deep underbrush.

General Wolfe elected to open the battle at dawn, and in the meantime, gave his tired invaders an opportunity to rest. Grateful for the chance, most of them fell asleep by their weapons and enjoyed a nap for nearly two hours.

Only the Seneca sentries remained alert. Ghonkaba reasoned that French replacements would come to relieve the men who had been killed. When they appeared, they, too, would have to be put out of the way swiftly and silently.

His expectation proved correct. About an hour before daybreak, four replacements did appear, each softly calling a password to the sentinels whom they were replacing.

Seneca tomahawks again became active, and the four French woodsmen were cut down instantly. They, too, suffered the final indignity of being scalped before their bodies joined those of their fallen comrades.

Dawn broke, and Ghonkaba and his sentries, relieved of their duties at last, were assigned to No-davo. As the sky grew lighter, the main body of Seneca warriors, which formed the advance guard, began to advance across the Plains of Abraham in the direction of the Citadel.

Directly behind the Seneca were Whiting's assault troops, followed by the colonials with the same function. The three units, about fifteen hundred men in all, crept across the exposed Plains of Abraham toward the high walls of the fortress. Wolfe, following them at the head of the remaining thirty-five hundred soldiers of his army, felt that victory was surely within grasp.

A French colonial, a recruit from Montreal seeing his first military service, was on guard duty in one of the watchtowers overlooking the Plains of Abraham. He saw the shadows creeping closer across the open field. Although a novice, he was no newcomer to the wilderness, and he knew instantly what was happening. He sounded an alarm, blowing as hard as he could on a sentinel's whistle suspended around his neck.

The sound of that whistle reverberated through the Citadel, and the attackers heard it, too. Ghonkaba realized that the advance would be forced to halt and that within moments the invaders would be engaged in a fight for their lives.

His prediction proved all too accurate. The French officer of the guard responded instantly, and the battalion of infantry kept on reserve duty for just such an emergency slipped out of a gate into the open and engaged the invaders.

Spreading out and allowing as much distance as possible between each man, rather than filing out in close formation as they would have done in Europe, the French troops opened fire on their adversaries. The crack of their rifles signaled the start of one of the most significant battles ever fought in the New World.

The outcome of the battle would influence, significantly and permanently, the development and history of North America. Yet it was strange that it was fought under conditions hardly typical of battles on the continent. Aside from a few scattered trees and a handful of large boulders, the Plains of Abraham provided virtually no cover. Foliage was inadequate to enable the Indians and the colonists to engage in their usual type of warfare, where they would seek cover and utilize the forests at every opportunity.

Men on both sides spread out, flattening themselves against the ground in order to reduce their visibility as targets. Their principal responsibility was to hold the ground they already occupied and not be pushed back.

Officers on both sides ordered their subordinates to absorb whatever punishment was meted out to them, and meanwhile to cling to every inch of territory in their possession. The carnage on both sides was tremendous, and Montcalm knew from reports that his troops were in for the fight of their lives.

Caught badly off balance, the French had not expected the enemy to appear on the Plains of Abraham. How the British had managed to find their way, undetected, to the heights remained a mystery for many years.

The French commander realized he had been outmaneuvered by a foe thoroughly familiar with his situation. Every artillery piece in the possession of the French faced the St. Lawrence and such heavy cannon could not possibly be moved quickly enough to thwart an attack from the Plains of Abraham. For all practical purposes, his artillery was useless except against a frontal assault from the St. Lawrence. The British force had brought no heavy guns, so the fight was being waged strictly by foot soldier against foot soldier in an attack from the rear.

Montcalm performed near miracles in averting a catastrophe. He sent unit after unit with remarkable speed and threw them into the fight. There were three cavalry units, and in addition, he was able to rally his Indian allies, particularly the more reliable of them, the Huron and the Ottawa. They poured out of the rear gate of the Citadel and took their places beside their buckskin-clad comrades.

The battle was in essence a slugfest, with both sides delivering their hardest blows simultaneously in an attempt to crumble the enemy lines. But neither side gave way. The entire future of North America was at stake, and no man in either force was willing to budge.

General Wolfe, committing battalion after battalion to the struggle in an attempt to maintain his initiative, could not help but feel severe disappointment. Somehow, the overall plans had gone awry. At this point, Amherst's army should arrive on the south bank of the St. Lawrence and attempt a crossing, thereby subjecting the French to pressure from both north and south.

Now, however, as Wolfe was all too painfully aware, something must have gone amiss with Amherst's timetable. It was useless to speculate on the possible reasons, or to wish for a speedup in his effort. The battle was joined, and Wolfe had to make the best of the situation without help.

In all, Wolfe knew that he had no cause for complaint. The battle was going well enough, thanks in large part to No-da-vo and his Seneca, and to the disciplined brigade commanded by Whiting. The two units, made up of about a thousand men in all, were performing superbly, as though they had fought side by side on many occasions. Even Wolfe found it difficult to realize that this was the first time they had ever entered combat together.

The Seneca, though they faced expert French riflemen, did not flinch or fade or retreat. Instead, they shot their long arrows steadily at the foe, making every shot count. Their war chiefs had no need to exhort them to exercise caution and make sure of their targets before they let loose an arrow. Their supplies of arrows were relatively limited, and they were determined not to needlessly waste any.

Whiting's brigade, however, using rifles, could afford to take a somewhat more aggressive stance. Equipped with ample quantities of ammunition, they fired round after round, and their long, rigorous training served them well as they picked off the enemy one by one. So far, at least, neither the Seneca nor Whiting's brigade had considered retreating. Holding their own, they weren't encountering much difficulty in keeping the terrain they occupied.

Ghonkaba was enjoying the experience of a lifetime. No longer forced to operate in the dark as a scout, he could be himself, a war chief of the Seneca. He sent arrow after arrow in the direction of the French, feeling great satisfaction each time he cut down an opponent. He knew at last the sheer exultation of fighting freely, of pouring his whole soul into the battle. And he understood now what his father and grandfather had meant when they spoke of battle fever. He was reckless, yet was endowed with a sense of cunning that permitted him to take no unnecessary risks. He did not know it, but he was already creating a legend for himself, having disposed of eight French soldiers and having wounded three others. He became a prime target for the enemy, but seemed to live a charmed life. His movements after each of his shots were just enough to spoil the aim of French sharpshooters taking a bead on him, and their shots missed him repeatedly.

The French units continued to pour onto the field from the Citadel. With relatively little space in which to maneuver, they were densely packed. They occupied no more than a third of the Plains of Abraham.

By the time the bulk of the French force had assembled on the field and had joined in the fray, they were still hemmed in closely by the two brigades. Montcalm realized that he would have to push them back in order to obtain his primary goal of clearing his foes from the Plains. So he directed his forces to attack the Seneca and the Regulars with all the might at their command.

The Ottawa, eager to gain renown for themselves as the conquerors of the invincible Seneca, advanced into combat, prancing, gesticulating, and uttering ferocious war cries.

The Seneca remained calm under the assault, and no one else maintained a more rigorous self-control than did Ghonkaba. He waited until the last possible moment to order his subordinates to open fire on the Ottawa. By this time, the enemy was so close that it was impossible to miss them, and they were mowed down as though a giant scythe, wielded by an oversize hand, had struck them.

The Ottawa retreated in wild disorder. Only the presence of other Indians and French troops behind them prevented them from fleeing from the field in even more disgraceful disarray than was the case.

The ranks of the Erie were thinner than the Ottawa, but their approach was more orderly and at the same time was carried out with the cunning for which their nation was renowned. They advanced with grim determination, hoping to use their show of valor as a means of expunging the stain that recently had been placed on their honor by the foolish behavior of one of their members. Again, as was the case with the Ottawa, they moved forward so far that it became almost impossible for the bowmen on either side to miss a target when it became available. However, the Seneca, having had a much greater opportunity to take concealed positions, had by far the best of the situation, and only occasionally did an Erie arrow find its mark in Seneca ranks. On the other hand, the Erie had to expose their entire front line, and as those warriors fell, others launched themselves into the fray seemingly without a qualm as they crept among their fallen comrades. The fury of the conflict raged on, but at no time was there any doubt as to what would be the outcome of the struggle. The courage of the Erie could not make up for the vulnerability of their position, and the skill of the Seneca took a very heavy toll.

Then, as it seemed that the Erie must retreat vanquished, though with less vainglory than the Ottawa, a lone figure emerged from among their increasingly disordered ranks.

Ghonkaba, in an excellent position to observe the progress of the conflict—the manner in which his braves were valorously standing their ground and turning back the enemy, as well as the devastating impact of their fire—saw with astonishment the Erie's wild dash to the forefront. Instantly, he recognized Ludona, the disgraced war chief who had been granted Montcalm's specific permission to make the murder of Ghonkaba in this battle his sole responsibility. Though Ghonkaba had no way of knowing of the dire mission on which Ludona now had launched himself, he quickly surmised that the brave's seemingly senseless appearance at this late juncture—when the fate of the Erie assault was virtually sealed—must have some special importance. He recognized, too, that his command posture was such that with the Erie brave approaching rapidly from an oblique angle, he would be exposed to Ludona's line of fire.

The Erie, having bided his time with growing impatience and frustration while the battle raged, had concentrated on spotting his archenemy's exact location. Having checked it and confirmed it to his full satisfaction, he was ready to stake his own life on this glorious chance of redeeming his honor and his nation's by taking the measure of the great warrior who had undone all his evil scheming. Now was the moment to avenge the dishonor he had sustained at Ghonkaba's hands, and he knew that he must seize it at whatever cost.

As he ran among the bodies of his fallen comrades and those of the slain Ottawa, he scorned the protection that was available and rushed straightforward into the melee, disregarding the numerous Seneca warriors who now took deadly aim at him.

With a gesture, Ghonkaba ordered his braves to withhold their fire. He recognized the confrontation as one that he himself must accept. He must not permit his own men to blunt the challenge to his personal honor and credibility as an unparalleled, fearless leader of men.

He had no time to bring his bow into action, but

with his tomahawk already in hand, he raised his powerful right arm in a reflexive motion and sent the weapon speeding on its way to the spot his instinct told him Ludona would have reached by the time the tomahawk arrived there. As usual, his judgment proved unerring, and the Erie crashed headlong into its edge with all his onrushing force. The effect was shattering. Ludona's wild whoops strangled in his throat as he plunged forward onto his face, now well ahead of the positions of any other attacking warriors. Seeking to assure that, without question, the arrow meant for Ghonkaba would hit home with undoubted fatal result, Ludona had delayed launching it a few seconds too long. The price for his determined, single-minded thrust to a surefire position had been his own life—and in his final moment of life he must have recognized that once more he had miserably failed. Ghonkaba, his hated rival, would survive—and with new heroic glory. Ludona was fated to join his ancestors with his honor unredeemed.

The failure of his mad dash took away all the remaining resolve from the hearts of the sparsely populated ranks of the Erie assault platoon, and they promptly fell back. Disaster had taken its toll on them once again.

And finally the Huron advanced, and as was their custom, they were more cautious. Dropping to the ground, they crawled forward before opening fire with their bows. They had no real chance to succeed. Their moves were all too plainly visible to the Seneca, who again waited and opened fire only when the Huron were within close, certain range. The Huron were forced to retreat, too, but managed to salvage their honor by keeping their ranks more or less intact as they drew back. It had become obvious that the Seneca could not be dislodged by any other Indian tribe.

During a brief respite that followed, Ghonkaba glanced to his right and was disconcerted to see Whiting's brigade being subjected to a severe pounding on three sides by the French troops. The English Regulars, trained in wilderness fighting, were holding firm, and it was evident that they had no intention of retreating. But as Ghonkaba watched, he saw Whiting himself crumble, struck by a French bullet. The man he had twice planned to kill had been felled by the enemy, and though still alive he was moving only feebly. Ghonkaba could not determine how severe his injury was.

Scarcely aware of the irony, Ghonkaba crawled to the nearby spot where No-da-vo had established himself. "Brigadier Whiting, the English leader, has been hit," he said. "May I take him to safety where doctors can care for him?"

"He has hundreds of his own men," the Seneca sachem replied curtly. "Let them look after him."

Ghonkaba shook his head. "They will never reach safety with him. That is a task that only a Seneca can perform."

"Go, then, but return rapidly. The French are certain to make another attempt to dislodge us."

Ghonkaba crawled as quickly as possible to the spot where Whiting lay very still on the ground, with a red stain on his shirt as well as other apparent wounds. His eyes were closed, his face was very pale, but he was still breathing, and Ghonkaba took heart.

Saying nothing to any member of the brigade, he gently hoisted Whiting onto his shoulders and, following an erratic, zigzag course, began to carry him toward the rear.

But the French immediately became aware of the attempt to remove the fallen brigadier from the battlefield, and made Ghonkaba a prime target. Quickly aware of the precarious situation, Ghonkaba promptly resorted to every trick he knew, sometimes dropping to his knees, lying prone and inching forward, and even leaping into an erratic, semidance as he continued to move toward the rear as best he could, meanwhile carrying or dragging Whiting as the situation required.

His tactics were so wildly unpredictable that they succeeded. But when he had moved about two-thirds of the distance through the area that Whiting's brigade held he suddenly felt a savage thrust in his left shoulder. It propelled him forward and knocked him to his knees. The blow was so unexpected that it took him a moment to realize that he, too, had been shot.

He discovered that he was still able to move, so he doggedly climbed to his feet and, still clutching his burden, continued to weave his way toward the rear.

Those who witnessed Ghonkaba's escape from the combat area never forgot it, declaring that in all their lives they had never seen such courage or such determination.

At last he reached an area occupied by a reserve battalion not yet in combat. Here, strong hands took Whiting from his shoulders. In spite of his protests, he was forced to lie down on a stretcher. Both young men were carried into the woods behind the Plains of Abraham to a makeshift medical center. There they were fed doses of laudanum, a liquid opiate that would lessen pain, and then, at the same time, they went under the knives of surgeons to remove the bullets lodged in their bodies. Whiting was given a block of wood on which to clamp his teeth, but Ghonkaba scornfully refused one and endured his agony in silence.

As his now-cleansed wound was being dressed, he was given more laudanum, and he drifted into a merciful sleep. The last thing he remembered was that Whiting's operation also had been terminated, and appeared successful.

In the meantime, the battle was waged with ever-increasing intensity. More and more men were committed by the British and French commanders in a futile attempt to tip the scale. In their desperation they killed their foes indiscriminately, hoping that the sheer numbers of casualties would discourage the enemy and turn the tide.

The troops on both sides fought tenaciously, giving no quarter, expecting none, and receiving none. The five hundred Seneca were badly outnumbered by Indian forces at least four times their number, but nevertheless they could not be dislodged. The myth of Seneca invincibility continued to expand that day.

Whiting's unit and the similar brigade from Massachusetts also distinguished themselves in action. Ignoring their frightfully high casualty rate, they dug in, and the most ferocious efforts of the enemy could not dislodge them. They were men of steel, determined to acquit themselves in a way that would be remembered for all time.

The French were similarly inspired. Paying no attention to the numbers of their comrades who were killed and wounded, they clung to the ground that they held and gave as good as they received, never flinching, never giving up the precious land they held.

The deadlock could not be broken by artillery on either side, as both commanders realized. They knew, too, that they would be encountering serious problems for the future if their casualty rate continued to mount so alarmingly. And so each of them, originally trained in the warfare of Europe's battlefields, came to the same conclusion: in order to break the deadlock, he must himself lead the sortie.

Their immediate subordinates, both English and French, were alarmed by the possibilities of such an engagement. One of the fundamental rules of combat insisted that the commander in chief of a force had to be protected at all costs. His was the brainpower, the motivating force behind an army's movements, and nothing could be allowed to unnecessarily endanger him.

But Wolfe was determined to lead the troops in a charge, hoping to overrun the French positions. Similarly, Montcalm could not be dissuaded from his plan to lead an attack on the English. Only his personal presence on the battlefield, he decided, might so inspire his men that they could hurl back the invader.

And so it happened that, in one of history's strangest coincidences, Generals Wolfe and Montcalm led their respective assault units at the same moment as their forces met and clashed on the field of battle.

No one on the field showed up with more conspicuous bravery than did the French and English generals. Leading a cavalry charge, Montcalm was knocked from his horse by a fusillade fired by British sharpshooters. An attempt was made to extricate General Wolfe from the field, but before this could be accomplished, French marksmen disposed of him, too.

The two commanders were killed at virtually the same time during the battle, and the combat ended shortly thereafter. Outmanned, and recognizing their impossible situation, the French promptly surrendered to the British and colonial colonels in charge of the invasion force. The battle was over, and the British occupied Quebec. Their ensign was raised over the Citadel, and civilian inhabitants of the city were informed they had become British subjects.

The process of disarming the Indian allies of the French was begun, but the savages, realizing they were about to lose their weapons, vanished into the forests and made their way by various routes to their homes. Meanwhile, Ja-gonh's Iroquois warriors and the British under General Amherst were still making their way northward after the prolonged engagements at Ticonderoga and Crown Point.

Royal Navy warships were dispatched in search of ships of the French fleet, which were then permitted to enter Quebec harbor, picking up captive French soldiers who would be transported back across the Atlantic to their native land, leaving behind the shattered aspirations of controlling a continent.

For all practical purposes, the conflict known in America as the French and Indian War had come to an end. Peace treaties still remained to be signed, and innumerable details had to be ironed out, but the basic results of the conflict were clear. England had won, and her colonies would remain under her rule. Quebec and the smaller town of Montreal were absorbed into the British Empire, along with vast tracts of Canada.

France was permanently eliminated as a major power in the northern New World, and aside from retaining several islands in the Caribbean, her only remaining possession was the large area known as Louisiana. Most of all, the liberty of the English colonials and of their Indian allies was assured, and they had real cause for rejoicing.

Never had the hospital at the Citadel been so crowded. Patients' beds lined the corridors, and the private rooms, reserved for higher-ranking officers, were crammed with two and three beds, making privacy impossible. The French and English were treated by their respective physicians, and the staffs had no direct contact with each other, but soon discovered that the art of healing knew no nationality.

Two bullets, lodged close together, had been removed from Ghonkaba's shoulder. No complications set in, and his recovery was smooth and rapid but not nearly fast enough to suit his impatient nature. Much to his disgust, he was required to remain in bed, and as the weeks passed, and summer turned to fall, the physicians were still unable to give him an idea when they might release him.

He shared a sickroom with Townsend Whiting, whose condition was far more serious as a result of wounds in a shoulder and a leg, as well as his chest. Whiting was depressed, additionally, by word from the doctors that his military career had come to an end. He always would walk with a decided limp, his physicians told him, and he was going to be placed on limited duty.

With time hanging heavy on their hands through the long hours of each passing day, the Seneca war chief and the British officer found themselves engaging in spirited conversation. They were gratified to learn that General Amherst finally had been able to reach Quebec after the unanticipated delay along his way north, and they looked forward to receiving information as to the cause of his inability to rendezvous at Quebec at the time of the great battle.

Much to their surprise, they discovered that in spite of the wide differences in their backgrounds, they held similar views on many subjects. Both, they learned, were passionately devoted to the principle of freedom of the individual, and both were willing to do what they had already done—risk their lives—for that cause.

Ghonkaba was surprised to hear that beliefs in liberty were more theoretical than practical in England. Many immigrants to the New World were impelled to move to the vast wilderness and start new lives for themselves because they sought freedom of religion, freedom to believe and practice their political and economic views, freedom to live and to rear their children as they saw fit.

"The only real democracy on earth exists right here in these colonies," Whiting observed one day. "The ideas of liberty that are expressed here originated in Great Britain, it is true, but they're not really practiced there."

Listening attentively, Ghonkaba felt that he was acquiring knowledge that he could have obtained in no other way.

"Since I'm being restricted to limited duty only," Whiting said one day, "Beth and I will face a very serious problem. We'll undoubtedly live—at least for the present—in a house that I own in London. But whether we stay in England permanently is a question that I'm not prepared to answer. I have a suspicion that both of us will want to return to live and raise our family on this side of the Atlantic. Once one has tasted the real freedoms that America offers, it's difficult, to say the least, to settle for anything less."

"I think I see what you mean," Ghonkaba told him.

Whiting smiled and shook his head. "I couldn't blame you in the least, old boy, if you didn't understand a word of what I'm saying. As an Indian—particularly a Seneca—you've known only freedom, and you comprehend completely the burden of responsibility that total freedom imposes on the individual. In fact, the contributions of the Indian to the outlook and attitudes of the settlers is one of the most fascinating aspects of life on this continent. Britain is riddled with class prejudices, religious prejudices, every sort of prejudice you can imagine. But those who have migrated here have had their eyes opened wide when they've seen nations, like you of the Seneca, who actually put their theories into practice."

"We have prejudices, too," Ghonkaba told him, "but they're less evident. For example, if I should marry Toshabe, who is a member of the Erie, I'm sure I'll meet strong opposition to such a union from many women of our own tribe."

Whiting smiled broadly. "I'm willing to wager any sum of money that you wish," he said, "that you'll marry Toshabe. If I had any doubts that you might still care for my wife, they were dispelled when they brought you into this room after they removed the bullets from your shoulder. As you recovered from the dosage of laudanum that you had drunk," he continued with a chuckle, "you began to talk. If you'll forgive the observation, old boy, don't let anyone ever tell you that Indians are silent people. You talked a solid blue streak, and your remarks were all on one subject—Toshabe."

Ghonkaba felt his cheeks burning and knew that he was reddening.

"If you like," Whiting said, "I'll be glad to refresh your memory and tell you what you had to say about her. All of it was highly complimentary, to say the least."

"That won't be necessary," Ghonkaba assured him quickly. "I'll take your word for it."

Again Whiting chuckled. "Rest assured," he said earnestly, "that I have absolutely no desire to embarrass you. Quite the contrary, I'm in your debt as long as I live. I can never forget that you saved my life at great risk to your own, and I can only hope that when you are married you'll pay us a visit at our London home. You'll be more than welcome whenever you arrive, especially as we can expect to be homesick for the people who live here."

Ghonkaba accepted the invitation in the same spirit in which it was given. "I've wanted to pay a visit to England," he said, "and gladly accept your invitation here and now. But we must leave the date open, as I'm not even certain that Toshabe will accept my proposal of marriage."

Whiting shifted his bandaged right side with some difficulty as he observed, "From your description of her when you were under the influence of laudanum, she's the most sensible of women alive. That being the case, how could she fail to accept your proposal?"

"I have not seen her in a number of moons," Ghonkaba said. "She's extremely attractive, and any warrior who sees her is sure to want her. Just as any settler who sets eyes on her will certainly yearn for her. For all I know, she's already married to someone else."

Knowing that his views had to be prompted in large part by his fears, Whiting wisely let the subject drop and did not refer to it again.

The following morning the convalescents were in for a surprise when General Amherst entered their room, accompanied by two aides and the senior physician of the expeditionary force. Dismissing the doctor and his aides, Amherst closed the door.

Ghonkaba and Whiting struggled desperately to achieve upright, sitting positions in their beds.

"Here, now," Amherst said. "We'll have none of that. This is a strictly informal visit. As you were!"

Both relaxed gratefully; the effort to achieve a degree of formality was too great for them.

"I understand that you two gave a splendid exhibition of how to conduct one's self in battle," he said.

Whiting smiled ruefully. "That's rather an exaggeration, General," he said. "At least as far as I'm concerned. I was wounded rather severely and Ghonkaba extricated me, carrying me from the front lines to safety at great risk to himself."

General Amherst smiled. "I've had a dozen reports of Ghonkaba's exploits," he said. "As for you, Brigadier, I've been told by witness after witness that you led your troops with great distinction."

"That's right, General," Ghonkaba said emphatically. "He furnished an inspiring example."

The general nodded, opened the door, and admitted his aides. "I'm not yet done with our private conversations, gentlemen, but I have some official business to which I must attend first. Brigadier Whiting," he said, handing the officer a velvet-lined box and simultaneously drawing his sword and tapping him lightly on the shoulder with it, "in the name of His Majesty, it gives me great honor to present you with a full membership as a knight in the Order of the Bath. Sir Townsend, I congratulate you."

The Order of the Bath was the highest military order in Great Britain, and membership in it was granted only to those who had distinguished themselves in battle. Townsend Whiting, flushing with pleasure, was momentarily overcome.

"Ghonkaba," the general continued, "only the fact that you are not a subject of His Majesty prevents me from awarding you a knighthood in the Order of the Bath also. I take great pleasure, nevertheless, in presenting you with the George Medal, the highest honor for valor that the Crown can give to an individual for courage beyond the call of duty in battle."

Ghonkaba opened the velvet-lined box he was handed and found himself looking at a medal bearing the portrait of the reigning monarch, King George II. To it was attached a red and blue ribbon, and a legend accompanying the medal said that on formal occasions he was entitled to wear a red and blue sash in lieu of the medal itself. The honor meant little to him, but it was significant in one respect. He was the first in a long line of distinguished Seneca fighting men who had received a British medal for valor.

Dismissing his aides again, Amherst questioned the pair at length on the development of the battle of the Plains of Abraham. No detail was too insignificant to attract his close attention, and he skipped nothing in obtaining a blow-by-blow recounting of precisely what had taken place.

"I regret deeply," he said, "my inability to keep my own appointment with General Wolfe and to have assisted in the fall of Quebec. Unfortunately, the French proved somewhat tougher nuts to crack than we had anticipated, and the reduction of their forts at Ticonderoga and Crown Point took rather longer than we had anticipated. However, I'm here at last, and the working out of a peace treaty by commissioners in London and in Paris is a mere formality. The governor-general of New France has already ceded all of Canada to me. I understand there's some talk in Montreal of putting up resistance to British occupation, but that will vanish by the time spring comes and the armies are able to take to the field again. I anticipate no more combat, and as I'm notifying London, the conquest of Canada is complete."

"May we offer our congratulations on the scope of

your victory, General?" Brigadier Sir Townsend Whiting asked politely.

"It's you lads who deserve the full congratulations and the gratitude of the entire British Empire," General Amherst told them firmly. "You and James Wolfe, who is no longer able to hear the cheers that ring out at every mention of his name."

Arriving in Quebec at the head of the large contingent of Iroquois allies serving directly under General Amherst, Ja-gonh went to the Citadel to visit his son. To the amazement of Sir Townsend Whiting, who was not accustomed to Indian ways, they greeted each other casually, and he gained only an inkling of the deep emotion underlying their reunion.

"When does my father lead our braves back to their homes?" Ghonkaba asked, speaking in English for the sake of courtesy to his roommate.

"In three days' time," Ja-gonh replied, "the sachems, including No-da-vo of the Seneca, should have completed reports of their activities in the war transcribed on paper and translated into English for General Amherst. So I intend to lead the march in three days. The weather is growing much colder now, and I am eager that we return to our homes before the heavy snows cover the fields and the wilderness of Canada and of our Iroquois homelands."

"In three days' time," Ghonkaba said, "I will march with you."

Sir Townsend thought that such optimism was quite unwarranted and could not help interrupting. "Forgive me for interfering in something that is none of my business," he said, "but I don't think the physicians will agree to allow you to leave the hospital that soon, Ghonkaba."

"My father marches, and I, too, will march," Ghonkaba said flatly—and that ended the discussion.

Ja-gonh took no part in the talk because his son, as a war chief, was capable of making his own decisions in matters of consequence.

The physicians, one from Boston and the other two from England, protested when they learned of Ghonkaba's decision, but he paid no attention to their protests. He insisted that he would accompany his fellow warriors on their march back to their homeland.

The Massachusetts doctor summed up the situation for his colleagues. "We may as well give our approval and release him," he said. "If we don't, I assure you, he'll go anyway, even if we post a guard to restrain him."

"But he's in no condition to walk hundreds of miles through forests at this season of the year," one of the Englishmen said. "He's had two bullets removed from his shoulder, and he's in a severely weakened condition."

The colonial doctor smiled. "I'm afraid you don't understand," he said. "Ghonkaba is a Seneca, and he's made up his mind. Nothing will stop him, and he will do precisely as he pleases."

So, seventy-two hours later, Ghonkaba was granted his release from the hospital and said good-bye to the British officer who once had been his enemy but now had become his close friend. "I'm sorry to desert you, Townsend," he said. "I hope you're not required to linger here overly long."

"I don't anticipate any delays," Whiting assured him. "Beth is due to arrive here on board a brig within the next few days, and it will set sail for London almost immediately."

"Give Beth my warm regards," Ghonkaba said, "and

tell her from me—from one who knows—that she has every reason to be very proud of the man she married."

"I'll certainly give her that message," Sir Townsend replied, and knew that any last lingering regrets on Ghonkaba's part that his wife had chosen to marry him rather than the Seneca were settled for all time.

They gripped hands, and Sir Townsend had the last word. "Remember," he said, "we're counting on a visit from you and Toshabe when you come to England."

An escort of senior Seneca warriors awaited Ghonkaba at the entrance to the Citadel, and as he and they made their way down through the town, he saw signs that indicated that the English occupation already was being felt. In numerous tailoring establishments, taverns, eating places, and shops, small placards in the windows stated that English was spoken there and that members of the conquering force were welcome.

The Iroquois contingent, numbering about three thousand men in all, already had boarded the ferries that would transport them across the broad waters of the St. Lawrence. When Ghonkaba appeared on the docks, all the Seneca broke the quiet with earsplitting war whoops.

Ghonkaba was pleased by the spontaneous tribute. Their opinion meant infinitely more to him than did the medal that had been awarded to him by the British. The exuberant cries of his brothers meant that they accepted him as a fighting man because of his own exploits, not because he was the son of the Great Sachem of the Iroquois or the nephew of the sachem of the Seneca. No accolade could mean more to him.

Battling a strong current, the bargemen fought for every yard as they struggled to pole the clumsy craft across the great river. The barges bobbed up and down like corks, and, much to their chagrin, a number of the braves became seasick. Ghonkaba was relieved that he felt perfectly normal and did not give in to a sense of seasickness.

When the group finally moved ashore on the south bank, he sought the company of the fifty men who had served so loyally and well as scouts.

But Ja-gonh quietly interfered. "These men," he said, "have earned the right to act as scouts for the entire body of Iroquois on our homeward journey. But another war chief has been appointed to lead them."

Ghonkaba was indignant. "Was my father not satisfied with the leadership I provided them?" he demanded.

Ja-gonh shook his head. "My son was injured in battle," he said, "and until he regained his feet today, he spent many days in bed. We will see what progress he makes on the march before we will permit him to assume command of the scouts once again."

Knowing no appeal was permitted from his father's verdict, Ghonkaba swallowed his indignation as best he could and joined the other war chiefs in the vanguard of the main column.

For a short time, as the Indians made their way through the deep forests, he was able to hold his own. He felt strong and confident, as healthy and vigorous as ever, and thought the precautions taken on his behalf were strictly unnecessary. Then the inexplicable happened. For no discernible reason, the wilderness seemed to swim before his eyes. His step became unsteady, and he was attacked by a dizziness that he had never known. With great difficulty he managed to regain his balance and prevent himself from falling.

No-da-vo had been keeping his nephew under quiet observation and immediately called a halt. A litter was provided, four braves promptly volunteered to be the first to carry it, and Ghonkaba was ordered to lie down. Feeling disgraced, he started to protest vigorously.

But his uncle refused to tolerate a word of nonsense. "Ghonkaba, a war chief of his people," he said, "has received a direct command from his sachem. He will do as he has been ordered."

Ghonkaba accepted the inevitable with bad grace. Brooding, feeling he was disgracing himself, his family, and the nation, he fell into a sullen silence, withdrawing far within himself as he was carried for the rest of the day.

He was still so disturbed that night that he could eat little of the venison prepared for supper. The hunters had shot a deer that very afternoon on the march.

Before the meal ended, his father came to him and spoke firmly. "Tomorrow and each day thereafter," he said, "Ghonkaba will be allowed to begin the day's journey on his own feet. Only if he falters will pallet bearers be called, and when this happens, he will submit to their ministrations properly and will allow himself to be carried for the rest of the day. This is not a subject for discussion. I have ordered this procedure to be followed, and none would dare to disobey my commands."

Ghonkaba felt that his cause was hopeless and saw no way he could regain his strength on the march. But gradually, almost in spite of himself, he showed a steady improvement. Little by little he became stronger, and by the time the Iroquois expedition left Canada behind, he was walking for three hours a day.

The war chiefs who had been ordered to keep watch over him obeyed the command scrupulously, and the moment he showed signs of faltering, they ordered the pallet bearers forward.

Ghonkaba was willing to admit that his shoulder ached, particularly in damp weather, when rain or snow threatened. But this was the first time he had ever suffered from a major wound, and he could not comprehend that considerable time was required for his recuperation.

The fact that he had been seriously incapacitated and would require many weeks to regain his full strength, and that until then he would require assistance, was beyond his ability to grasp. As soon as he was placed on a pallet to be carried, a marked change took place in his personality. He fell silent, brooded, and barely replied when spoken to. He contemplated giving up his three hawk feathers of a war chief, at least until he could function at full capacity.

The homeward march was long and tedious but uneventful. Ghonkaba was not the only wounded warrior being carried by his comrades, and his state of mind did not improve when he discovered that they felt just as he did. They suffered from a sense of shame, as though being wounded were their fault. No Seneca ever expected to be wounded in battle.

Ghonkaba was aware of the history-making exploits he had performed in the battle. He was more responsible than anyone else for the British victory because he had led his comrades up the slopes to the Plains of Abraham. That, coupled with his deeds in saving the life of Townsend Whiting, not to mention the furious fight in which he had engaged while holding the enemy at bay, marked him as one of the primary heroes of the engagement.

The knowledge that he had every right to feel proud of his accomplishments in no way relieved his pervading sense of gloom. He was the first in his family ever to be felled in battle, and he convinced himself that in being wounded he had let the family down.

The Iroquois marched rapidly, without needing to make an allowance for the inability of the wounded to keep up their rapid pace. And so, ultimately, the expedition reached the land of the Seneca. Their arrival was announced by the beating of sentries' drums through the deep forest. The army drew ever closer to the main town of the nation, and to Ghonkaba's disgust, he was required to accept a ride on a pallet for the final stage of the journey. His mortification was complete.

Wallowing in gloom mingled with self-pity, he scarcely looked up when the pallet bearers approached the palisade. He heard the excited cheers of the inhabitants, but he assumed they were greeting others, and he waved feebly, not bothering to look up at the celebrants.

"Ghonkaba!"

He heard his mother's familiar voice calling his name. Raising his head, he found himself returning Ah-wen-ga's concerned stare, and he raised a hand in salute to her, not realizing that he was remaining wooden-faced and withdrawn. Beside his mother was Toshabe, looking even lovelier and more desirable than he had imagined her in his countless daydreams. But his sense of shame was so overwhelming that he could not return her gaze for more than a moment, either, and he greeted her as he had greeted his mother, raising a hand to his forehead in a vague salute, and then dropping his head back onto the pallet again, not even realizing that the emotional stress of the encounter had exhausted him.

His shame so great that he could not face either the woman he loved or his mother, he took refuge in sleep before he was deposited at the home of his parents.

When Toshabe and Ah-wen-ga arrived at the house, they found him sleeping soundly. Not knowing the extent of his ailment, they made no attempt to awaken him, but impatiently awaited Ja-gonh.

When the Great Sachem came into the house a short time later, he explained his son's situation in detail. It was Ghonkaba's contributions that made possible the capture of Quebec, he said. He had been granted the highest decoration that the British could give.

"What about his health?" Toshabe demanded impatiently.

Ja-gonh smiled soothingly and spread his hands. "He was wounded when he saved the life of Whiting in battle," he said, "and the removal of the bullets from his body left him in a weakened state. He's very much ashamed of his condition and feels that he has failed to live up to the tradition of a Seneca warrior."

"That's nonsense!" Ah-wen-ga declared.

"It certainly is. It's total rubbish," Toshabe agreed. "Is that why his greeting to us was so remote?"

"I'm afraid," Ja-gonh said, "that he doesn't want to face either of you."

Neither woman had ever faced such a problem, and they looked at each other uncertainly.

"I suggest," Ja-gonh said gently, "that you leave the solution of that particular problem to me."

His wife, who had faith in his judgment, readily agreed. Aware of the difficulties for some time, he undoubtedly had been thinking of a possible solution, she assumed.

Toshabe, however, was less certain. Waiting so long and so anxiously for Ghonkaba, his cool, almost remote greeting had struck her like a sharp blow across the face.

Ja-gonh understood her hesitation and sympathized.

"Have faith in me, my daughter," he said. "It is my fondest wish, as it is the wish of my wife, that you truly become our daughter. Subject yourself to my authority now, as though you and Ghonkaba were already married, and I think I can almost assure you that all will work out as all of us wish."

Realizing she had no real choice, she bowed her head and folded her hands across her breasts. "I will do as you direct, my father," she said quietly.

Pleased by her willingness to subject herself to his will, Ja-gonh said firmly, "Station yourself at the other end of the house from where Ghonkaba sleeps. When he awakens, do not go to him and do not speak to him, but instead come straight to me. I will be waiting outside the house, and I will handle the matter."

Almost allowing her curiosity to overcome her, Toshabe nevertheless knew better than to ask questions and simply accepted his orders. She took a place across the room from Ghonkaba's bed, and only when he stirred did she look in at him. His appearance had changed in the campaign he had just undergone, but she supposed it was only natural that he should look older, thinner, and more mature. In fact, his appearance was no longer youthful. He was a seasoned warrior now, with deep lines etched in his forehead, at the corners of his eyes, and around his mouth. She could not be sure from a distance, but she suspected that the hair of his scalp lock was beginning to turn slightly gray.

Ghonkaba stirred, groaned lightly, and opened his eyes.

Toshabe conquered her desire to speak with him, to embrace him, to welcome him home, and instead she withdrew instantly and reported to his father, who was sitting outside the house with Ah-wen-ga.

"He is awake now?" Ja-gonh asked.

Catching her breath, she nodded tensely.

The Great Sachem was on his feet instantly and took his leave. "I think," he said, "that the trouble will soon be cured." Ah-wen-ga looked at the younger woman as if to say that she knew nothing of what her husband had in mind.

Ja-gonh seemed cheerful as he entered the house, sat down cross-legged in a corner on the floor, and slowly began to pack a short Indian pipe, one used for pleasure smoking, rather than for ceremonials. "You are home now, my son," he said.

"I wish to discuss with you a matter of the gravest importance," the Great Sachem went on. "Toshabe has been on my mind of late, and much on the mind of your mother. We have grown very fond of her during the months that she has made her dwelling with us."

No answer was required, so the young war chief merely moved his head enough to show he had heard and understood.

"As is the way with older people," Ja-gonh continued casually, "Ah-wen-ga and I assumed that the day would come when you and Toshabe would marry. But as so often happens in matters of the heart, we were totally mistaken. You have not mentioned her name to me in the times we have been together, and she has not spoken of you to us."

In spite of himself, Ghonkaba was miffed.

"Although she is part French by birth and part Erie by training, she has adapted to the ways of our people with miraculous ease, and for all practical purposes, she has become a true Seneca," Ja-gonh said, and this time a ring of utter sincerity was in his voice. "So it is not surprising that she has attained a great popularity with the braves of our nation. Many clamor for her

255

hand, among them, several distinguished war chiefs and senior warriors who have covered themselves with honors. Due to your previous association with her and your rescue of her from captivity in Quebec, your mother and I assumed that your interests came first, and consequently we have not yet encouraged other suitors for her hand."

A look of alarm crossed Ghonkaba's face.

His father pretended not to notice it. "It is not fair to her or to the men of our nation who seek her hand, to hold her apart, to reserve her for one who does not want her," Ja-gonh said, his voice still matter-of-fact. "Therefore, I considered it only fair and fitting to tell you that I intend to solve this small problem as an early order of business now that I have returned home."

Clenching his fists, Ghonkaba looked stricken and sought in vain for appropriate words to stem the tide of his father's decision.

"She will make a fine Seneca wife," Ja-gonh said blithely, "for the warrior who is fortunate enough to marry her, and I see no reason to procrastinate any longer." He looked innocently at a spot in the air above his son's head.

"My father is intending to arrange Toshabe's future tonight?" Ghonkaba asked in a strangled voice.

Still showing no concern, the Great Sachem said only, "No, many moons have passed since I have been absent from home, and my first duty is to my wife. I will let the problem of Toshabe wait until tomorrow morning."

At least a respite would be granted, and that was all to the good. "Where is Toshabe now?" Ghonkaba asked. "I have not yet greeted her."

Puffing slowly on his pipe, his father rose. "If I happen to see her somewhere, you can be sure that I'll tell her that you asked for her." He strolled from the house, a perfect picture of unconcern. Only when out of sight of Ghonkaba did his expression change, and then he hurried outside, where Ah-wen-ga and To-shabe were waiting impatiently. "My son is awake," he said, "and has the strength to feed himself dinner and to walk about the house. Incidentally," he said, glancing at Toshabe, "he expressed a desire to see you in order to greet you."

She leaped to her feet and would have raced into the house, but the Great Sachem halted her. "Heed my words, Toshabe," he continued, "and do as I say. Let your eagerness to see Ghonkaba be concealed and present to him a calm and tranquil attitude."

She halted, steadied herself, and took his words to heart. Ah-wen-ga instantly realized that the advice was sound, and as Toshabe looked at her, she lowered one eyelid in a solemn wink.

Toshabe laughed aloud, then sobered and walked into the house, her manner demure and her attitude one of earnest seriousness.

She had noted that Ghonkaba was thinner and had aged, but these were quick, surface impressions. Most of all, she realized, he was highly agitated. Nevertheless, she spoke to him coolly and sweetly. "I offer a welcome to Ghonkaba on his return from the wars," she said. "I understand he performed many valorous deeds, and I am pleased for him."

"I will permit you to marry no Seneca except me," Ghonkaba said immediately, "and no warrior of any other nation."

Whatever his father had told him had been jarring, and she had the good sense to remain cool. "By what right does the son of Ja-gonh and Ah-wen-ga dare to

257

give me orders?" she demanded. "By whose authority does he forbid my marriage to any brave whom his father may choose for me?"

"I seek no authority, and I accept no authority in this matter other than my own. I have loved you for too long and have yearned to make you my wife for too long to tolerate the interference of any other man in our relationship. Rather than accept the presence of a rival, I will challenge him to a fight to the death and will present you with his scalp."

Having heard the words that she had longed so desperately to have him speak, she relaxed, her smile angelic as she looked at him.

Ghonkaba was still too distraught to be aware of her reaction. He caught hold of her shoulders and was about to shake her, but she seemed so helpless that he could not take advantage of any weakness.

Instead, becoming aware of her smile, he thought she might be laughing at him. "You have not answered me properly," he said accusingly.

"You've given me little chance to speak," she replied, suddenly coming to life and showing spirit. "But for whatever interest this may have for you, I have long awaited a declaration of your love, because I can scarcely remember a time when I failed to love you."

He looked at her in wonder, and suddenly his anger was gone and he was so filled with love for her that he swept her into his arms and kissed her.

She clung to him, noting his lack of physical strength. He would need much food, exercise, and other care in order to return to normal.

Neither could remember much of what they said thereafter. Defying Seneca custom, they walked hand in hand outside the house, where Ah-wen-ga was busy preparing dinner and Ja-gonh sat in the late afternoon sunlight smoking his pipe. The expressions of pure joy on the faces of Toshabe and Ghonkaba told the older couple all they needed to know and wanted so badly to see.

The wedding of Toshabe and Ghonkaba was the most prominent event of the early winter season. Not only was the bridegroom an authentic hero, but as the son of the Great Sachem, he had unmatched status.

His head freshly shaved on either side of his scalp lock, he wore a new shirt of buckskin and new winter trousers of the same leather material. In his belt he carried a new knife, sharply honed, that he himself had made for the part it was to play in the ceremony.

With her face scrubbed clean of makeup, Toshabe wore a simple doeskin dress, and with it a headband that Ah-wen-ga had given her. On it were burned various Seneca symbols, all signs that the wearer would have the protection of the manitous all of her days.

So many people were in attendance, including delegations from the other Iroquois tribes, that the ceremony was held out-of-doors in the natural amphitheater. Fortunately, the weather was mild, with a weak sun shining overhead. The heat created by the cooking fire in a huge pit, where a pair of buffalo were being roasted for the occasion, emitted enough warmth to make everyone comfortable.

A huge throng had gathered by the time the medicine men of the town appeared, wearing the Great Faces for the roles that would be required of them during the ceremony. The drums began to throb very softly at first, then with subtle, ever-increasing intensity, and finally Ghonkaba and Toshabe appeared, walking hand in hand. Ordinarily, the man was expected to carry his bride to the scene of the nuptials, but Ghonkaba still lacked the strength for such strenuous effort, so it was decided that he would walk beside her.

Ashamed of his weakness, he was nonetheless unwilling to wait until he was stronger in order to be married. "We have waited long enough," he said flatly, "and we will be married now!"

The medicine men gathered around the couple and began to dance. Their gyrations were sedate at first, but as the rhythm increased they began to spring up and down and gesticulate more wildly.

Some spectators, moved by the spectacle, felt compelled to join in the dance, and they were welcome to do so. No formal steps or gestures were part of the wedding dance, a spontaneous expression of joy in which anything a couple did was considered right.

In the center of the celebration, Toshabe and Ghonkaba found the rhythm contagious and began to gyrate with it, taking care only to avoid touching each other, which was forbidden, even in a wedding dance.

"Don't exert yourself unduly," she told him above the throbbing of the drums. "Remember, you're still recuperating."

Annoyed at being reminded of his disability, he frowned. Saying no more about it, Toshabe deliberately slowed her pace and did not engage in violent exertions, thus compelling him to move more slowly, conserving his energies.

Ja-gonh and Ah-wen-ga arose from their honored positions in the first row and joined the dancers, too. Sharing in the happiness of the young couple gave them a greater contentment than either had known in years. "You know," Ah-wen-ga said, as she and the Great Sachem began to dance, "I have the strange feeling that Renno and Betsy, and Ghonka and Ena, are watching this celebration from the far shores of the great river."

"They're doing more than that. Much more, I think," Ja-gonh answered quietly. "Unless I'm very much mistaken, they, like we, are joining in the dance and are celebrating the most important event in the life of Ghonkaba."

Chapter XII

When Seneca youngsters married, their contemporaries delighted in playing pranks on them, just as the New England colonists enjoyed the same rituals. But Ghonkaba and Toshabe were spared, largely because of his high rank. It would not have been appropriate for the warriors to engage in tricks at the expense of someone who held the exalted position of a war chief. What was more, the subordinates who had served under him in the Quebec campaign knew of his volatile, fiery temper, and none wanted to be on the receiving end of a blast of disapproval.

The feasting went on at great length, with ordinarily abstemious braves and squaws gorging themselves on the special holiday fare. The merrymaking went on at length, too, and those who thought of the Seneca as a taciturn people would have been very much surprised to see them laughing, singing, and joking.

At a signal from Toshabe, Ghonkaba rose to dance with her again, somewhat surprised by her request because she had seen to it that he did not overly exert himself. When they reached the base of the amphitheater where couples were gyrating wildly, a slight nod of her head gave him a message: the time had come for them to take their leave silently from the wedding festivities. So they danced to the section farthest from where the diners were still seated, gorging themselves, and then quietly slipped off into the shadows.

Hand in hand, they made their way back to the town, where a new house had been constructed for their use. Ghonkaba was filled with dread; he had been awaiting the moment with grave anxiety.

Toshabe understood what he was suffering and knew the reasons behind his feelings, although she gave no indication of her knowledge. By now she knew this man far better than he knew himself, and she felt completely capable of handling any contingency.

As the couple approached their new dwelling, the holiday spirit seemed to drain from Ghonkaba, and by the time he held the door flap aside for his bride and then lighted a large candle with a tinder box and flint, an invention of Western civilization of which he was very fond, his air had become gloomy.

Toshabe pretended to be unaware of his mood as she fastened the leather flap over the door to insure privacy and then lighted a wood fire for warmth in the stone pit in the center of the main room.

"I think," she said, "that we got away without anyone noticing that we were leaving."

Ghonkaba kicked a stray log back into the heart of

the mounting fire. "I hope you're right," he said. "I'm in no mood for childish tricks tonight."

"There will be none; you may be sure," she assured him.

"How can you speak so positively?" he demanded.

"Your mother told me in so many words that the pranksters would leave us strictly alone tonight. They are afraid of your temper."

He kicked hard at a slab of wood that was beginning to flare up; for some reason, it offended him. "It's far more likely," he said in self-disgust, "that they're going to leave us alone because they feel sorry for me, and if there's anything on earth I hate, it's the pity of my brothers."

Toshabe knew precisely what was troubling him, but she feigned surprise. "Why in the world should anyone pity you?" she wanted to know.

Ghonkaba faced her resolutely, a trifle defiantly. "I was wrong," he said. "Very wrong to rush our wedding. I should have waited until I completely recovered from the wounds I received at Quebec. I am not yet myself, and it was wrong of us to be married before my injuries were completely healed. I am ashamed to admit to you that I lack the physical strength and the stamina to make love to you as you deserve to be made love to."

Toshabe astonished him by bursting into laughter. Her reaction was so surprising that he could only stare at her.

"You and I," she told him softly, "have no ordinary marriage. We have already undergone trials together that would make most warriors and squaws flinch. But Ghonkaba and Toshabe did not flinch."

He had no idea what she was leading up to, but he agreed that everything she had said was true.

"We are partners in all that we do," she said flatly. "If you lack the physical strength at present to make love to me, then it is my duty and my pleasure to make love to you." Giving him no chance to protest, she went to him, unfastened the loops that held his shirt closed, and pressed against him, raising her face to his.

Ghonkaba's only conscious thought as his mounting passion swept him up in its surging tide was that he should have known he had married a woman who would find the answers to whatever question troubled him.

Before Major General Jeffrey Amherst returned to England at the end of the Quebec campaign, he wrote a long, secret, and candid letter to Ja-gonh. Everyone in the land of the Seneca knew of such a letter, but its contents had remained a secret.

The sachems who comprised the Council of the Iroquois ordinarily would have been summoned to an emergency meeting, and would have spent two days in the heavily guarded council chamber of the Seneca discussing whatever problem was presented in the communication. But Ja-gonh, in consultation with No-da-vo, decided that he must expedite action, accepting full responsibility.

It appeared that only one person in all the land, Ah-wen-ga, the wife of Ja-gonh, had been told the message in the letter. Ghonkaba thought that was a logical conclusion to draw. "My father always has trusted in the judgment of my mother," he said to Toshabe when he returned home from fishing in the lake, where he had made a hole in the ice in order to drop a baited hook into the water.

Toshabe took the string of three large fish from him. "It is necessary," she told him, "that we place these in the woodshed to freeze and save them for use on another evening. Your mother has invited us to supper at the house of the Great Sachem tonight, and she was very insistent that we come."

Ghonkaba was puzzled. "That's rather odd," he said.

"I think not. From the way your mother hinted, I think that—for whatever their reasons—they're going to confide the secret of General Amherst's letter."

They arrived early for the evening meal at the largest of the private residences in town, and Toshabe immediately pitched in, helping prepare the meal. Even though Ghonkaba held an exalted rank in the nation, his squaw, like every other married woman, had homely, everyday activities to perform, and did so as a matter of course.

The Great Sachem was amiable and pleasant, as he always was, but he seemed preoccupied.

"You have no doubt heard that I have received an important communication from General Amherst," he said. "That is true. Although both of you can read English, he discusses many confidential matters with me, so I will go through the letter for you and will give you the gist of what he says."

Ja-gonh began reading aloud:

"Not only have we captured all of Canada from the French, but the winter of 1760 will be known as a time when the Royal Navy took a terrible toll on French shipping, particularly in European waters. Consequently, France is at last on the verge of suing for peace, and the safety of the British colonies on this continent is assured."

So far, Ghonkaba had learned nothing he didn't already know.

"The situation has been slightly complicated in England because King George the Second has died, and his young grandson, George the Third, has ascended to the throne in his place."

"General Amherst has written to me in confidence," Ja-gonh said, "that the new king is not the most attractive of monarchs. He is grossly overweight, and the royal physicians say that he has a disease of the blood that causes fits of madness."

Ghonkaba frowned. How could the English allow themselves to be ruled by such a man, one who was so weak and sickly and who could not even be held responsible for his actions? Hearing this about the king, Ghonkaba's estimation of the English immediately went down a notch.

"Even when he is sane, George the Third is said to be a thoroughly disagreeable man," Ja-gonh went on. "While he is the first of the Hanoverian monarchs to speak English as his primary language, he is nevertheless very German in his tastes and his ways of life.

"He is argumentative and will dispute any subject with anyone, even though he may know nothing about it. He's heavily sarcastic in his dealings with others, and if there were not a crown upon his head, he'd be challenged to duels every day of his life. He also has a stubborn streak that makes him unbearable, and General Amherst writes that when he takes a position on any matter, it is impossible to budge him from it."

"He sounds thoroughly disagreeable," Toshabe commented.

"I'm sure he is," Ja-gonh said. "His accession to the

throne has created a flurry here in the colonies, and each of them has sent, or is sending, representatives to London to declare their fealty and their total loyalty to the crown. King George puts a great store by such acts of symbolism, and General Amherst has urged that we, too, should send a delegate from the Iroquois to meet the king and to renew our treaty of alliance with the British Crown."

Ghonkaba was puzzled. "Is such a renewal of the alliance truly necessary?" he wanted to know.

"The ways of the English are not our ways, and I must take the word of General Amherst in such matters," Ja-gonh answered.

In his son's opinion, the formality was a waste of time, but the young war chief kept his opinion to himself.

"Our principal concern in our talks with our brothers of the Iroquois and our own people of the Seneca has been the identity of the representative whom we should send to England. The sachems are in agreement with me that this is of primary importance. King George appears to be a difficult young man and we want to make a good impression on him for the sake of maintaining amicable relations in the years ahead."

Ah-wen-ga interrupted gently. "It has long been a tradition," she said, "for the men in our family to represent our own nation and the Iroquois League in meetings at the courts of Europe."

Ghonkaba recalled the story of the prowess with Indian arms displayed at the court of King William by Renno when he was a young man. He had made a lasting impression on the monarch and on his court.

He mentioned the incident, and Ja-gonh smiled. "It is true," he said, "that that occasion will live for many years in the annals of the Seneca. It is also true that Ah-wen-ga and I have visited the court of the French king, and that even Ghonka paid a token visit on one occasion to the Royal Court in England."

Ghonkaba realized that his parents were looking at him strangely, but he had not guessed what they had in mind.

Toshabe, however, was aware of what they were leading toward, and she had to curb her excitement.

"My own election to the high post of Great Sachem of the Iroquois is too recent for me to be able to take the time away from my duties here and to go to England," Ja-gonh said. "No-da-vo would be a natural selection to take my place, but he can speak only a few words of English and would need to rely on his wife as a translator. The sachems of the other Iroquois nations also are very limited in their command of English, and from what General Amherst has written about George the Third, we cannot afford to take needless risks. We must send someone who is fluent in his tongue."

Finally comprehension dawned and Ghonkaba began to smile.

The twinkle in his father's eyes belied his solemn manner. "At last you have drawn the right conclusion, my son," he said. "Your mother first suggested that you and Toshabe go as our representatives to London. I know opinions of the sachems and of the Seneca council will also concur."

"When is it the wish of my father that Toshabe and I sail across the Great Sea?"

"It is needful," his father replied, "that you go at once, without delay of any kind. The representatives of the various English colonies will have made their obeisances to the king soon, and if we are too late in acknowledging his sovereignty, he might take offense. General Amherst has written in his letter that a cabin is reserved on a warship of the Royal Navy, one that sails in twelve days' time, and you will make it your business to be on board that vessel in Boston in time to set sail for England."

Ghonkaba nodded in satisfaction, knowing that he and his wife could reach Boston easily in the allotted time.

But Toshabe's temper flared and she was much concerned. "How can we possibly be ready to go to England and meet the king?" she demanded. "That is impossible!"

Father and son looked at her blankly.

Ah-wen-ga, however, understood the problem immediately. "My daughter," she said, "is thinking of the clothes that she and her husband will wear when they go to Whitehall Palace to meet King George."

"Exactly so!" Toshabe said. "We cannot wear the attire of Indians at the grand court of the English king."

"I have to agree that you are correct, my daughter," Ja-gonh said. "I must admit that *I* see no reason why it should be needful for you and Ghonkaba to wear the attire of the English when you call on the king. But General Amherst stresses strongly in his letter that this is a necessary precaution."

"He is our friend and would not mislead us," Ghonkaba said thoughtfully, "and I believe I can sense his reasoning. If King George thinks of his colonists as barbarians, then we of the Indian nations must seem like savages. If we speak his tongue and dress as he and his subjects dress, perhaps he will not see us in such an alien light."

"The fact remains," Toshabe said, "that we shall have very little time in which to obtain an appropriate wardrobe."

Familiar with the tempo of life at a court of the Old

World, Ah-wen-ga hastened to reassure her. "You'll have time," she said, "provided you place your order for clothing as soon as you reach London. The ways of kings are very strange, and one would think that a monarch would receive immediately a person who has traveled many thousands of miles to see him. But that is not the way of European kings. They are so afraid of losing their precious dignity that they will force you to wait many days for an audience, for no reason other than that of showing that they are superior to you."

Toshabe shook her head in wonder. "This journey," she said, "will not be lacking in interest."

Ghonkaba wrote a hasty letter to Townsend and Beth Whiting, telling them that he and his wife would be arriving in London in approximately four to six weeks' time and expressing the hope that the offer of accommodations in London made by Brigadier Whiting was still good. He sent the communication off by special messenger.

Working assiduously on a declaration of loyalty to the British Crown, Ja-gonh read it to his son, insisting that he take it and read it aloud to King George.

Then the young couple set out for Boston forthwith. At Ghonkaba's insistence, no ceremony marked their departure, and he and Toshabe left quietly.

A spell of unseasonably cold weather, accompanied by snow and high winds, made travel difficult and slowed them on the trail. Consequently, they reached Boston only hours before their ship was scheduled to depart, and they went directly on board.

The captain informed them that because of the inclement weather the ship's departure was delayed, and he urged them to buy fresh fruits, bread, jam, honey, and any other luxuries that would make the journey more pleasant.

Ghonkaba immediately arranged to go to the marketplace adjacent to the waterfront for the purchases that he needed. Toshabe, however, was delighted by the delay and intended to spend the entire time until sailing acquiring a wardrobe for herself and her husband that would be suitable for wear when they went to Whitehall Palace.

The *Intrepid,* officially listed as a war frigate, was almost as large as a ship of the line. It mounted fifty guns, twenty-five on each side. The arrival of Ghonkaba and Toshabe created an immediate stir among the crew, particularly because he had been one of the heroes of the battle of Quebec.

His ability to speak a flawless English made him even more of a curiosity, but by the time he returned from his shopping expedition, the furor had quieted down. The highly disciplined officers and men of the *Intrepid* were careful in their approach to a man who was going to London to visit George III.

A flushed, triumphant Toshabe arrived back at the *Intrepid* just in time to join her husband and the majority of the ship's officers in the wardroom for supper.

She was too excited to eat the meal of oxtail soup, steamed fresh fish, and apple turnover that the chef had prepared. Ghonkaba put a lid on his own curiosity, knowing that she would reveal the details of her day at the first opportunity.

After supper, the couple retired to the private chamber that two senior lieutenants had vacated for them. Ghonkaba and Toshabe had no idea that the cabin was regarded as underfurnished and Spartan. All they knew was that it was far more luxurious than anything that they had ever enjoyed in the land of the Seneca.

The hammock that swung freely from side to side was too hazardous and too much of a novelty, and so they arranged to share the single, built-in bunk that the cabin boasted. The mattress and pillow of down were far too soft for people accustomed to sleeping on beds of pine branches and corn husks, but they were happy to make do as best they could.

"I knew," Toshabe said gleefully, "that all I needed was an opportunity to find the clothes we'll want for our introduction to the Court in London."

Ghonkaba chuckled. "I suspected as much."

"I found a shop near the waterfront that could make exactly the kind of dress I sought," she told him. "I was fitted for two dresses, which will be ready tomorrow. I also purchased stockings and earrings and everything else I'll need. I asked where I could find the right clothes for you, and they directed me to another shop that was every bit as good. I gave them your approximate measurements, and you're going to be the best-dressed man at the Whitehall Court."

Ghonkaba was pleased. "I'm glad you've found what you wanted," he said. "If I were you, I'd go to the shop no later than noon tomorrow and get the merchandise as soon as it's available. There's nothing to prevent the captain from changing his mind and sailing anytime tomorrow on the spur of the moment."

Toshabe took his advice and shortly after noon the following day she returned to the *Intrepid*, laden down with bundles.

Precisely as Ghonkaba had anticipated, they sailed almost immediately after a midday meal of smoked haddock and ginger beer.

Toshabe subsequently claimed that the smoked fish had disagreed with her, but her husband realized that was not the real cause of her malaise. The weather was

273

foul, and in spite of the ship's size, it rolled and pitched. Even before making its way out of Boston Harbor everyone on board realized that they were in for a rough voyage.

Faced with the unpleasantness of a bout of seasickness, the first she had ever encountered, Toshabe was miserable and insisted on being alone in the cabin. Only after several days did she finally acquire her sea legs, and her malaise was receding as suddenly as it had arisen.

She insisted on celebrating her recovery that night by wearing one of her new outfits to the supper table, which she and her husband shared with the ship's officers. Ghonkaba entered into the spirit of the occasion by wearing one of his new suits, and although he couldn't quite place his finger on what was amiss, he knew that something wasn't quite right about it. As a matter of fact, the suit was too sharply tailored and in too vivid colors to be suitable for wear by conservative English gentlemen.

As for Toshabe, she wore her hair piled high on her head, as she had in the Quebec bordello, and her makeup was intensified as a result of her experiences of that period. She had no idea that the gowns she had selected were far too flamboyant, cheap, and tawdry for wear by any lady.

When Toshabe appeared in the wardroom with Ghonkaba directly behind her, the reaction of the assembled officers seemed to be precisely what she had anticipated. Her change from a simple-looking squaw into an outrageously provocative wench was so startling and dramatic that the officers could only stare at her in a moment of embarrassed silence. Similar silences had greeted her appearance before customers in Quebec, and she accepted the quiet as a tribute to her beauty.

It was, of course, a tribute to her striking appearance, but unfortunately it was far more than that. They had seen her briefly, at one meal, as a pleasant Indian woman who spoke a good English, and whose manners were certainly acceptable. Suddenly she was transformed into a ravishing, mysterious beauty, complete with an undefinable but definitely naughty sense of mystery, and the transformation was as bewildering as it was dramatic.

Ghonkaba, taken aback by the officers' reaction, misunderstood the reasons for it.

He saw covetousness combined with desire shining in the eyes of many of the officers and felt a surge of intense jealousy. Only after deliberation was he able to remind himself that these men were absent from their wives and sweethearts for a long time, and that naturally they would react in this way to someone as lovely as Toshabe. Instead of feeling jealous, he thought, he had every reason to be proud of her. And finally pride won the day over jealousy.

Customary English good manners were observed at the supper table, and as a consequence not one unpleasant word was said to either Toshabe or Ghonkaba. No one was willing to intimate, or even suggest, that Toshabe bore too strong a resemblance to the higher class trollops of London and that her appearance was inappropriate for polite company.

With childlike naiveté, she assumed that her new wardrobe was a smashing success, and Ghonkaba thought the same. Neither saw any reason to suspect or even imagine that they resembled caricatures more than real people.

Satisfied that her wardrobe and her husband's were

successes, Toshabe was content to put them aside and enjoy herself for the rest of the voyage. This she did, and her health continued to improve rapidly until her bout with seasickness was purely in the past.

The frigate crossed the Atlantic in her customary three and a half weeks, and then slowly made her way up the River Thames to the great city of London.

Never in their wildest dreams had the young couple from the North American wilderness imagined a city the size and complexity of London. They stood on the deck, gaping openly at the countless spectacles that swept in and out of view as the great ship maneuvered through heavy river traffic.

What struck them most was the teeming mass of people they saw everywhere. Great ladies and gentlemen drove in carriages and were borne in sedan chairs on the shoulders of humans in livery; horsemen were everywhere, as were the countless pedestrians. Ghonkaba had always considered Boston to be big, but here was a community that outnumbered it by a million persons to a scant ten thousand. Small wonder, he thought, that Great Britain was a huge nation and a major world power.

Toshabe expressed disappointment when she could see from the deck that neither Townsend nor Beth Whiting was on hand to greet them. "It may be," she said, biting her lower lip, "that now that they are at home in England they prefer not to mix with such simple folk as you and me."

Ghonkaba shook his head violently. "Never!" he exclaimed. "Townsend and I at last became good friends, and he is loyal to the core. You see that captain in scarlet and gold on the dock?"

She nodded, uncertain how he could be so sure about the captain, but refrained from asking.

"He wears the credentials of a staff member of Townsend's brigade," Ghonkaba told her, "so I'll be very much surprised if he wasn't sent here with a message of some sort for us."

The couple said their farewells to officers with whom they had been particularly friendly on the voyage, and then proceeded ashore, a seaman carrying their baggage. The dock was crowded with relatives of seamen and officers who had been absent from home for a long period, and Ghonkaba and Toshabe had to make their way slowly through the rejoicing crowds.

The captain, recognizing the pair by their deerskin garb, approached and saluted. "War Chief Ghonkaba?" the officer asked. "Captain Mercer, aide-de-camp to Brigadier Whiting. He and Lady Whiting regret their inability to be here but have asked me to deliver this note to you."

Ghonkaba broke the seal, then held the parchment in such a way that Toshabe could read it simultaneously with him. Its message was short and to the point.

The Whitings had been unexpectedly called north to Derbyshire because of a severe illness of Sir Townsend's father. They insisted, however, that the newly arrived couple make themselves at home in the Whitings' townhouse and promised to join them there as soon as possible. The Whitings felt certain, the brigadier added, that they would be back before the interview with George III took place.

Captain Mercer was available for the convenience and comfort of Ghonkaba and Toshabe and was under orders to attend to their various needs. He was already proving his value by rounding up their luggage and having it placed in a brigade cart. To the relief of Toshabe, who was unfamiliar with horseback riding, a carriage was made available, and that meant that she would be carried rather than be required to ride to their destination. The captain rode with them to their destination and busied himself in describing various spots of historical and geographical interest.

Only when they rode past Whitehall did Ghonkaba's interest spark at the sight of the handsome, vast stone building. Here, he knew, the kings of England lived with their queens, their children, and their mistresses. His mind reeled.

"How many people live in that place with the king and his family?" he wanted to know.

"For the present," the captain said rather stiffly, "Their Majesties still have no children. But I daresay that with the chamberlains, the lords and ladies-in-waiting, the military and other aides, and so on, the household staff comprises many hundreds of persons."

Toshabe's eyes grew round with wonder. She couldn't imagine any two people requiring the services of so very many others in order to live comfortably. She could not understand the ways of European royalty, and her husband's expression showed that he felt as she did.

"Quite possibly," the aide said primly, "you're tired after your long voyage and you'd like several days to rest. If so, the servants at the house will know where to fetch me when you're ready for a somewhat more active existence."

"What do you mean by more active, Captain?" Ghonkaba demanded bluntly.

"London has many fascinations," Captain Mercer said, with a slightly condescending note in his voice. "Not the least of them is our theater, which is renowned and unparalleled in all the world. Then there are private clubs for dining, gaming, and the like, that also may amuse you. And so on. The list is endless."

He hesitated a moment, and then took a steep plunge. "Brigadier and Lady Whiting," he said, "were a bit fearful that your clothes might not be appropriate for city life. If so, they've already recommended you to their own tailors and dressmakers, and I urge you to make your very first order of business here a visit to those persons and to the haberdashers, bootmakers, and the like."

"We shall follow your suggestions, sir," Toshabe replied, feeling a trifle superior to him, "although it isn't really essential that we do so. We were fortunate in obtaining a quite satisfactory wardrobe for ourselves in Boston for our visit here."

Captain Mercer, agile and adept at dissembling, knew how to keep his thoughts to himself and made no comment, though he was thinking that surely these oafs from the colonies who were only partly white and certainly reflected their part-Indian ancestry weren't suggesting that it was possible to obtain a wardrobe in Boston suitable for one's presentation at the king's Court at Whitehall! "You'll find their names and addresses on a list that Lady Whiting made up for you," he said. "Just let me know and I'll gladly make appointments for you."

"Good!" Ghonkaba said emphatically. "As for requiring several days to rest, that will be strictly unnecessary. We did nothing on board ship for the better part of a month, and our time in London is limited, so we'll want to see and do all that is possible."

Idly amused, the aide wondered what this self-confident Seneca would say after waiting in vain for a royal summons for four or five months. George III had already demonstrated repeatedly that when people might bore him, he didn't care how long he kept them on the waiting list.

The Whiting home proved to be an impressive white building of wood, four stories high, located in the most fashionable district of London, known as Belgravia. It had a bewildering number of rooms, and an equally bewildering group of servants were on hand to wait on the residents.

Captain Mercer showed the visitors through the dwelling before he departed and arranged to pick them up later for theater, supper, and perhaps a glimpse of a gaming club.

"I can't believe it!" Toshabe exclaimed as she sank onto a heavily brocaded chaise. "I tried to keep count of the rooms, but I was totally lost after we reached forty. Does everyone in London live this way?"

"I think not," Ghonkaba told her. "I know his father is a very wealthy man of very high estate, so the family undoubtedly lives accordingly. I'm sure that most people here are too poor to live on such a scale."

"I counted a staff of many more than fifty who have nothing to do in all this world but wait on Sir Townsend and Lady Whiting. So if a low-ranking knight, as you say he is, has that many in attendance—well, it's small wonder, then, that the king and queen have hundreds on their staff at Whitehall."

Ghonkaba smiled knowingly at her. "You would like to have servants of your own, no doubt."

Toshabe promptly threw a pillow at him; her aim was poor and she missed, but that did not deter her in the least.

"I would not like it!" she insisted. "Such a useless life would bore me, and I would feel no reason to live. You lead a most useful existence in our own land, where you hunt and fish and tan skins and protect our nation in times of trouble. I hope I serve you well by keeping your house for you and making your clothes out of skins you provide me, and cooking your meals and growing your vegetables. If we did not have these activities to keep us busy, and one day to instruct our young in how to handle these duties for themselves when they grow to be of age, what use are we as men and as women? We would be like the squashes that rot on the vine if they are not picked when their time is ripe."

Ghonkaba went to her and squeezed her shoulder affectionately. "Do not upset yourself," he said. "The English ways are not our ways, and we are not like them. We are far more like the colonists, who live on our side of the ocean and who have learned to think and act much as we do."

"Yes, I think you're right," she agreed. "It will interest me to see how Lady Whiting has changed since she married, and now makes her home in England. But we must accept her advice and take advantage of the opportunity to visit their tailor and dressmaker so we have a larger choice to our wardrobe."

That evening when Captain Mercer appeared to escort the couple to the theater and an evening of festivities afterward, a series of shocks awaited him. First and most unexpected was Ghonkaba's appearance. The Seneca was dressed in a gaudy suit that was so startling Mercer could merely blink at him. He wore a purple swallowtailed coat with gilt buttons, a yellow waistcoat, and cream-colored breeches. He looked even more conspicuous because of the incongruity of the apparel with his scalp lock.

Mercer debated whether to recommend that Ghonkaba wear a powdered wig to conceal his scalp lock, but on second thought he decided that a wig would make his appearance even more absurd.

An even greater shock awaited Mercer, however,

when Toshabe came into the room. Wearing an extremely low-cut, tightly fitting gown, she bore a strong resemblance to the town's most beautiful and popular trollops, who paraded up and down the promenades outside London theaters and opera houses.

Horrified and alarmed, the captain nevertheless took some comfort in the realization that neither of the couple seemed to have any idea of the sensation they were sure to cause. Perhaps an unpleasant incident could be avoided.

They took the Whiting carriage to the Drury Lane Theater, where David Garrick was starring in a new, popular melodrama. Precisely as Mercer had anticipated, the patrons of the theater gaped and gawked at the beautiful woman and the handsome but odd-looking man, both of them resembling American Indians, but both of them obviously at least partly white themselves.

Ogled and jostled by the crowds at the theater, Ghonkaba and Toshabe tried to follow the custom of strolling up and down the aisle outside their box during the first intermission. But the crowds were so great, the interest in them so intense, that Captain Mercer nervously suggested they return to their seats.

They did, exchanging frequent glances that expressed their sense of shock at the crass behavior of the English theatergoing public. Never had either encountered such rudeness, and it did not surprise them that some of the curious pushed aside the curtains of their box in order to view them more clearly.

Captain Mercer quietly breathed a sigh of relief when he managed to escort the couple safely, without undue incident, to their waiting carriage. Their public appearances were ended for the night, and hereafter they would be enclosed within the solid walls of the

Byblos Club, one of London's oldest and most distinguished private clubs, where they would be received as the guests of Sir Townsend Whiting.

He soon discovered his error. Though attendance at the club seemed sparse, every member present was as nosy and as curious as were the mobs at the theater. Not only was the young couple instantly surrounded as they entered the elegant main salon of the club, but various members repeatedly tried to dangle before them the bait of an evening's adventures on the town.

"Could I interest you in the sport of cockfighting, perhaps?" a high-ranking official of the Foreign Office inquired as he ogled Toshabe.

"What is cockfighting?" she asked blankly.

He explained in detail that two roosters who had been trained for the purpose were equipped with steel spurs and a steel prod attached to their foreheads. They were let loose at each other and usually fought until one or the other died.

"How barbarous," she murmured. "I'm afraid I should feel too strongly inclined to come to the aid of the poor birds."

A retired lieutenant colonel of the Grenadier Guards broke the somewhat embarrassed silence that followed. "You might be interested in watching a most unique sport," he said. "We call it bearbaiting."

"What is that?" Ghonkaba asked politely.

The lieutenant colonel, not sensing his subtle disapproval, went on to explain at some length that a bear was tormented to the point of madness and when it launched into a full attack, it had to be killed for the protection of the patrons of the "sport."

"In my homeland," the Seneca said firmly, "my family have been members of the Bear Clan for many generations. In fact, my grandfather established a great friendship with a bear when he was a boy, and they remained close friends for many years. My father was given the bear's name and uses it to this very day. So I'm afraid that if I saw any man, regardless of his person or his rank, who tormented a bear, I should be forced to come to the defense of my clan and attack."

"Attack, sir?" The lieutenant colonel was startled.

"Precisely what I would do," Ghonkaba assured him, "would depend on the cruelty that had been shown to the bear. If the animal had been mistreated too badly in my opinion, I would merely incapacitate the man and give the bear the privilege of finishing him off. If he had shown any spark of humanity, however, I would perhaps take pity on him and put him out of his misery myself, quickly and decisively."

No sport was more popular with England's upper class than bearbaiting, and Ghonkaba's calm discussion of doing away with anyone who dared to torment a bear horrified his listeners.

Throats were cleared, feet were shuffled, and men suddenly found themselves unaccountably unable to meet the steady gaze of the Seneca. Most rapidly lost their appetite for further contact with the young Indian couple, who obviously were as primitive and uncivilized as they were reputed to be.

One who remained undiscouraged, however, was the Earl of Buccleigh, one of the most dissolute and degenerate of young noblemen in the kingdom. He was a philanderer and gambler who drank to excess. In fact, his one redeeming virtue that granted him instant entry into any upper-class home in Great Britain was his close personal friendship with the new king. They had been intimates for years.

"Madam," he said, bowing to Toshabe, who fascinated him, "I wonder if you would do me the honor

284

of accompanying me to the gaming tables, where your beauty is certain to bring me good fortune." He extended an arm to her.

Toshabe could not refuse the offer without being unnecessarily rude. So she smiled broadly at her husband, placed her hand lightly on the earl's arm, and allowed herself to be led into an adjoining chamber, where several high tables, each covered in green baize, were located. Buccleigh drew up two stools, making certain they were very close together. After ordering a drink for himself and another for her, he settled down to a game of high-low-jack.

Drinks of potent Dutch gin, accompanied by beakers of a strong French claret wine to be used as "chasers," were set in front of them, with a dealer on a stool opposite.

"The rules are very simple, m'dear," Buccleigh explained, unable to keep his eyes from wandering to Toshabe's low-cut décolletage. "You shall play on my behalf and draw a card from a deck that the dealer will extend to you. He then has the choice of choosing high or low. That is, if the card he then draws is higher than that which you have taken, he wins, provided he has stated his position clearly in advance. If he chooses low, he must draw a lower card than yours. You understand, I trust?" He picked up a glass of gin and handed it to her.

She took a drink, coughed violently, and had to down some of the claret in order to calm her throat. "I'm afraid I know nothing about playing cards," she said. "I wouldn't know what was higher or lower."

"I'll teach you," the earl said soothingly, "and never fear, you'll catch on quickly enough."

It was not accidental that they were seated around a

bend in the gaming room that made it impossible to see them from the barroom, to which Ghonkaba, Captain Mercer, and the few others who had remained with them had gone.

Ghonkaba's lifelong training in controlling his emotions enabled him to conceal his feelings when the earl so summarily whisked his wife away, without even asking permission. But he was seething inwardly, nevertheless, and Captain Mercer, recognizing a far more dangerous situation than had arisen earlier in the evening, decided to take no risks.

Having previously noted Ghonkaba's dislike of strong drink, he deliberately ordered tankards of mild, sweet ale for everyone, and sought to defuse the situation. "After we've finished our ale," he said to Ghonkaba, trying to sound jovial, "we'll pick up your wife and go on to the dining room. I imagine we can all stand something substantial in the way of food."

The suggestion that the present situation involving Toshabe would not be allowed to continue indefinitely had an appropriately soothing effect on Ghonkaba, who relaxed somewhat. In fact, he found the ale, the first he had ever tasted, much to his liking and now began to enjoy himself.

Meantime in the gaming room Toshabe, much to her own surprise, found herself intrigued with the game of high-low-jack. Latching onto the principles of it, she was now engrossed in the game.

The Earl of Buccleigh was thoroughly enjoying his unexpected run of good fortune. Usually he lost at cards, but thanks to this glamorous creature he was winning handily. He sat so close to her that their bodies touched, and he continually urged her to drink more of her gin.

She didn't like the taste of the beverage, but did take frequent sips of wine, and that was enough to satisfy him.

Overcome with both liquor and the emotion of being a winner at last, the earl placed his chips in two piles and pushed one of them in front of her. "Here, m'dear," he said a little thickly. "You deserve this! From now on I'm splitting my evening's winnings with you!"

Toshabe realized that this fat, ungainly English nobleman wanted her; she was more than sufficiently experienced in men and their ways to recognize so obvious a situation. But she didn't know quite how to handle his sudden, generous gesture, and she temporized by murmuring, "That's very kind of you, sir."

The earl was elated, and was convinced that she had understood his subtle advance. Any woman who would accept money from a man was signaling him that she was making herself available to him. He was wildly excited. He had bedded women of many nationalities in his career, but never had he gone to bed with such a sultry beauty, who combined the eroticism of a foreign race with the piquancy of the French.

Suddenly the subdued quiet of the Byblos Club was shattered by the loud, terrified scream of a woman. To the best of the knowledge of the group sitting in the bar, the only woman on that floor of the establishment was Toshabe.

On his feet instantly, Ghonkaba raced pantherlike into the adjoining gaming room, with Captain Mercer and several others at his heels. The sight that confronted them was so unexpectedly shocking that it brought them up short.

The Earl of Buccleigh, his face florid and eyes slightly glazed but with an alcoholic's manic gleam in them, had plunged a hand deep inside the front of To-shabe's gown.

She was trying to fight him off with both arms and, like a creature possessed, was kicking, biting, scratching, using every weapon at her command.

In spite of his dissolute condition, the earl was proving surprisingly strong, and was even enjoying the struggle. "That's it, m'dear," he said. "I like a wench with spirit!"

Ghonkaba did not waste a second. His wife was under attack and he reacted accordingly. Reaching beneath his swallowtailed coat, he drew his tomahawk, which he had concealed in his belt, drew back his arm, taking instant aim, and let fly.

Only prompt reaction by Captain Mercer saved Buccleigh's life. Under such circumstances, the killing of a high-ranking nobleman, a close friend of George III, would create a scandal that would not be lived down for years. He reached out and managed to jar Ghonkaba's arm just in time so that the tomahawk missed the earl's head by no more than a fraction of an inch. It buried itself in the weathered, paneled oak of the wall directly behind him.

Having been foiled in his initial attempt, the young war chief nevertheless persisted. Leaping forward, he seized Buccleigh by both shoulders. He hauled him off Toshabe, bore him to the floor, and repeatedly bashed his head against the hard wood.

Since it was evident that he would soon succeed in killing Buccleigh, again Captain Mercer, along with four other members of the party, swiftly intervened. After exerting a great effort and marveling at the physical strength of the white Indian, they were able to pull him off his opponent.

Mercer's one idea was to bring the whole nightmarish incident to an end. "If you please, sir," he said, "don't attack again. That sort of thing simply isn't done here; this gentleman is an earl and a close friend of His Majesty."

Ghonkaba was still firmly in the grasp of the five men, and rather than try to wrench free, he bided his time. "Is this whole country rotten?" he demanded. "This low creature assaulted my wife, and I will not rest until he's been punished for it."

"We have ways of handling such disputes in this country, if you'll just be reasonable," the captain informed him.

Straightening his attire with difficulty and shaking his head in an attempt to clear it, the earl was feeling very much abused. The woman had led him on, and so far as he was concerned he had done nothing to her that was unexpected. Then, for some reason, she screamed and this wild savage in an Englishman's gaudy attire had appeared out of nowhere and attacked him. "I demand satisfaction," he shouted angrily.

Toshabe managed to put the front of her dress together in such a way that it would not fall open. The significance of the earl's comment about demanding satisfaction totally escaped her.

"There! You see!" Captain Mercer was somewhat relieved because the problem gave promise of being contained within civilized channels. "His Lordship has now challenged you to a duel."

"A duel?" Ghonkaba replied promptly. "I accept!" He looked ready to begin a fight without delay, and Mercer realized that he knew nothing about the rules of dueling. "As the challenged party," he told him patiently, "you have the choice of weapons."

"That is perfect!" Ghonkaba replied grimly. "We will have a fight to the death with knives. We will strip to our breechclouts, and we will fight until one or the other of us no longer lives." He reached into his belt and produced two knives, each with a thin, eight-inch blade and a sharp point capable of doing incalculable damage.

Two of the Englishmen gasped, and the entire group stared at the Seneca in silent horror. They found it hard to believe that he could mean such a barbarous fight as a serious duel, but it was apparent that he was in earnest.

The Earl of Buccleigh, looking pale and shaken, somehow found his voice. "If this is a sample of North American humor," he said, "I don't share in the sense of humor of such people. I'm willing to engage in a duel in any standard way, with any standard weapons, including pistols and swords. But I will not resort to the sheer butchery of savages! I hereby call off the duel!"

Ghonkaba seemed ready to leap forward again and finish the task he had started. But Toshabe distracted him by putting a hand on his sleeve. "Please, Ghonkaba, take me home," she said in a thin, almost childlike voice. "I'm very tired."

Her desires took precedence over everything else, and he smiled reassuringly at her. "Of course," he said. Then, his manner changing, he wheeled on the earl, snatched his wig from his head, and caught hold of him by a handful of his thick hair. "Hear me, O English noble. It seems the manitous have decided that your time on earth is not yet ended, so I will not press the fates to dispose of you now. But you have become the enemy of Ghonkaba and of his woman. So I give you fair warning: stay out of my sight! It does not matter whether we should arrive at the same public place or at some private house. I will not tolerate your presence anywhere! If you do not remove yourself immediately from my vision, I will kill you at once and will present your scalp to my wife to wear on her belt as a warning to any other man who would dare to dishonor her!"

He flung Buccleigh from him with such force that the earl, who had completely lost face and was disgraced by the incident, slipped and fell to the floor.

Then, putting one arm around Toshabe, Ghonkaba retrieved his tomahawk from the wall, and left the room with her without another word. Captain Mercer, shirt soaked with perspiration, followed close after, grateful that the incident had ended without bloodshed, but knowing all too well that it would be the talk of London tomorrow. Ghonkaba had created a first-rate scandal that would be certain to survive for many years to come.

Wanting to make certain that no further incidents were created that night, he took the precaution of escorting the couple back to the Whiting house in their carriage and depositing them safely there.

The seclusion, privacy, and security of the interior of the well-furnished carriage began to restore Toshabe's spirits, and she was much improved by the time she reached the house.

Ghonkaba, however, brooded in a tense, silent mood, and Captain Mercer, afraid of arousing his ire again, said nothing until they reached the house. "I beg you, sir," he said, "for the sake of the mission that brought you to our shores in the first place, stay indoors and don't go anywhere until Sir Townsend and Lady Whiting return to act as your escorts. I shall write to them immediately and tell them of tonight's happenings, and I'm sure they'll hurry back to the city at the very first opportunity. Until then, you're going to become the most notorious couple in the city, and rather than tolerate future disruptions and misunderstandings, which would be very likely to occur, I beg you to keep to yourselves!"

Ghonkaba began to relax in the private suite he shared with Toshabe, and as they undressed, preparing for night in the soft featherbed that they despised, he began to express his thoughts aloud. "I am sorry we were sent to this terrible land," he said. "They call us savages and look down their noses at us, but it is they who are savages. They even eat their meat half raw! They torture friendly bears and innocent roosters for their own entertainment. Their poor live in squalor, always hungry, and their rich live in huge and sumptuous homes like this, served by so many helpers that no one can find enough for all of them to do. Every woman one sees can be had for a price, and the people know no virtue, so that even respectable marriage is unknown, and the honorable women are not safe from the depredations of the greedy."

"I cannot help but reflect," Toshabe said, "on how different people are here in England from those with white skins whom we met in Boston."

"Of course they are different," Ghonkaba explained eagerly, "because the colonists have been subjected to the Seneca and the other Iroquois and scores of other tribes of Indians, as well. They have learned our ways, and they have adopted our thoughts. They may be whites, like the whites of England, but their souls more nearly resemble the Indians of the wilderness. Do you know why? Because the manitous have seen fit to admit the wilderness and its influences to their souls, and it has made them a new people, a breed apart!"

Before Captain Mercer retired for the evening, he wrote a letter in full detail to his superior, explaining all that had happened in the shocking incidents that evening. He was careful to cast no blame but intimated that it would be well if Sir Townsend and Lady Whiting could return to guide their guests through the maze of complicated London living.

Before the post was even picked up, sorted, and the letter sent on its way north, the story of the evening's events had spread like wildfire throughout London, and the details inevitably were exaggerated in each retelling.

Coffeehouses and private clubs, and the corridors of Parliament, all buzzed with the story, as did even the floors of the great money and commodity exchanges in that part of London known as the City.

The late editions of newspapers printed bawdy versions of the tale, carefully disguising the identities of the participants, but in such a way that their identity could not be mistaken. Eventually, word even traveled through the long, gloomy halls of Whitehall Palace, where the king was enjoying a late breakfast of sausages and German pancakes that he preferred to English food. One of his chamberlains sighed and, steeling himself, gave the monarch an account of the incident.

George III sat in his chair scowling and drumming his fingers as he listened. As it happened, the incident struck him in the worst of all possible ways, at the poorest of all possible times. Late the previous afternoon Prime Minister Pitt had taken upon himself the painful and delicate, but—in his opinion—highly necessary duty of informing the king that he was rapidly losing the popularity and friendship that he enjoyed from his subjects and that he would have to change his ways.

The people were tired after three generations of German being spoken as the official Court language. Granted that King George spoke English, but he still preferred to converse in the tongue of his Germanic ancestors. It was said that he ate no English foods and preferred German dishes exclusively, and it was well-known that his closest friends were Germans who had come to England from Hanover and had been given titles and large estates. Particularly resented was the Earl of Buccleigh, who rode roughshod over the wishes of his tenants, and Pitt urged the monarch to drop his friendships with men like Buccleigh and instead to cultivate Englishmen of taste, distinction, and valor.

It was evident that this latest incident would reflect badly on the king's choice of his friends, and the realization sent George III into a typical rage. "Send at once for Buccleigh," he said, "and let me be attended also by some of the other gentlemen who witnessed this absurd and disgraceful scene last night." He downed the better part of a full pint of breakfast beer without pause.

"As it happens, Your Majesty," the chamberlain replied, "the earl and several of his companions of last night already crave an audience with you and await your pleasure."

The king pounded furiously on the gleaming mahogany-topped table. "Send them to me at once," he shouted, "so that I may hear a true account of last night's events. Don't keep them waiting any longer."

The chamberlain hastily withdrew.

By the time the group reached the dining room,

George III had helped himself to another stack of pancakes and was now demolishing what was left of the sausages. He offered them neither food nor drink, but instead demanded sharply, in both German and English, "Sit down! And tell me about this incident of last night in which you became a laughingstock!"

Buccleigh was well prepared for such a demand. He told his story with only a few embellishments and changes. For the sake of clarity, he spoke exclusively in German.

The woman, he said, obviously was a professional courtesan accomplished in luring men. He had found her so exotic and the circumstances so unusual that he had made the mistake of conceiving a great desire for her. But he had paid for that error.

Dissatisfied with the sum of money that he had offered her, she had called to her consort in an adjoining chamber in the hopes of browbeating the earl into paying her a larger sum for her favors. This he had refused to do, and she subsequently claimed that he had assaulted her, which was anything but the truth.

Her consort, a wild Indian, as savage a man as had landed on these shores in countless hundreds of years, had demanded a barbarous duel—and here the earl hardly needed to exaggerate. He told the actual truth, then ended by saying that he had been unable to countenance such behavior and hence had rejected the idea of a duel. Thereupon, he added, he had been told that if his path should ever cross the Indian's again, the savage would kill him and give his scalp to his wife to wear.

Blinking angrily, King George turned to the other members of the party and knew at a glance that they had not understood a word. This suited his purposes perfectly, and he asked them to offer their versions of what had happened.

They knew to a man what was expected of them. The Earl of Buccleigh had already taken the precaution of telling them in detail his version to avoid any discrepancies. They realized that if he emerged from this scrape with his standing at Court intact, he would be more powerful than ever and in a better position to dispense favors. So the witnesses took care to repeat his story one by one, and those with better memories told it almost precisely as Buccleigh had.

George III heard these identical tales repeated a total of four times and was satisfied that Buccleigh's account of the affair was accurate. He made up his mind at once, though with typical Hanoverian abstruseness, he confided his plan to no one. His intention was apparent only to himself. Rather than give up Buccleigh as a friend, he intended to turn the earl from the goat of an unsavory tale into the hero of the occasion. The cost would be small, involving only the feelings of a pair of savage Indians from the forests of North America.

Captain Mercer was badly disconcerted when he reached the Whiting house at noon the following day to find a coach bearing King George's coat of arms on the doors and footmen and drivers in royal livery on the box. Inside the house was one of the monarch's gentlemen-in-waiting, intending to escort the Indian couple to Whitehall Palace. They had been summoned there for an interview with His Majesty.

The captain's heart sank. He assumed that beyond doubt the king had heard of the previous night's incident, and that, for whatever reason, he wanted to judge the couple for himself. Unfortunately, the return of the Whitings was now out of the question, nor was there an opportunity for Mercer to coach Ghonkaba and Toshabe on their behavior in meeting the surly, bad-tempered, and mercurial king.

"May I accompany you?" he asked, trying to keep the note of despair from his voice.

"By all means," the equerry replied cheerfully. "As far as I know, the audience isn't going to be private. Far from it."

At that point, Toshabe and Ghonkaba came into the room, and Mercer had to curb a long shudder. Toshabe was more outrageously attired than on the previous night. Her gown was even more revealing, and she had lavished cosmetics on her face. But she still seemingly had no realization that as a result she had made herself look like a courtesan.

As for Ghonkaba, he even more closely resembled a caricature of an English gentleman. His suit was more garish, if that was possible. With it, incongruously, he had a quiver of arrows and a bow over one shoulder, and he carried a tomahawk and a knife in his belt. In spite of his English attire, his scalp lock gleamed with grease, and he wore the war paint of his nation on his face.

Captain Mercer tried to find the right words, but could not bring himself to say anything to cause them to realize they would be sure to make themselves the laughingstock of the entire Royal Court. They were so naive and sincere that he felt he was dealing with children. They would only be severely hurt by their inability to understand what he was trying to tell them. So, for better or worse, he had to accept them as they were. By the time the Whitings returned, the damage would have been done. All he could do was take a fatalistic view of the events that were unfolding and assure himself that powers other than human were deciding the fate of the envoy from the Iroquois.

The couple presented so strange an appearance that the equerry lost his customary ability to make light conversation. He struggled in vain to overcome his silence on the ride in the royal carriage to the palace. Captain Mercer did a little better and managed to eke out a semblance of small talk.

Ghonkaba was curious. "I was surprised to be called so soon to the presence of the king," he observed. "I assumed from all I had been told that I might have to wait for many weeks."

"He's heard of you, no doubt," the captain told him, "and no doubt he's sufficiently curious that he wants to meet you."

At last they drove past sentries armed with muskets stationed at the palace entrance and pulled up before a courtyard entrance. A young lieutenant of the Grenadier Guards who came forward to greet them stopped short at the sight of Ghonkaba's weapons. Somewhat flustered, he could not help stammering. "I b-beg your pardon, sir," he said, "but it's an inviolable rule of Whitehall that anyone attending a royal audience is allowed to carry only his side arms."

Ghonkaba looked mystified.

"He means your sword," Captain Mercer prodded.

Ghonkaba shook his head with finality. "I own no sword and do not wield one," he said. "These are the weapons of my people, and I thought it might amuse the king to see an exhibition of their use." When he stalked past the lieutenant, his attitude and appearance were so bizarre that the Guards officer failed to make an issue out of disarming him. This strange-looking savage would object, and it was best not to create a scene on a day when George III was in a particularly unpleasant mood.

At last they entered a large, spacious chamber that had a slightly faded red carpet running down its center toward an oversize chair on a dais at the far end. George III was perched there, and the ladies and gentlemen of his court filled the room.

"Ghonkaba of the Seneca, the envoy of the Iroquois League, and his wife, Toshabe, are here to present their respects to His Majesty," a majordomo announced.

Captain Mercer had time only to whisper some last-second instructions. "Walk up the length of the red carpet until you reach the platform where the king is sitting," he murmured. "And be sure you bow low before him. Then you wait for him to address you first."

The couple started up the remainder of the carpet and were watched in a dazed silence by lords and nobles, generals and admirals, and other high-ranking members of the ruling class required to be in attendance at these levees.

The crowd watched in a stupefied silence. Some were inclined to laugh, but Toshabe, in spite of her gaudy appearance, was too provocatively beautiful to cause amusement. As for her husband, the onlookers took note of his weapons, remembered what they had heard about his encounter with the Earl of Buccleigh the previous evening, and again decided to contain any laughter.

Making his way slowly down the length of the carpet as he approached the dais, Ghonkaba was genuinely shocked by King George's appearance. The man was moon-faced, with a fat, flabby body, and although he was gorgeously arrayed in a suit festooned with lace, food spots marred the cuffs and the front of his amply cut waistcoat. He could not help but contrast this weak-looking buffoon with his stately, awe-inspiring grandfather and his powerful, wise father. They, too, were monarchs and gave off an instant aura of substance, power, and dignity.

Walking proudly three paces behind her husband, Toshabe could feel the waves of admiration that went up from the onlookers as they stared at her. But more than admiration was in those looks, and she became uneasy. Feeling hostility from the women, she realized, too, that in recognizing her sex appeal, the men were also revealing a leering contempt.

The Seneca reached the foot of the dais, halted, and raised his left arm in a stiff, formal greeting. Without intending to be disrespectful of Captain Mercer, he was unconsciously ignoring his instructions.

He anticipated that, at the very least, the king would respond in kind and quite possibly would even stand and either beckon his guests to join him on the dais, or would come down to their level. He did neither, but returned the visitor's gaze without expression.

Ghonkaba began to speak in an unaccented English, much clearer than the king's. "I, Ghonkaba of the Seneca," he declared proudly, "bring greetings to George from his brother, Ja-gonh, Great Sachem of the Iroquois League."

His Majesty was known to be ever conscious of his rank and the protocol surrounding it. In fact, it was rumored that in private even his mistresses addressed him as "sire."

An equerry stationed behind his throne whispered in a loud voice that this Indian was descended from three generations of leaders of the Seneca nation and of chiefs of the Iroquois. In other words, the equerry pointed out, he held the comparable rank of a prince, son of a king.

Displaying his customary callous disregard for the feelings of others, King George replied in a voice that everyone in the chamber could hear. "I don't much care who he is. He looks like a bloody fool to me."

A wave of suppressed laughter ran through the chamber.

Ghonkaba's eyes blazed, but he managed to keep his temper under control. Regardless of his personal opinion of this gross caricature of a ruler, he must not fail in his diplomatic duty. The identity and person of George III meant nothing to him, but he was conscious of the mission on which he had been sent. He could not permit his temper to be responsible for a break in the alliance between the Iroquois and the English.

He had the responsibility of formally delivering to this Englishman in full the friendly greeting of his father, Great Sachem of the Iroquois. Ja-gonh was not only the physical and moral superior of such a repulsive person, but his stature in his domain granted him equality with the royalty of England, no matter what pretensions they took upon themselves.

Accordingly, Ghonkaba removed from an inner pocket of his dress coat the folded paper that he had brought all the way from the land of the Seneca. It contained his father's message to the king expressing loyalty to the crown and, in the present difficult situation among nations, his avowal that the Iroquois League would stand steadfast beside their friends, the British. Ja-gonh's message was simple indeed but in its straightforward language his true majesty of character shone through. Ghonkaba read from it faithfully, in order to impress upon the king the fact that the words were not his but those of another ruler, even though he already knew them virtually by heart. Even as he spoke, giving proper emphasis to the most important portions, he realized that King George's attention seemed to have wandered. The effect on everyone present was as though he had dismissed the message as insignificant and its reading as merely an irritating waste of time. By the time Ghonkaba finished reading aloud and refolded the paper, he was aware that the words had made no impact on the arrogant-looking king. It was just as if the entire incident had never happened. The king's reaction was a blatant insult to the Great Sachem of the Iroquois and to his son, and he hardly could help but recognize that fact. In every way, the king gave the appearance of taking pleasure in the stiuation he had created.

Beginning now to genuinely enjoy himself through his familiar device of humiliating individuals who could not fight back, the monarch beckoned Toshabe forward. She advanced several paces closer to his chair and stood beside her husband.

"I must compliment you on your shoulders, which are very pretty indeed," the king told her with an expression slyly approaching a smirk, "and I admire the svelte litheness of your body."

He had to be aware that his remarks were entirely out of place and reflected unfortunately on his regard for the Indian nation that these callers represented.

"But," he continued tongue-in-cheek, "as you're unfamiliar with our English winters, allow me to give you a word or two of advice."

Here he paused, as if to make certain that the attentive audience received the full impact of his next slighting words.

"You'd be very wise," the king said with a slight chuckle at his own crude humor, "to avoid drafts and to wear much heavier clothing to protect you from the cold. We wouldn't wish to send you back home . . . ill, would we?"

Again the courtiers laughed, this time more openly, for they avidly sought their king's favor.

Ghonkaba and Toshabe knew that he was making sport of them, but they could do nothing about it. Suddenly, the king pointed to Ghonkaba's weapons and demanded brusquely, "What are those strange objects?"

"They are my weapons, and my nation's skill with them has kept us predominant among all the tribes of North America for many hundreds of years," Ghonkaba replied coldly. "When Renno, my grandfather, first came to England as a young man, he demonstrated their use to William, your predecessor on the throne here, and his prowess made them good friends. I thought you might like to see a demonstration with them."

This was even better than King George had anticipated. "By all means," he said. "I'd be delighted!"

Ghonkaba quickly took charge. Noting several stands, each about five feet high, clustered beneath tall, austere windows, he requested that several be placed about a hundred feet down the length of the red carpet.

They were quickly placed where he directed. "Good," he said. "Now I wonder if you'd be good enough to provide me with some fruits from your larder."

"By all means," George III replied, chuckling silently until his shoulders heaved. "Would you prefer grapes or melons?"

"Melons are far too large for my purposes, but grapes may be a trifle too small." Ghonkaba remained

303

in full command of his dignity. "Perhaps some apples?"

"By all means," the king replied. "Fetch a basket of apples," he ordered.

After the fruit was brought, Ghonkaba directed that one apple be placed on each of the small platforms. Then, standing directly below the dais, he pointed down the length of the carpet, with an expectant grin.

The courtiers who had curiously been crowding forward on either side of the four-foot wide carpet suddenly realized that he intended to shoot down its length, and they began to back away.

Ghonkaba was not forgetting that these were the people who had laughed at him and—even worse—his wife. "There's no need to back away," he called. "You can stand anywhere you please, but I prefer that you keep the carpet itself clear."

With great reluctance the members of the Court began to move forward again. George III suspected this was unnecessary and frowned, which pleased Ghonkaba a great deal, and he grinned even more amiably.

"We of the Seneca," Ghonkaba said, his voice becoming a shade harsh, "allow our deeds to speak for themselves." He seized his bow, which he strung, took an arrow from his quiver, and after taking quick, careful aim, let fly. Without even waiting to see the result, he snatched another arrow from the quiver and sent it at the second apple in the line.

A ripple of applause broke out when the startled courtiers saw that the arrows had split in half both apples.

But Ghonkaba was not yet finished with his remarkable exhibition. Removing his tomahawk from his belt, he let fly with it and split a third apple in half. Then, with only his knife remaining undemonstrated, he plucked it, balanced it in the air for an instant, and threw it hard. It sliced deeply into the flesh of the final apple, which remained on its shelf, the knife blade still quivering.

The courtiers broke into spontaneous applause.

King George scowled; the savage had won the hearts as well as the plaudits of the crowd.

Ghonkaba retrieved his weapons, wiping them off carefully on his sleeve before dropping them back into place. Then, sauntering up the carpet again toward the dais, he munched on an apple that he had cut, and said casually, "Now, my brother, George, knows, perhaps, how we Seneca won our repute for prowess."

King George felt he was losing the battle of words and deeds. "That was rather impressive, considering the primitive nature of the weapons you used, young man," he said. "I'm sure, however, that any one of our Grenadier Guards could have done the same with his rifle."

Ghonkaba's eyes narrowed, but he agreed equably. "To be sure," he replied. "A battalion of Grenadiers served beside us in our recent campaign against the French, and they acquitted themselves in battle well, once they learned to acclimate to the special fighting conditions of the New World."

He had scored again, and his boldness, combined with the king's obvious dislike, had unexpectedly turned the crowd in his favor. They laughed even more openly at his latest remark.

It was almost inconceivable that George III, ruler of Great Britain and of a far-flung empire that virtually stretched around the world, should be outsmarted by a crude savage.

As he always did when he was thwarted, the king immediately cut himself off from the source that had annoyed him. "We accept the gesture of fealty from our Indian subjects in the New World," he said, thereby causing much distress among the officials who knew that the Indians of the British colonies were not his subjects. "And we greet them in return. We've enjoyed your exhibition, and you'll be glad to hear that we have a warship leaving London in the next forty-eight hours for the New World, on which accommodations will be found for you and your wife."

Two lords of the admiralty exchanged quick glances. No warship was scheduled to make such a voyage soon. But the king's wishes had to be obeyed, so a vessel would have to be quickly made ready for sea in order to fulfill his expectation that the Indians leave England forthwith.

Showing no emotion, Ghonkaba raised his hand in a gesture of farewell, though he did not expect to be rewarded with a similar gesture of civility in return. As he walked out of the chamber he was overcome by a feeling of relief. It was almost too good to be true that they soon could be leaving this dissolute, degenerate land for the clean, fresh air of the New World.

He neither knew nor cared that a warship would have to be provided for the exclusive purpose of carrying him and Toshabe across the Atlantic. All that mattered was that they were leaving the shores of England behind them.

It was astonishing, he reflected, that the difference between the British and their colonists in North America should be so great. Come to think of it, they were totally different breeds. They spoke the same language and had a common heritage, but they were in effect two vastly different people. The British were aliens in the forests of the New World, where they might never be at home. The Americans already were as at home as were their Indian allies.

Almost all the white men whom he admired and respected were Americans. Chief among them was Colonel Washington of Virginia. He had not liked Townsend Whiting when they first met, and had begun to enjoy the officer's company only after Whiting had been in the New World long enough to acquire new ways of thinking.

"The manitous are showing their favor to us once again," he said softly to Toshabe in the tongue of the Seneca once they had reached the security of the corridor outside the chamber. "They are allowing us to leave this terrible land and to go home to a place where men may live in freedom and dignity!"

Once aboard the British warship that had been so quickly ordered into service in ferrying the Seneca couple back to the shores of North America, Ghonkaba had further time to assess in detail their experiences since leaving Boston.

One of his first orders of business after the ship cleared the English Channel and passed beyond the point known as Land's End was to drop overboard the uncomfortable and unwanted clothing that they had worn in London. The garments no longer were necessary and they served only as unwelcome reminders of a most unhappy episode. For the rest of the voyage and on their overland journey home, he and Toshabe would be content to wear their own clothes. The weeks of the long voyage home would give them a pleasurable period of time together, away from the cares of the warring nations, and entirely relaxed and happy in each other's company, with nothing expected of them.

He reflected on these things as he stood at the rail gazing at the dim horizon of England as it slipped gradually into the distance.

"We did exactly the right thing at each step," he had told Toshabe as they sat alone in their small cabin, "and have nothing to regret. We held our heads up while we were there, and we can hold our heads high now, even though we did not experience all that we had expected and were disappointed in many of the things that we did experience."

"That is true," Toshabe agreed loyally, "though I am afraid that your friends, the Whitings, will be shocked that we did not even stay long enough to see them but hurried away after accepting their hospitality. It does seem strange, even to me."

Ghonkaba was quick to reassure her. "I, too, am unhappy that we did not have the privilege of spending some time with Beth and Sir Townsend and that you therefore did not have the opportunity of coming to know both of them much better. That would have been most enjoyable, you may be sure. But regrettable as the circumstances proved to be, I made use of the occasion before we left to write a note describing fully the facts of what had happened and thanking them for their generous arrangements to have us made comfortable." He chuckled. "I wonder what Captain Mercer's account of it all will be!"

Then he had gone on to discuss much more significant recollections of their visit to England. Not only had he noticed the considerable difference between those rather strange island people and the expansive colonists of North America, but when he pondered particularly the attitude of George III and his Court he could see grave and disturbing distinctions.

And, standing as he now was with the refreshing

ocean winds whipping about him, bearing as they did
those insistent sea gulls who still followed the vessel, he
gave further thought to the stirring insights he had
gained in the past several days. The gulls, he thought,
somehow reminded him of the English people—free,
but unable or unwilling to take full advantage of that
freedom; rather, they were content to live an almost
parasitical existence. They must be, it seemed to him,
among the least happy of winged creatures—and the
least admirable, especially compared with the birds of
North America, such as the proud hawks with which
his own history, and future, were so closely allied.

"Freedom!" he exclaimed aloud. That was what he
cherished most of all the precious Seneca traditions. It
was a sentiment that seemed to pervade all of America,
and now was reinforced by the defeat of the French
colonists.

As he looked at the green sea, now changing subtly
to a royal blue, he contemplated the possibility of a
most difficult decision in the days and years ahead.

The experience with King George and his cohort
had proved to be so deeply distasteful that he could
not now imagine being closely allied with such people.
The Iroquois League did indeed have a treaty with
those very English people whom he disliked and dis-
trusted, and his father had just restated it forcefully.
Ghonkaba could accept such a liaison only by closing
his eyes and his mind to what he believed the king to
represent, and focusing instead on an alliance with
such American colonists as General Strong and Colonel
Washington. With them, he was willing to think of
himself and his people as allies.

And if those people ever had a major difference of
opinion with the lords in London, Ghonkaba knew in-
tuitively on which side his sympathies and his support

would fall. He would do his best, under those circumstances, to persuade his father and the other leaders of the Iroquois that they should take their place beside the colonists, reviewing and perhaps renouncing their long-standing ties to the British Crown. As Indians they were the first Americans, and they should recognize and honor the role of all those people—English and others from Europe—who had voluntarily joined them in America. They were all Americans, though originally of vastly differing backgrounds and traditions.

His thoughts strayed to one further, disquieting idea. If he were to prove unable to persuade his fellow Seneca and Iroquois of the views he now held so strongly, he might one day find it necessary to separate himself again from them and aid the white Americans in whatever way was possible at such a time. The concept of disloyalty was distressing in the extreme, for he took most seriously his emerging role as a future leader of all his people, but he believed that he understood his values fully and maturely now, and was prepared to make such a painful decision if confronted with it.

With the hope that such a day might never come, he stepped away from the rail to return to Toshabe's side. He was filled with the glow of satisfaction in knowing that he had performed well despite the difficult conditions imposed by British royalty, and he took pride in having carried out to the fullest extent the mission his father had entrusted to him. Now he would return with a full heart to his own people, where he belonged.

★ WAGONS WEST ★

This continuing, magnificent saga recounts the adventures of a brave band of settlers, all of different backgrounds, all sharing one dream— to find a new and better life.

☐	26822	**INDEPENDENCE! #1**	$4.50
☐	26162	**NEBRASKA! #2**	$4.50
☐	26242	**WYOMING! #3**	$4.50
☐	26072	**OREGON! #4**	$4.50
☐	26070	**TEXAS! #5**	$4.50
☐	26377	**CALIFORNIA! #6**	$4.50
☐	26546	**COLORADO! #7**	$4.50
☐	26069	**NEVADA! #8**	$4.50
☐	26163	**WASHINGTON! #9**	$4.50
☐	26073	**MONTANA! #10**	$4.50
☐	26184	**DAKOTA! #11**	$4.50
☐	26521	**UTAH! #12**	$4.50
☐	26071	**IDAHO! #13**	$4.50
☐	26367	**MISSOURI! #14**	$4.50
☐	27141	**MISSISSIPPI! #15**	$4.50
☐	25247	**LOUISIANA! #16**	$4.50
☐	25622	**TENNESSEE! #17**	$4.50
☐	26022	**ILLINOIS! #18**	$4.50
☐	26533	**WISCONSIN! #19**	$4.50
☐	26849	**KENTUCKY! #20**	$4.50
☐	27065	**ARIZONA! #21**	$4.50
☐	27458	**NEW MEXICO! #22**	$4.50
☐	27703	**OKLAHOMA! #23**	$4.50
☐	28180	**CELEBRATION! #24**	$4.50

Bantam Books, Dept. LE, 414 East Golf Road, Des Plaines, IL 60016

Please send me the items I have checked above. I am enclosing $_____ (please add $2.00 to cover postage and handling). Send check or money order, no cash or C.O.D.s please.

Mr/Ms _____

Address _____

City/State _____ Zip _____

Please allow four to six weeks for delivery.
Prices and availability subject to change without notice.   LE-3/90